SELECTED S...

BY GUY DE ...

GUY DE MAUPASSANT (1850–1893). A prolific and notable French writer, Maupassant is best remembered for his wide-ranging, original and satirical short stories.

Guy de Maupassant was born in Normandy in 1850. After his parents separated he stayed with his mother, who was a close friend of Gustav Flaubert. He served in the army from 1870 to 1871 and then became a Government office clerk, a job which he performed conscientiously, but for which he never showed much enthusiasm or ambition. He was more interested in outdoor sports, such as boating, fishing and shooting, and in writing, under the guidance of Flaubert. He was thus introduced into literary circles, where he met Emile Zola, who, among other writers, formed the *groupe naturaliste* in 1880. Maupassant contributed to their collection of short stories, *Les Soirées de Médan*, with his own *Boule de suif*, which made him a huge success virtually overnight. He left the Civil Service in 1882 and devoted the rest of his life to literature. He wrote over 300 short stories, which were extraordinary for the time. Pessimistic, nihilistic and sadly disillusioned, his writing greatly reflected his dissatisfaction with the world. However, there was also a positive response to life in his stories, as he presented vivid and charming images of the countryside, complete with the joys of rowing and fishing, although these scenes never quite achieved an idyllic state. In addition to the stories he wrote six novels, the best known being *A Woman's Life* (1883), *Bel-Ami* (1885) and *Pierre and Jean* (1887). Maupassant's last ten years proved to be prodigiously fruitful and earned him much money, which he spent extravagantly on his luxuriant and salacious lifestyle. A notorious womanizer, he suffered as a result from mental disorders, which were syphilitic in origin. This strain, combined with overwork, eventually led to his ruin and from 1890 his reason began to fail. An abortive suicide attempt in December 1891 was followed by eighteen months in a mental home in Paris, where he died in 1893.

Guy de Maupassant's *Selected Short Stories* contains all his best-loved works. They vary in style, locale and the message conveyed, with *Boule de Suif*, which tells of a prostitute from Rouen; *A Vendetta*, the story of a mother's revenge; and a light-hearted, comic tale about *Madame Husson's May King*.

PENGUIN POPULAR CLASSICS

SELECTED SHORT STORIES

GUY DE MAUPASSANT

PENGUIN BOOKS

PENGUIN BOOKS

Published by the Penguin Group
Penguin Books Ltd, 27 Wrights Lane, London w8 5tz, England
Penguin Putnam Inc., 375 Hudson Street, New York, New York 10014, USA
Penguin Books Australia Ltd, Ringwood, Victoria, Australia
Penguin Books Canada Ltd, 10 Alcorn Avenue, Toronto, Ontario, Canada m4v 3b2
Penguin Books (NZ) Ltd, Private Bag 102902, NSMC, Auckland, New Zealand

Penguin Books Ltd, Registered Offices: Harmondsworth, Middlesex, England

Published in Penguin Popular Classics 1995
5 7 9 10 8 6

Printed in England by Cox & Wyman Ltd, Reading, Berkshire

CONTENTS

BOULE DE SUIF

FOR several days in succession remnants of a defeated army had been passing through the town. They were not disciplined units, but hordes of stragglers. The men were unshaven and unwashed, their uniforms were in rags and they slouched along without colours or order. All seemed dazed and exhausted, marching mechanically, beyond thinking or planning, and collapsing from fatigue whenever they stopped. The reservists in particular, men of peace, who had lived quietly on their private means, were staggering under the weight of their rifles; there were the excitable militia-men, whose morale was easily lowered and as easily raised, as quick to attack as to run away. Mixed up with them came a few red-coats, the remains of a regular division that had been cut up in a big battle; gunners in their dark uniform marched alongside all these different infantrymen; and here and there appeared the polished helmet of a dragoon, whose heavy step had difficulty in keeping up with the brisker pace of the men of the line.

Guerrilla units with high-sounding names, the Death or Glory Boys, the Diehards, the Legion of Death, passed through, looking like brigands.

Their officers, ex-drapers or corn-merchants and men who had sold lard or soap, were soldiers only by force of circumstances; chosen to command owing to the length of their bank-balances or of their moustaches, armed to the teeth, wearing the red flannel waist-band of their rank and plastered with stripes, they spoke in loud confident voices, discussing strategy and boasting loudly that only they stood between France and destruction. But they were often afraid of their men, thorough-paced scoundrels, often amazingly brave but given to looting and all kinds of excesses.

People said that the Prussians would soon be in Rouen.

The National Guard, who for the last two months had been patrolling the neighbouring woods with extreme caution, sometimes shooting their own sentries and preparing for action whenever a rabbit moved in the undergrowth, had gone home. Their arms, their uniforms, all the panoply of war, with which they had recently been terrorizing every mile-stone on the main roads for ten miles round, had suddenly disappeared.

The last French soldiers had just crossed the Seine and occupied Pont-Audemer, moving through Saint-Sever and Bourg-Achard; bringing up the rear between two aides plodded the general. He was in despair, unable to do anything with this riff-raff, himself dazed by the catastrophe that had overtaken a people accustomed to victory and now hopelessly defeated in spite of their traditional bravery.

And now a deep calm, a dumb terrified foreboding had settled down upon the city. Many of the shopkeeper class, grown portly and enervated in business, awaited the conquerors anxiously, fearing that their roasting-spits or their big kitchen knives might be mistaken for arms.

Life seemed to have stopped; the shops were closed and the streets deserted. Sometimes one of the townspeople, terrified by the silence, slunk along keeping close to the walls.

The agony of waiting made everyone long for the arrival of the enemy. On the afternoon of the day following the departure of the French troops, a few uhlans, suddenly appearing from nowhere, rode rapidly through the town. A little later a dark column of men marched down St. Catherine's Hill, while two other detachments of the enemy appeared on the roads from Darnetal and Boisguillaume. The advance guards of the three bodies, arriving at exactly the same moment, met on the square in front of the Town Hall;

and along all the neighbouring streets the German army began to arrive, the cobble-stones ringing under the heavy rhythmical tread of the marching battalions.

Orders were shouted in an unintelligible guttural language outside the houses, which seemed dead and deserted, while behind the closed shutters peering eyes watched the conquerors, now masters of the town and of the lives and fortunes of its people by right of war. The townsfolk in their darkened rooms were dazed as if by some cataclysm, some devastating earthquake, against which all wisdom and all resistance is of no avail. Such a feeling is produced every time the established order of things is upset, when security is destroyed and everything hitherto protected by the laws of man or nature is suddenly at the mercy of wild unreasoning brutality. The earthquake crushing a whole people beneath collapsing houses, the river in flood which sweeps away the drowned peasantry along with the bodies of cattle and beams torn from the roofs, or the victorious army massacring all who resist and carrying off the rest as prisoners, looting by right of the sword and thanking their God with the roar of cannon—these are all scourges of the same kind which destroy belief in eternal justice and all the confidence we have learned to feel in the protection of heaven and the rationality of man.

Soon small parties were knocking at every door and then disappearing into the houses. Occupation was following invasion. It now became the duty of the conquered to show themselves accommodating to their masters.

After a short time, when the first panic had subsided, a new calm descended on the town. In many houses the Prussian officer ate at the family table. He was not infrequently a gentleman, and out of politeness expressed sympathy with France, saying how much he disliked having to take part in the war. People were grateful to him for this sentiment; moreover, one day they might need his protection. If they were nice to him, they might perhaps have fewer men to feed. And why make things unpleasant for him, when they were entirely at his mercy? This would be rashness rather than bravery. And rashness is no longer the fault of the Rouen shopkeeper, as it had been in the days of heroic defence, which had on so many occasions in the past shed glory on the city. They put forward traditional French good manners as their final justification; they reflected that politeness inside their own houses was quite permissible, provided they did not fraternize in public with enemy soldiers. In the streets they cut each other, but at home they chatted freely, and every evening the German stayed later, warming himself at the fire with the family.

Even the town gradually resumed its normal appearance. The French still mostly stayed at home, but the streets swarmed with Prussian soldiers. Moreover, the officers of the Blue Hussars, arrogantly trailing their long sabres on the pavement, did not show noticeably greater contempt for the ordinary civilian than the French Light Infantry officers, who had been drinking at the same cafés the year before.

But there was nevertheless something in the air, something subtle and mysterious, a strange unbearable atmosphere like some penetrating smell, which one could only call the smell of invasion. It filled private houses and public places alike, affected the taste of food, and made everyone feel as though he was in a foreign country, far from home, among dangerous and savage tribes.

The conquerors demanded money, a great deal of money; the population was always having to pay. It is true they were rich; but the richer a Normandy shopkeeper becomes, the more any sacrifice hurts, and the less he likes to see any fraction of his wealth passing into other hands.

Nevertheless, six or eight miles below the city downstream in the direction of Croisset, Dieppeville or Bissart, bargees or fishermen often brought up from the river bottom

the swollen body of a German in uniform, stabbed or kicked
to death or pushed over the parapet of a bridge, or with his
head beaten in with a stone. The slime of the river hid
these unknown acts of revenge, barbarous but legitimate,
secret deeds of heroism, silent attacks, more dangerous than
fighting in the open, and without the reward of fame.

For hatred of the foreigner always inspires a few brave
men, ready to die for an ideal.

At last, as the invaders, though they subjected the town to
their stern discipline, had not perpetrated any of the atrocities
attributed to them by rumour all along their triumphant
line of march, people plucked up courage, and the urge to
do business again stirred in the hearts of the local tradesmen. Some had considerable interests at Havre, which was in
the hands of the French army, and they wanted to get to that
port by going overland to Dieppe and taking ship there.

They made use of the influence of German officers, whose
acquaintance they had made, and a permit to leave Rouen
was granted by the Commander-in-Chief.

Accordingly, a large four-horsed coach was engaged for
this journey and ten passengers booked seats with the owner;
it was decided to start one Tuesday morning before dawn
to avoid arousing the curiosity of a crowd.

After several days' frost the ground was like iron; on the
Monday about three o'clock great dark clouds from the
north brought snow, which fell continuously all that evening
and through the night.

At half-past four in the morning the travellers met in the
courtyard of the Hôtel de Normandie, where they were to
board the coach. They were still sleepy, shivering under
their wraps. They could hardly see each other in the darkness; they had all piled on heavy winter clothes, till they
looked like portly priests in long cassocks. But two of the
men recognized each other and a third joined them; they
got into conversation: "I'm taking my wife away," said

one. "That's just what I'm doing." "And so am I." The first speaker added: "We shan't be coming back to Rouen, and if the Prussians get near Havre, we shall cross to England." All had the same intention; they were that sort.

Meanwhile the horses were not being put in. At intervals a small lantern carried by a groom came out of one dark door and disappeared immediately into another. The stamping of horses' hoofs, deadened by the manure of their litter, and a voice talking to the animals and swearing came from inside the stable. A faint tinkle of bells suggested that harness was being put on. This faint tinkle soon became a loud, continuous sound, following the animals' movements, sometimes stopping and then starting again with a sudden clatter accompanied by the dull clang of a horse's shoe on the ground. Suddenly the door closed and all was silence. The freezing passengers had stopped talking; they just stood there stiff and motionless.

An unbroken curtain of shimmering flakes continued to fall; contours were obliterated, and everything was covered with a coating of white cotton-wool; in the deep silence of the town swathed in its winding-sheet of snow no sound was audible except the faint indefinable swish, felt rather than heard, of the falling feathery particles, which seemed to fill the sky and cover the earth.

The man reappeared with the lantern, leading a miserable reluctant horse by a halter; he made it stand alongside the pole and fastened the traces, walking round and round it adjusting the harness, for he could only use one hand, as the other held the lantern. As he was going back to fetch the second horse, he noticed all the passengers standing there, already white with snow, and said: "Why don't you get into the coach? You'd at least be under cover."

Presumably the idea had never occurred to them, and they made a rush for the door. The three men settled their wives at the far end and seated themselves. Then the other vague shadowy figures in their turn occupied the remaining places without a word.

Their feet sank into the straw that covered the floor. The ladies at the far end lit the small copper foot-warmers they had brought with chemical fuel and for some time enumerated in whispers the advantages of these contraptions, with which they had all long been familiar.

At last the coach was harnessed, with six horses instead of four, owing to the heavy roads, and a voice enquired: " Is everyone in? " A voice from inside answered: " Yes! " and they started off.

The coach travelled very slowly indeed; the wheels sank into the snow and the whole body groaned and creaked. The horses slipped and panted and steamed, and the driver's enormous whip cracked all the time, darting in every direction, tying itself into knots and uncoiling again like a writhing snake, or suddenly tickling the hind-quarters of a horse, which then strained forward with greater efforts.

Imperceptibly the light increased. The snow, which one passenger, a typical Rouen man, compared to a rain of cotton, had ceased. A feeble glimmer came through the heavy leaden clouds, showing up more brilliantly the whiteness of the countryside, against which stood out, now a line of big trees thickly coated with hoar-frost, now a cottage under a cowl of snow.

In the coach the travellers scrutinized one another in the depressing dawn twilight.

In the best places at the far end M. and Mme. Loiseau, wholesale wine-merchants from the Rue Grand-Pont, were dozing opposite each other.

Once clerk to a wine-merchant who had failed, Loiseau had bought the business and made his fortune. He sold very inferior wine very cheap to the small retailers round about, and had the reputation among his acquaintances and friends of being a crafty scoundrel and a typical Norman in his combination of joviality and guile.

His reputation as a crook was so well established that one evening at the Prefecture, M. Tournel, an author of lampoons and satirical ballads, and celebrated locally for his mordant wit, suggested to the ladies, who seemed to want waking up, that, as Loiseau was present, a game of " Beggar my neighbour " would not be amiss; and the witticism was repeated in the Prefect's reception rooms, and spreading from there to the town, had made the whole province laugh for a month.

Besides this, Loiseau was famous for his practical jokes of all kinds, good-natured and the reverse; no one could mention his name without immediately adding: " Loiseau is a priceless fellow."

He was short, with a protruding stomach and a red face framed in side-whiskers, now greying.

His wife, tall, powerfully built and determined, with a shrill voice and a decisive manner, was responsible for the organization and accountancy of the firm, while he kept it alive with his cheery energy.

Next to them, more dignified as belonging to a superior social class, sat M. Carré-Lamadon, a man of substance with an assured position in the cotton trade, the owner of three spinning mills, an officer of the Legion of Honour and member of the General Council. All through the period of the Empire he had remained at the head of the benevolent opposition simply in order to extract a higher price for his support of a policy which he opposed by all methods open to a gentleman, as he put it himself. Mme. Carré-Lamadon, considerably younger than her husband, was still the one consolation of the officers of good family quartered in Rouen.

She sat facing her husband, tiny, attractive and pretty, muffled up in her furs, gazing at the depressing interior of the coach with a woe-begone expression.

Her neighbours, the Comte and Comtesse Hubert de Bréville, bore one of the oldest and most honoured names in Normandy. The Comte, an old nobleman of distinguished appearance, took considerable trouble by the cut of his clothes to accentuate his natural resemblance to King Henri IV, who, according to the story of which the family was very proud, had had a child by one of the de Bréville ladies, whose husband had been rewarded with a title and the Governorship of the province.

Serving with M. Carré-Lamadon on the General Council, Comte Hubert represented the Orleanist party in the Department. The story of his marriage to the daughter of a small ship-owner from Nantes had always remained a mystery. But as the Comtesse had distinction and was an excellent hostess, and moreover was reputed to have been the mistress of one of Louis-Philippe's sons, she was warmly received by the nobility, and her receptions were the smartest in the district, the only ones where the old courtly manners survived and to which an invitation was hard to get.

The de Brévilles' income, all from real estate, was said to amount to half a million francs.

These six occupied the front seats of the coach, representing the leisured moneyed class, self-assured and solid, respected and dictatorial, pillars of the Church and morality.

By a strange accident, all the women were on the same side; and the Comtesse had next to her two nuns, who told their beads interminably, mumbling Paternosters and Aves. One was an old woman, pitted with smallpox, as if she had received a charge of buckshot at close range full in the face. The other was frail and pretty in a delicate sort of way, obviously consumptive, eaten up by the devouring faith which makes martyrs and fanatics.

Opposite the two nuns were a man and woman, who were the objects of general interest. The man, whom everyone knew by sight, was Cornudet, the Radical, the

terror of all respectable people. For twenty years he had
been plunging his long ginger beard into mugs of beer in
all the democratic bars. With the help of his brothers and
friends he had run through a considerable fortune inherited
from his father, a retired confectioner, and he was waiting
impatiently for the Republican Government to reward him
with the position he had earned by so many revolutionary
potations. On the Fourth of September, as a result perhaps
of a practical joke, he thought he had been appointed prefect,
but, when he tried to take up his duties, the office staff, left
in sole charge, refused to recognize him and he was forced
to retire. He was, however, a kindly soul, good-natured
and obliging; and he had devoted himself with exemplary
enthusiasm to organizing the defence of the district. He
had had trenches dug in the flat country and all the young
trees in the neighbouring forests cut down, he had scattered
booby-traps on all the roads, and then, on the enemy's
approach, had hurriedly retired to the town, satisfied with
his preparations. He thought he could now be more useful
at Havre, where new trenches would be needed.

The woman, one of those usually called " gay ", was
famous for her youthful stoutness, which had earned her
the nickname of Boule de Suif, the Dumpling. She was
short and rotund, as fat as a pig, with puffy fingers con-
stricted at the joints, like strings of miniature sausages; in
spite of her shiny, tightly stretched skin and an enormous
bust, which stuck out under her dress, she was nevertheless
desirable, and was in fact much sought after, so attractive was
her freshness. Her face was like a red apple or a peony bud
about to burst into flower. She had magnificent dark eyes,
shaded by long thick lashes, and below a fascinating little
mouth, moist to kiss, with tiny white teeth.

She was said moreover to possess many other attractions
not visible to the eye.

As soon as she was recognized, the respectable women

began to murmur, and the words " prostitute " and " public scandal " were whispered so loud that she looked up. She cast such a bold challenging glance at her neighbours that there was a sudden silence and everyone dropped their eyes, except Loiseau, who kept an admiring stare fixed on her.

But conversation soon started again between the three ladies, whom this woman's proximity had suddenly made friends, almost intimates. It was their duty, they thought, to pool their united dignity as married women in face of this shameless hussy; for legitimate love is always scornful of its free-lance sister.

The three men, too, brought together by their conservative instincts in the presence of Cornudet, were talking finance with the natural contempt of the rich for the poor. Comte Hubert was describing the damage he had suffered from the Prussians, his cattle stolen and crops destroyed, in the confident tone of the great land-owner, rolling in money, who would recover from all his losses within the year. The cotton industry having been hard hit, M. Carré-Lamadon had been careful to send six hundred thousand francs to England, so as to have something put by for a rainy day. As for Loiseau, he had made arrangements to sell to the French Commissariat Department all the cheap wine he had left in his cellars, so that the State owed him considerable sums, which he hoped to draw at Havre.

Friendly glances passed between the three men. Though they belonged to different social classes, money made them brethren of the great freemasonry of the wealthy, who always have gold to jingle in their trouser-pockets.

The coach went so slowly that by ten o'clock they had not covered twelve miles. The men got down three times to walk up hills. They were beginning to get worried, for they were to have lunched at Tôtes, and now there was no hope of getting there before dark. They were all looking out for an inn on the road, when the coach stuck in a snow-drift, and it took two hours to get it out.

Their spirits sank as their hunger increased; there was not anywhere they could get a bite or a sup, as the approach of the Prussians and the passage of the starving French troops had frightened away all business. The gentlemen looked for food at the farms on the side of the road, but they could not even find any bread, as the suspicious peasants were hiding their stocks for fear of being robbed by the soldiers, who, having no rations, were forcibly requisitioning any-thing they found.

About one o'clock Loiseau announced that he had an aching void in his stomach. Everyone had been in the same condition for some time; and the longing for food, becom-ing more acute every minute, had killed conversation.

At intervals first one would yawn, then another. Each one in turn according to his character, his manners and his social position opened his mouth noisily or politely put his hand before the gaping, steaming chasm.

Boule de Suif bent down several times, as if feeling for something under her skirts. She hesitated a moment, looked at her neighbours, then quietly straightened herself. Every-one looked pale and drawn. Loiseau declared that he would give a thousand francs for a knuckle of ham. His wife made a sign of protest and then subsided. The mere men-tion of money wasted always worried her; she could not even see jokes on the subject. "I admit I'm beginning to feel pretty rotten," said the Comte. "Why didn't I think of bringing food?"

Everyone was blaming himself for the same omission.

However, Cornudet had a flask of rum; he offered it round, but was met with a cold refusal. Loiseau alone accepted two sips, and as he handed back the flask, he ex-pressed his thanks: "Anyhow, it's good stuff; it warms one and takes the edge off one's hunger." The alcohol

cheered him up, and he suggested imitating the sailors in
the lifeboat in the song and eating the fattest of the passengers.
This indirect allusion to Boule de Suif shocked the more
refined members of the party. There was a chilly silence;
only Cornudet smiled. The two nuns had stopped mumbling over their rosaries, and, with their hands buried in their
wide sleeves, were sitting motionless, keeping their eyes
carefully on the ground, no doubt offering up to heaven
the discomfort they were enduring.

At last at three o'clock, while they were in the middle of
an interminable stretch of flat country, without a village
in sight, Boule de Suif, bending down quickly, brought
out from under the seat a large basket covered with a white
napkin.

She took out first a small china plate and a slender silver
drinking-cup, then a great pie-dish containing two whole
chickens in aspic, ready carved; there were also visible in
the basket other good things wrapped up—meat pies, preserved fruits and sweet biscuits, enough food for a three
days' journey without having to rely on hotel meals: the
necks of four bottles of wine protruded from the parcels
of food. She took the wing of a chicken and began to eat
it delicately with one of the small rolls called Regency rolls
in Normandy.

Every eye was turned towards her. The smell of the
food spread, tickling every nostril and making every mouth
water, inducing a painful twitching of the muscles of the
jaw under the ear. The ladies' contempt for the harlot
increased in intensity, till they would have liked to kill her
or throw her out of the coach into the snow, with her
drinking-cup, her basket and her food.

But Loiseau could not take his eyes off the chicken-pie.
He said: "That's something like; Madame had more fore-
sight than the rest of us! Some people always think of
everything." She glanced at him: "Will you join me,

Sir? It's no fun having nothing to eat since breakfast."
He bowed: "I really can't refuse; I'm at the end of my
tether. In Rome one must do as the Romans do, mustn't
one, Madame?" And glancing round the coach, he added:
"At a moment like this one is glad to find a Good Samaritan."
He had a newspaper, which he spread out so as not to dirty
his trousers, and on the point of a knife, which he always
carried in his pocket, he speared a leg in its covering of
jelly, stripped the meat off with his teeth and then ate
it with such obvious relish that there was a great sigh of
longing all round.

Thereupon Boule de Suif in a low respectful voice suggested to the nuns that they should share her repast. They
both accepted unhesitatingly, and without raising their eyes
began to eat very quickly, after stammering their thanks.
Cornudet did not refuse his neighbour's offer either, and
the two of them made a sort of table with the nuns by
spreading newspapers over their knees.

Their mouths continued to open and shut, as they chewed
and swallowed, attacking the food ravenously. Loiseau in
his corner was making great efforts in a low voice to persuade his wife to follow suit. She refused for some time,
but at last, unable to endure the agonies of emptiness, she
gave way. Then her husband with formal politeness asked
"his charming neighbour" if he might offer his wife a mouthful; she replied with a pleasant smile: "But of course, Sir,
do," and handed him the pie-dish.

An awkward moment occurred, when they had opened
the first bottle of claret; there was only one drinking-cup.
They passed it round after wiping it. Only Cornudet, no
doubt out of mere politeness, put his lips on the place still
wet from his neighbour's mouth.

Surrounded by the others eating and suffocated by the
smell of food, the Comte and Comtesse de Bréville and
M. and Mme. Carré-Lamadon suffered the excruciating

torment associated with the name of Tantalus. Suddenly the manufacturer's young wife uttered a sigh, which made everyone turn round; she was as white as the snow outside. Her eyes closed and her head fell forward; she had fainted.

Her distracted husband appealed for help. No one knew what to do, till the elder of the two nuns, supporting the fainting lady's head, slipped Boule de Suif's drinking-cup between her lips and made her swallow a few drops of wine. The lady stirred, opened her eyes, smiled and declared in a weak voice that she was feeling quite well now. But, to prevent a repetition of the incident, the nun forced her to drink a cupful of claret, adding, " It's nothing but hunger."

Boule de Suif, getting very red and uncomfortable and looking at the four passengers who had eaten nothing, stammered: " Really, if the ladies and gentlemen wouldn't mind my offering them something . . ." Then she stopped, fearing they would be insulted. Loiseau broke in: " Dash it all, in a case like this we are all in the same boat, and we must pull together. Come, ladies, don't stand on ceremony; hang it all, accept her offer. Are we even sure of having a roof over our heads to-night? At our present pace we shan't get to Tôtes before midday to-morrow." There was a pause; no one dared to take the responsibility of being the first to accept.

But the Comte settled the question. He turned to the fat, shy girl and said in his most impressive manner: " We accept gratefully, Madame."

It was only the first step that was difficult. The Rubicon once crossed, they set to heartily. The basket was emptied; it had still contained a *pâté de foie gras*, a lark pie, a piece of smoked tongue, some Bergamot pears, a slab of Pont-l'Évêque cheese, some fancy biscuits and a cupful of gherkins and pickled onions, for Boule de Suif, like all women, adored strong flavours.

They could not well eat the prostitute's food and not

speak to her. So they began to talk, at first guardedly, then, as she showed admirable taste, they let themselves go more freely. Mme. de Bréville and Mme. Carré-Lamadon, whose manners were perfect, made themselves tactfully pleasant. The Comtesse in particular showed the affable condescension of the true patrician, proof against all vulgar contacts, and was charming. But the powerfully built Mme. Loiseau, who had the soul of a policeman, remained surly, saying little and eating heartily.

They talked about the war, of course. They told stories of Prussian atrocities and deeds of French heroism; and all these people, who were bent on saving their own skins, paid tribute to the courage of others. Soon they got on to personal experiences, and Boule de Suif told, with unaffected emotion and that command of vigorous phrase which such girls often possess to express their primitive feelings, how she came to be leaving Rouen. "I thought at first I should be able to stay," she said. "I had the house full of food, and I preferred to feed a few soldiers rather than leave home for some strange place. But, when I saw these Prussians, I couldn't stick it. Everything in me revolted, and I cried with shame all day. Oh! if only I were a man! I used to look at them out of the window, the fat swine in their spiked helmets, and my charwoman had to hold my hands to prevent my pitching the furniture out on to their heads. Then some were billeted on me; I went for the first one who came. They're no harder to strangle than anyone else! I'd have done for that one, if I hadn't been dragged off by the hair. After that I had to hide. At last I got a chance to leave Rouen, and here I am."

She was warmly congratulated. She was going up in the estimation of her companions, who had not shown such courage; and Cornudet, as he listened, smiled with the benevolent approval of a Father of the Church, just as a priest listens to the devout praising God; for bearded Radicals have the monopoly of patriotism as churchmen have of religion. He went on talking as if addressing a public meeting, in the exaggerated language of the proclamations posted up every day on the walls, and ended with an eloquent peroration, in which he soundly trounced " that scoundrel Badinguet ", as he called Napoleon III.

But Boule de Suif immediately fired up, for she was a Bonapartist. She got redder than a cherry, and, stuttering with indignation, she cried: " I should like to have seen you fellows in his place; that would have been a great sight, that would. It is you who betrayed him. There'd be nothing to do but get out of France, if the Government got into the hands of rotters like you."

Cornudet, unruffled, preserved his smile of disdainful superiority, but it was obvious that fur would soon be flying, when the Comte intervened, and with some difficulty pacified the exasperated harlot, laying it down with the full weight of his authority that all opinions sincerely held were deserving of respect. But the Comtesse and the manufacturer's wife, having in their heart of hearts the upper classes' unreasoning hatred of the Republic and an instinctive soft spot for the plumes and gold lace of a despotic government, felt attracted in spite of themselves to this dignified prostitute, whose sentiments bore such a strong resemblance to their own.

The basket was empty: the ten of them had finished it up without difficulty, only regretting that it had not been larger. Conversation went on for some time, though in a slightly chillier atmosphere after the end of the meal.

Night was coming on, the darkness was gradually increasing, and the cold, to which the process of digestion rendered them more sensitive, made Boule de Suif shiver, fat as she was. Mme. de Bréville offered her foot-warmer, the fuel in which had been renewed several times during the day,

and she at once accepted, for her feet were freezing. Mmes.
Carré-Lamadon and Loiseau gave theirs to the nuns.

The driver had lit his lamps; their bright lights shone on
the cloud of steam over the haunches of the sweating trace-
horses, and on both sides of the road lit up the snow,
which seemed to be streaming past under the moving
reflections.

It was pitch dark inside the coach; but suddenly there
was a sharp movement between Boule de Suif and Cornudet,
and Loiseau, peering into the blackness, thought he saw the
bearded man start back, as if he had received a good noiseless
kick.

Little points of light appeared in front on the road. It
was Tôtes. They had been travelling for eleven hours, and
the four half-hour halts, which had been allowed for the
horses to eat their oats and recover their wind, made thirteen
hours in all. They entered the little market town and
stopped in front of the Hôtel du Commerce.

The door opened and all the passengers started at a well-
known sound, the tapping of a sword-sheath on the ground.
Immediately a German voice shouted an order.

Although the coach had stopped, no one got out, as if
they all expected to be murdered as they stepped down.
Then the driver appeared, holding one of the lanterns,
which cast a sudden beam of light right down the coach,
revealing two rows of frightened faces with mouths open
and eyes staring in surprise and terror.

By the driver's side in the lantern light stood a German
officer, a tall young man, very slim and blond, in a uniform
as tight as a woman's corset, wearing on the side of his head
a flat shiny cap, which made him look like a page-boy in
an English hotel. His exaggerated moustache, with its long
straight hairs thinning out imperceptibly towards each end
and finishing in a single fair hair so thin that one could not
tell where it stopped, seemed to depress the corners of his

mouth and by stretching the skin of the cheek imparted a downward curl to the lips.

He invited the passengers to alight, in French with an Alsatian accent, saying curtly: "Get out, please!"

The two nuns were the first to carry out the order, with the docility of holy women trained to implicit obedience. The Comte and Comtesse emerged next, followed by the manufacturer and his wife, then by Loiseau, pushing in front of him his better—and larger—half; as he set foot on the ground, he wished the officer "Good evening", from motives of policy rather than politeness. The latter, with the insolence of the autocrat, stared at him without a word.

Boule de Suif and Cornudet, though near the door, were the last to get out, dignified and contemptuous in face of the enemy. The fat prostitute was trying hard to preserve her self-control and calm; the Radical was tugging furiously at his long reddish beard with a hand that trembled. They wanted to maintain their dignity, realizing that in encounters of this sort everyone is in some measure his country's representative, and both shocked by their companions' obsequiousness; the woman was anxious to show that she had more self-respect than her neighbours, the respectable women, while the man, feeling that it was up to him to set an example, made his whole attitude carry on the task of resistance he had begun by blocking the roads.

They made their way into the huge kitchen of the inn, and the German demanded the permit to travel, signed by the Commander-in-Chief, which contained the name, description and profession of each passenger; he scrutinized them all carefully, comparing their appearance with the written particulars.

Then he said shortly: "All correct," and disappeared.

Everyone breathed again. They were still hungry, and supper was ordered. It took half-an-hour to get it ready

and, while two maids bustled about attending to it, they
went up to their rooms, which were all off a long passage
ending in a glass door with a number indicating its function.

At last they were ready to sit down, when the proprietor
himself appeared. He was an ex-horse-dealer, a fat asthmatic
man, with a permanent wheezy huskiness, which made it
necessary for him to be always clearing his throat. His
father had saddled him with the name of Follenvie.

He inquired for Mademoiselle Élisabeth Rousset.

Boule de Suif started and turned round:

" Yes, that's me."

" Mademoiselle, the Prussian officer wants to speak to you
at once."

" To me? "

" Yes, if you are Mademoiselle Élisabeth Rousset."

She hesitated, thought for a moment and then said with
emphasis:

" Perhaps he does, but I'm not going."

There was a general stir; everyone was talking, wondering
what was the reason for the order. The Comte went up to
her:

" You are wrong, Madame. Your refusal may cause
considerable trouble not only for yourself, but for all of us.
It is always a mistake to withstand superior force. I am sure
there can be no risk in complying with this order; some
formality has probably been omitted."

Everybody seconded him; they begged, urged, lectured
her and finally overcame her reluctance, for they all feared
the consequences of obstinacy. At last she said:

" Well, I'm only doing it for your sakes."

The Comtesse took her hand:

" And we are very grateful to you."

She left the room, and they awaited her return before
sitting down. Everyone regretted that it was not one of
the others who had been sent for instead of this quick-

tempered, uncompromising harlot; and they began mentally to rehearse the commonplaces they would utter in case they were all sent for in turn.

But in ten minutes she returned, breathing hard, scarlet, choking with rage; she stammered:

" Ah! the blackguard, the blackguard! "

Everybody was curious to know what had happened; and, as the Comte was insistent, she replied with considerable dignity:

" No, it's nothing to do with you; I'm not talking about it."

They sat down round a large soup-tureen, from which the smell of cabbage rose. In spite of the shock they had had, supper was a cheerful meal. The cider was good; the two nuns and the Loiseaus took it because it was cheap; the others called for wine, while Cornudet demanded beer. He had his own method of uncorking the bottle, to give the contents a good head, and examining the liquor by tilting the glass, which he then raised between the lamp and his eye in order to appreciate the colour. While he was drinking, his full beard, which retained the tint of his favourite beverage, seemed to quiver with emotion and his eyes squinted in order not to lose sight of his mug; he seemed to be discharging the one function for which he had been born. He looked as though he was mentally bringing together and, as it were, establishing a connexion between the two great passions of his life, Pale Ale and the Revolution; he certainly never tasted the one without thinking of the other.

M. and Mme. Follenvie were having their dinner at the far end of the table. The man, wheezing like a worn-out steam-engine, had too much congestion in the chest to be able to speak while eating, but the woman talked continuously. She recounted all her impressions of the arrival of the Prussians, what they did and what they said, cursing them first of all because they cost her money, and secondly because she had two sons in the army. She addressed her remarks mainly to the Comtesse, flattered at having a real lady to talk to.

Then she lowered her voice, as she touched on more delicate subjects, and her husband from time to time interrupted her: " You'd better keep your mouth shut, Madame Follenvie," but she paid no attention and went on: " Yes, Madame, the creatures do nothing but eat potatoes and pork, and pork and potatoes. And don't you believe they're clean; not a bit of it, they make messes everywhere, if you'll excuse my mentioning it. You should see them drilling hour after hour and day after day; they're all out there in the field, they advance, about turn, right turn, left turn. If only they were working on the land or road-making in their own country! No, Madame, these soldiers are no use to anybody. The wretched people have to feed them, and all they are taught is how to kill! I'm just an old uneducated woman, I know, but, when I see them wearing themselves out foot-slogging from morning to night, I says to myself: ' When people are making useful discoveries all the time, why must others take so much trouble to destroy things?' Why, isn't it a shame to kill people, whether they are Prussians or English or Poles or even Frenchmen? If you murder someone who has injured you, it's bad, because you get punished; but if you kill young men with rifles, like game, that's good, because the one who kills the most gets a medal. No, I just can't understand it."

Cornudet raised his voice:

" War is barbarism when it is aggression against a peaceable neighbour, but it is a sacred duty when it is in defence of one's country."

The old woman cast down her eyes:

" Yes, it's quite a different thing to defend oneself; but wouldn't it be better to kill all the kings, who make war for their own amusement?"

Cornudet's eye flashed: "Bravo, Comrade!" he cried.

M. Carré-Lamadon was thinking hard. Though he was an enthusiastic admirer of the great military leaders, this peasant woman's common-sense made him think of all the wealth that would be created in a country by so many hands now unemployed, and consequently wasted, of all this man-power kept unproductive, while it might be set to great industrial tasks needing centuries to complete.

But Loiseau, leaving his seat, entered into a whispered conversation with the innkeeper. The fat man laughed, coughed and spat. His huge stomach heaved with laughter at his neighbour's jokes, and he bought from him six quarter-casks of claret for the spring, when the Prussians would be gone.

Immediately after supper everyone, being tired out, went to bed.

However, Loiseau, who had kept his eyes open, got his wife into bed, and put first his ear and then his eye to the keyhole to try to discover what he called "the secrets of the passage".

After about an hour he heard a rustling sound, looked quickly, and saw Boule de Suif, fatter than ever in a blue cashmere dressing-gown edged with white lace. She had a candle in her hand, and was making for the lavatory at the end of the passage. But the next door opened a chink, and when she returned a few moments later, Cornudet in his shirt-sleeves was following her. They were talking in whispers; then they stopped. Boule de Suif seemed to be trying hard to keep him out of her room. Loiseau unfortunately could not hear what was being said, but at last, as they raised their voices, he caught a few words. Cornudet was being very pressing: he was saying: "Look here, you're being a fool; what difference does it make to you?"

She seemed annoyed and replied:

" No, my dear man; there are times when you simply can't do it. Besides it would be shameful here."

He apparently failed to understand, and asked why. Then she lost her temper, raising her voice still more:

" Why? You want to know why, when there are Prussians in the house, perhaps in the next room ?"

He was silenced. This patriotic modesty on the part of a prostitute, who would not submit to caresses in the neighbourhood of the enemy, must have awoken in his heart the remnants of his self-respect, for after merely giving her a kiss he tiptoed back to his room.

Loiseau, all lit up, left the keyhole, skipped across the room, put on his bandana night-cap, and, pulling back the sheet covering his wife's bony frame, woke her up with a kiss, whispering: " Do you love me, darling? "

Then silence reigned in the house. But there soon arose from some undefined direction, which might have been attic or cellar, a powerful, monotonous, regular snore, a long-drawn muffled sound, like the vibrations of a pressure boiler; M. Follenvie was asleep.

As it had been decided to start at eight o'clock, everybody met early in the kitchen; but the coach, with its roof covered with snow, stood deserted in the centre of the yard without horses or driver. They looked for him in the stables, the hay-lofts and the coach-houses. Then the men made up their minds to search the town and went out. They found themselves in the main square, with the church at one end, and along the sides, low houses, in which Prussian soldiers could be seen. The first man they saw was peeling potatoes. The second, further on, was scrubbing out the barber's shop. Another, bearded up to the eyes, was kissing a crying baby, rocking it on his knees and trying to stop its tears; and the stout peasant women, whose husbands were in the army fighting, were explaining by signs to their obedient conquerors the various jobs to be done—the wood to be chopped, the soup to be prepared, the coffee to be ground; one of them was even doing the washing for his hostess, an old woman who couldn't do anything for herself.

The Comte, in surprise, questioned the verger, who was coming out of the priest's house. The old church servant replied: " Oh! these fellows aren't so bad; they say they aren't Prussians; they come from farther away, I don't quite know where from, and they've all left a wife and children at home; the war's no fun for them, you see! There'll be just as much distress in Germany as here. Besides, we're not too badly off at the moment, because they don't do any harm, and they work as if they were in their own homes. You see, poor people must help each other. It's the rich who make wars."

Cornudet, shocked at the pleasant relations that had been established between conquerors and conquered, turned back, preferring to shut himself up in the inn. Loiseau made a joke: " They're restocking the country." M. Carré-Lamadon put it more politely: " They're making reparations."

But they couldn't find the driver. At last he was discovered in the village café, sitting quite friendly at the same table as the officer's batman. The Comte tackled him: " Weren't you told to have the horses harnessed to start at eight o'clock?"

" Yes, but that was countermanded later."

" What do you mean?"

" I was ordered not to put the horses in at all."

" By whom?"

" The Prussian Town Major, of course."

" Why?"

" I don't know; go and ask him. I've been told not to harness the horses, so I'm not doing it; that's that."

" Did he give you the order himself?"

" No, the innkeeper gave me the order from him."

" When?"

" Yesterday evening, just as I was going to bed."

The three men returned, much disturbed.

They asked for M. Follenvie, but the maid replied that the master never got up till ten on account of his asthma; she had been expressly forbidden to wake him earlier except in case of fire.

They wanted to interview the officer, but that was entirely out of the question, though he was billeted at the inn, M. Follenvie alone having access to him on civilian matters. So they waited. The women went up to their rooms again and busied themselves with various little jobs.

Cornudet settled himself in the chimney-corner in the kitchen, where a good fire was blazing. He had one of the little tables brought in from the café and a bottle of beer, and he took out his pipe, which in Radical circles enjoyed a respect almost as great as his own, as if its service to Cornudet was service to the country. It was a magnificent meerschaum, beautifully coloured, as dark as its master's teeth, and fragrant, curved, gleaming, a joy to handle, an integral part of his face. He sat there motionless, his glance fixed now on the glowing ash in the bowl, now on the froth on the top of his glass; and after each drink he ran his long thin fingers through his thick greasy hair, while he sucked at his moustache with its fringe of foam.

Loiseau, on the pretext of stretching his legs, went out to sell some wine to the local retailers. The Comte and the manufacturer began talking politics, looking forward to the future of France. The one believed in the Orléans family, the other in some unknown saviour, a hero who would appear at the last desperate moment, a du Guesclin, a Joan of Arc perhaps, or another Napoleon I. If only the Prince Imperial were not so young! As he listened to them, Cornudet smiled like a man for whom the future held no secrets. His pipe scented the whole kitchen.

As ten o'clock was striking, M. Follenvie appeared. They questioned him at once, but he could only repeat the same words two or three times over: "The officer says to me, 'M. Follenvie, you will forbid the horses to be harnessed for this party to-morrow. I do not wish them to start without orders from me. You understand? That is all'."

Then they demanded to see the officer. The Comte sent in his card, to which M. Carré-Lamadon added his name with his full titles. The Prussian sent word that he would see the gentlemen after his lunch, about one o'clock.

The ladies reappeared and, in spite of their anxiety, did fair justice to the meal. Boule de Suif seemed out of sorts and extraordinarily upset.

They were just finishing their coffee, when the orderly came to fetch the gentlemen.

Loiseau joined the original pair. When they tried to persuade Cornudet to go with the deputation to add to its impressiveness, he proudly announced that he refused to have any dealings with the German; and he returned to his chimney-corner, calling for another bottle of beer.

The three men went upstairs and were shown into the best room in the hotel, where the officer received them, lounging in an arm-chair with his feet on the chimney-piece, smoking a long porcelain pipe and wearing a gaudy dressing-gown, doubtless looted from some middle-class home deserted by its Philistine owner. He did not rise or greet them, or even look at them. He presented a perfect example of the overbearing offensiveness of the typical soldier in the moment of victory. After a pause he finally said:

"What do you want?"

The Comte acted as spokesman:

"We are anxious to start, Sir."

"Well, you can't."

"May I venture to inquire the reason for this refusal?"

"Because I forbid it."

" I should like to point out, Sir, with all respect, that your Commander-in-Chief gave us a permit to travel to Dieppe. I do not think we have done anything to deserve your severity."

" I forbid it, that's all; you may go."

The three men bowed and retired.

They spent a wretched afternoon. They could not understand the cause of the German's capricious refusal; the strangest explanations were offered. Everyone stayed in the kitchen, and the discussion went on interminably; the most improbable suggestions were made. They were being held as hostages—but why? They were to be taken away as prisoners or, more likely, a large ransom would be demanded. They were panic-stricken at this idea. The richer ones were the more frightened, seeing themselves already compelled, in order to save their lives, to empty sackfuls of gold into the hands of this insolent soldier. They racked their brains for convincing lies to conceal their wealth, and be taken for the poorest of the poor. Loiseau took off his watch-chain and hid it in his pocket. Night was falling, and this increased their apprehensions. The lamp was lighted and, as there were still two hours before dinner, Mme. Loiseau proposed a game of Trente et Un; it would take their minds off their troubles; the suggestion was adopted. Cornudet himself put out his pipe out of politeness and took a hand.

The Comte shuffled and dealt. Boule de Suif had thirty-one in her first hand; and soon interest in the game made them forget their anxiety. But Cornudet noticed that the two Loiseaus were systematically cheating.

As they were sitting down to dinner, M. Follenvie reappeared and, clearing his throat loudly, he announced:

" The Prussian officer wishes to know if Mademoiselle Elisabeth Rousset has changed her mind yet."

Boule de Suif remained standing, very pale; then, suddenly flushing a fiery red, she became speechless with fury. At last she burst out:

"Tell this blackguard, this skunk, this filthy swine of a Prussian, that I won't do it; you understand, never, never, never!"

The fat innkeeper left the room. Boule de Suif was surrounded and questioned and pressed by everyone to reveal the mystery of her visit. At first she refused, but she was soon carried away by her rage: "What does he want? What does he want? He wants to go to bed with me!" she shouted. So keen was their indignation that the crudity of the language shocked nobody. Cornudet brought his mug down on the table so hard that it broke. There was a chorus of execration against this contemptible soldier, a burst of anger which united the whole party to resist, as if each was involved in the sacrifice demanded. The Comte declared with disgust that these Germans were behaving just like the Huns of old. The women in particular expressed to Boule de Suif their warm and affectionate sympathy. The nuns, who only appeared at meal-times, kept their eyes on the ground and said nothing.

Nevertheless they all had their dinner, when their first indignation had subsided; but there was little conversation; everyone was thinking.

The ladies retired early; and the gentlemen, as they enjoyed their smoke, got up a game of écarté, to which M. Follenvie was invited, the intention being to question him tactfully as to the means to be employed to overcome the officer's obstinacy. But his attention was so concentrated on his hand that he heard nothing and did not answer any of their questions, repeating continually: "Let's get on with the game, gentlemen!" His concentration was so great that he even forgot to spit, with the result that his chest got congested from time to time and his wheezy lungs sounded the whole asthmatic scale, from low deep notes to the high-pitched huskiness of a prentice cockerel.

He refused to go upstairs, even when his wife, who was

dropping with sleep, came to fetch him. So she went off alone, for she was an " early bird", always up with the sun, while her husband was a " late bird ", always ready to sit up at night with his friends. He shouted after her : " Put my egg-flip in front of the fire ", and went on with the game. When they saw there was nothing to be got out of him, they declared they must be going and went off to bed.

Next morning they were up fairly early with vague hopes and an ever-increasing desire to be off, terrified at the prospect of having to spend another day in this horrible little inn.

Alas ! the horses were still in the stable and the driver nowhere to be seen. Having nothing to do, they hung about round the coach.

Lunch was a depressing meal. A certain coolness towards Boule de Suif was noticeable, for the night, with its opportunity for reflexion, had somewhat modified their attitude. There was now a feeling almost of annoyance with the prostitute for not having gone secretly to the Prussian, in order to have a pleasant surprise for her companions in the morning. What could have been simpler? Who would have been any the wiser anyhow? She could have saved her face by getting the officer to say that she had acted solely from pity for their predicament. It couldn't have made any difference to her.

But no one was yet prepared to confess to such thoughts.

In the afternoon, as they were bored stiff, the Comte proposed a stroll round the village. Everybody wrapped up carefully, and the little party set off, with the exception of Cornudet, who chose to stay by the fire, and the nuns, who spent all day in church or in the priest's house.

The cold, which was becoming more severe every day, stung nose and ears cruelly ; feet became so painful that every step was torture, and when the country came into view, it looked so dreadfully depressing under the unbroken shroud of snow that they all immediately turned tail, their blood frozen and their spirits paralysed.

The four women walked in front, with the three men a little behind.

Loiseau, gauging the general feeling, suddenly asked if "that bitch" intended to make them stay much longer in such a hole. The Comte, with his usual gallantry, said that so distressing a sacrifice could not be demanded of any woman, and that the offer must come from herself. M. Carré-Lamadon observed that, if the French launched a counter-attack through Dieppe, as was suggested, the clash must take place at Tôtes. This thought worried the others. "Suppose we escaped on foot," said Loiseau. The Comte shrugged his shoulders: "How can you think of such a thing in all this snow, with our wives? Besides, we should at once be pursued, and caught in ten minutes and brought back prisoners at the mercy of the soldiers." It was true, and nothing more was said.

The ladies were talking clothes, but a certain constraint was perceptible between them. Suddenly at the end of the street the officer appeared. His tall figure in the wasp-waisted uniform stood out sharply defined against the background of snow; he was walking with his knees wide apart, the gait affected by soldiers anxious not to dirty their carefully polished boots.

He bowed as he passed the ladies, and glanced contemptuously at the men, who for their part retained enough self-respect not to take off their hats, though Loiseau made a half-hearted movement with his hand in the direction of his head.

Boule de Suif had blushed up to the roots of her hair; and the three married women were conscious of a feeling of humiliation at being seen by this soldier in company with the prostitute, whom he had treated so scandalously.

Then they began to discuss him, his figure and his looks.

Mme. Carré-Lamadon, who had known a great many officers and judged them with the eye of an expert, pronounced him quite presentable; she even expressed regret that he was not a Frenchman, because he would make a very good-looking Hussar, who would certainly captivate any woman's heart.

Once back at the inn, they didn't know what to do with themselves. Sharp words were even exchanged over trifles. Dinner, eaten in silence, was soon over, and everyone went up to bed, hoping to kill time by sleeping.

When they came down next morning, they looked tired and irritable; the women hardly spoke to Boule de Suif.

The church bell rang; it was for a baptism. The fat prostitute had a child that was being brought up in a peasant family in Yvetot. She scarcely saw him once a year, and never worried about him, but at the thought of the baby to be christened a sudden overpowering affection for her own child awoke in her heart, and she insisted on attending the ceremony.

As soon as she had gone, they all looked at one another and chairs were pulled up, for they realized that the moment had come when a decision must be taken. Loiseau had an idea; he proposed to suggest to the officer that he should detain Boule de Suif alone and let the others go.

M. Follenvie again acted as intermediary, but returned almost at once. The German, knowing human nature, had refused to listen to him. He insisted on keeping the whole party till his demand was complied with.

Then the strain of vulgarity in Mme. Loiseau came out: " But we don't want to die of old age here. Since it is the slut's job to do this with any man, I don't consider that she has any right to refuse one man rather than another. Why, I ask you, she took anybody she could get in Rouen, even coachmen! Yes, Madame, the Prefect's coachman. I know all about it; he gets his wine at our place. And to-day, when it's a question of getting us out of a hole, she picks and chooses, the wretch! Personally I think this officer has behaved very well. He may have had to go without for a long time; and there were three of us here whom he would doubtless have preferred. But no, he is content with a common whore. He respects married women. Just think, he could have done as he liked. He had only to say 'I insist,' and he could have taken us by force with the help of his men."

The two women shivered slightly. The eyes of pretty Mme. Carré-Lamadon shone and she went a little pale, as if she felt herself already being raped by the officer.

The men, who had been discussing the matter by themselves, now joined the ladies. Loiseau was raging, and wanted to hand over the hussy to the enemy bound hand and foot. But the Comte, scion of three generations of ambassadors and himself looking every inch a diplomat, favoured the use of tact. "We have got to convince her," he said.

So a plot was hatched.

The women moved closer and voices were lowered; the discussion became general, each one giving an opinion. But the proprieties were carefully observed. The ladies in particular found delicacies of phrase and charming subtleties of expression for the coarsest ideas. It would have conveyed nothing to a stranger, so punctiliously were the conventions of polite conversation followed. But the thin veneer of modesty, the armour of every society woman, is skin-deep, no more; so they revelled in their equivocal subject, really tremendously thrilled. They felt quite in their element, stimulated with the sensual pleasure of an epicure chef, at work on another's supper.

They quickly recovered their spirits, so entertaining did the discussion become in the end. The Comte told a few smoking-room jokes, and told them so well that everyone smiled. After him Loiseau produced some even more questionable stories without giving offence; and the thought brutally expressed by his wife convinced them all: "Since it's this woman's job, why should she refuse one man rather than another?" The good-looking Mme. Carré-Lamadon was inclined to opine that in her place she would have refused this particular man less sternly than most.

Detailed plans were laid for the blockade as if against some besieged fortress. Everyone agreed to his or her part, to the arguments to be used and the tactics to be employed. The plan of attack was drawn up, the stratagems to be elaborated and the surprise attacks to be launched, in order to compel this citadel of flesh and blood to admit enemy penetration.

Cornudet, however, remained aloof, refusing to have anything to do with the plot.

Everyone was so intent on the matter in hand that they did not hear Boule de Suif return. But the Comte whispered a low "'Sh!" which made them all look up. There she was. A sudden silence fell, and a certain feeling of embarrassment at first prevented anyone speaking to her.

At last the Comtesse, more accustomed than the rest to the hypocrisies of polite society, asked her: "Did you enjoy the christening?"

The fat prostitute, still under the influence of her emotion, gave them all the details, what everyone had looked like and how they had stood, even describing the church. She added: "It's so helpful to pray sometimes."

Up to lunch-time the ladies confined themselves to being pleasant to her, in order to lull any suspicion and render her more amenable to their suggestions.

But as soon as they were seated, the scouting began. First of all the subject of self-sacrifice was casually introduced into the conversation. Instances from ancient history were quoted—Judith and Holofernes—and then, as if accidentally, Lucretia and Sextus, and Cleopatra inviting the Roman generals to her bed in order to reduce them to slavish obedience. Then came at some length an entirely fictitious account, hatched in the imagination of these uneducated plutocrats, of the way in which Roman matrons went to Capua to lavish their charms on Hannibal, his officers and his hordes of mercenaries. They cited all the women who have checked conquerors by making of their own bodies a battle-field, a symbol of power, a weapon; women who by their heroic caresses have overcome some hideous or hated enemy and sacrificed their chastity on the altar of vengeance or devotion. They even referred allusively to the well-born English lady who had allowed herself to be inoculated with a horrible contagious disease in order to infect Bonaparte, who was only saved by sudden impotence at the moment of the fateful meeting.

And all these stories were told in polite language, which never outraged conventional propriety, though enthusiastic approval calculated to inspire emulation was sometimes allowed to appear.

The final conclusion might have seemed to be that in this imperfect world a woman's only duty was the continual sacrifice, the perpetual surrender of her body to the lust of a licentious soldiery.

The two nuns were apparently not listening, lost in deep meditation; Boule de Suif was silent.

All the afternoon she was left to her own reflexions. But instead of calling her Madame, as they had done hitherto, they now simply addressed her as Mademoiselle, no one quite knew why, as if they wanted to take her down a peg from the pinnacle of respect she had gained and make her realize her shameful situation.

As the soup was being served, M. Follenvie appeared again with the same message as on the previous day: "The Prussian officer wishes to know if Mademoiselle Élisabeth Rousset has changed her mind yet."

Boule de Suif replied curtly: "No, Sir!"

At dinner the concerted attack faltered. Loiseau made three unfortunate remarks. Everyone was cudgelling his brains for fresh examples without success, when the Comtesse, perhaps on the spur of the moment from a vague desire to pay homage to religion, questioned the elder of the nuns about the great exploits in the lives of the saints. Certainly many of them had done things which we should consider criminal; but the Church is always ready to grant free absolution even for heinous crimes committed for the greater glory of God or for the good of one's neighbour. It was a strong argument, of which the Comtesse made the most. Then, either by one of those tacit understandings, that unconfessed desire to please so characteristic of all who wear the uniform of the church, or simply as a lucky result of pure stupidity, which is always eager to oblige, the old nun powerfully reinforced the attack. They had thought her shy, but she proved outspoken, long-winded and downright. She was not worried by the tentative arguments of the casuist: doctrine, as she knew it, was cast-iron; her faith knew no reservations, her conscience saw no difficulties. She considered Abraham's sacrifice perfectly natural, for she would have slain father or mother without a qualm on an order from on high; and in her view nothing could fail to please the Lord, if the intention was praiseworthy. The Comtesse, exploiting the sacred authority of her unexpected ally to the full, elicited from her an edifying paraphrase of the moral axiom " the end justifies the means "

She put the question:

" So, Sister, you think that God accepts any means and pardons any deed, when the motive is pure? "

" Who can doubt it, Madame? An action, blameworthy in itself, often becomes meritorious by virtue of the intention which inspires it."

And so they went on, elucidating the will of God, anticipating His judgments and attributing to Him an interest in many things which were strictly not His business at all.

It was all allusive, very tactful and discreet. But every word from the nun in her coif made a breach in the prostitute's desperate defence. Then the conversation took a different turn; the nun with the rosary spoke of the houses of the order, of her Mother Superior, of herself and of her attractive companion, Sister Saint Nicephorus. They had been sent for to Havre to nurse the hundreds of soldiers in hospital there with smallpox. She described the men's miserable plight, with details of the disease. And, while they were delayed on the way by the caprice of this Prussian, a large number of Frenchmen, whose lives they might have saved, might die. She specialized in nursing soldiers; she had been in the Crimea, in Italy and in Austria, and, as she told the story of her campaigns, she suddenly revealed herself as one of those fife and drum Sisters, who seem cut out to follow camps and pick up the wounded in the ebb and flow of battle, and are more competent than an officer to keep tough undisciplined soldiers in order with a word. A typical, hard-bitten Army Sister, with a face scarred and pitted with innumerable pock-marks, she seemed a living illustration of the ravages of war.

Her words seemed to make a great impression and no one had anything to add.

As soon as the meal was over, they went up at once to their rooms, and did not come down next morning till late. Lunch was uneventful. The seed sown the day before was being allowed time to sprout and bear fruit. The Comtesse suggested a walk in the afternoon; and the Comte offered Boule de Suif his arm, according to plan, and let the others go on in front.

He talked to her in the confidential fatherly tone, slightly condescending, adopted by respectable elderly gentlemen in conversation with such girls; he called her " My dear child ",

and talked down to her from the height of his commanding
social position of undisputed superiority. He plunged
straight into the heart of the matter:

"So you prefer to keep us here, exposed like yourself to
all the dangers which would result from a check to the
Prussian troops, rather than agree to grant a favour which
has so often been a matter of routine in your life: am I
right?"

Boule de Suif made no answer.

In the end he overcame her resistance by his gentle reasonableness and his appeal to her better feelings. He had the
knack of remaining the Comte all the time, though he could
be attentive at need and flattering, in fact thoroughly agreeable. He emphasized the service she would render them and
spoke of their gratitude; then, suddenly dropping the formal
mode of address, he said cheerfully: "And you know, my
dear, he would be able to boast of having enjoyed an unusually attractive girl, the like of whom he won't easily find
in his own country."

Boule de Suif did not answer and rejoined the party.

When she got back, she went straight to her room and
did not reappear. Anxiety was acute. What was she going
to do? If she still refused, what was to happen?

Dinner-time arrived; they waited for her in vain. Presently M. Follenvie came in and announced that Mademoiselle Rousset was not feeling well and that they were to
start dinner. They all pricked up their ears; the Comte
approached the innkeeper and whispered: "Is it all right?"
"Yes." For the sake of propriety he said nothing to his
companions, merely giving them a slight nod. Immediately
a great sigh of relief came from every heart and joy was
depicted on every face. Loiseau shouted: "Three cheers!
I'll stand champagne, if there's any to be had in this place."
Mme. Loiseau had a shock when the proprietor returned
with four bottles. Everyone suddenly became noisily

talkative, full of ribald joviality. The Comte appeared for the first time conscious of Mme. Carré-Lamadon's charms, and the manufacturer paid flattering attentions to the Comtesse. Conversation became animated and vivacious, full of witty sallies.

Suddenly Loiseau, looking worried, raised his hand and shouted: "Silence!" Everyone fell silent, surprised, almost frightened. Then, straining his ears and beckoning for silence with both hands, he raised his eyes to the ceiling, listened again, and then said in his natural voice: "Don't worry, it's all right."

They were slow to understand, but soon there was a general smile.

A quarter of an hour later he went through the same performance again, repeating it at intervals throughout the evening. He pretended to be questioning someone on the floor above, giving equivocal advice of the kind that passes for wit among commercial travellers. From time to time he assumed an expression of sadness, sighing: "Poor girl!"—or else he murmured angrily between his teeth: "Ugh! The Prussian swine!" Sometimes, when the subject had been forgotten, he would repeat several times in ringing tones: "Now that's enough, that's enough!" adding as though to himself: "I do hope we shall see her again; I hope he won't kill her, the wretch!"

Although these witticisms were in the worst possible taste, they went down and shocked no one, for indignation, like other things, depends on circumstances, and everyone was conscious of an atmosphere gradually becoming heavily charged with suppressed sexual excitement.

Over the dessert even the women made discreetly risky allusions. Eyes were bright, for they had drunk a good deal. The Comte, who even in his most questionable remarks preserved his air of patrician gravity, amid general applause compared their present position to the joy of shipwrecked sailors, who see their way of escape southwards opening before them at the end of the arctic winter.

Loiseau, who was by now very talkative, got up with a glass of champagne in his hand, crying: "Here's to our rescue!" Everyone stood up and applauded. Even the two nuns, on the invitation of the ladies, consented to take a sip of the sparkling wine, which they had never tasted before; they pronounced it like fizzy lemonade, but nicer.

Loiseau summed up the situation.

"It's a pity there isn't a piano; we might have had a bit of a hop."

Cornudet had not said a word or made a movement. He seemed deep in serious meditation, tugging furiously at his full beard from time to time, as if he wanted to make it still longer. At last, towards midnight, as the party was on the point of breaking up, Loiseau, who was by now unsteady on his legs, dug him suddenly in the ribs and said in a thick voice: "You're pretty glum this evening; you don't say much, comrade."

But Cornudet raised his head and, casting a piercing glance fiercely round the company, said: "I tell you, you've all done a shameful thing to-night." He got up, went to the door, repeating "a shameful thing," and disappeared.

This chilled the atmosphere for a moment. Loiseau, taken aback, stood dumbfounded; but he soon recovered himself and suddenly roared with laughter: "Sour grapes, old man, sour grapes!" As no one knew what he meant, he told them about "the secrets of the passage." There was a renewed outburst of merriment; the ladies were terribly tickled. The Comte and M. Carré-Lamadon laughed till they cried; they refused to believe it.

"Really? Are you sure? He wanted to . . ."

"I tell you, I saw him."

"And she refused. . . ."

"Because the Prussian was in the room next door."

" I don't believe it ! "

" I swear it's true."

The Comte was choking with laughter, and the industrialist was holding both his sides. Loiseau went on :

" So, you see, this evening he wasn't amused, not a bit."

And the three of them started off again, roaring with laughter, till they were gasping for breath.

Then they separated. But Mme. Loiseau, who had a bitter tongue, observed to her husband, as they were getting into bed, that the laugh of that prudish little Carré-Lamadon woman had rung false all the evening. " You know, when a woman loses her head over a uniform, it doesn't matter a bit whether a Frenchman or a Prussian is inside it. My God ! I'm sorry for that sort of woman."

And all night in the dark passage there were little rustling noises, barely audible, like breathing, the patter of bare feet, and faint creakings. They certainly did not go to sleep till very late, for lines of light were long visible under the doors. Champagne is apt to produce this result ; it is said not to encourage sleep.

Next day the snow was dazzling in the bright winter sunshine. The horses, ready harnessed, were standing at the door, while a flock of white pigeons, with their thick plumage all puffed out and their pink eyes with a black speck in the centre, were strutting about between the legs of the six horses, scratching at the steaming dung in their search for food.

The driver, swathed in his sheepskin coat, was puffing at his pipe on the box, and all the light-hearted passengers were getting food wrapped up for the journey.

They were only waiting for Boule de Suif. At last she appeared.

She seemed worried and shamefaced, and came forward shyly towards her companions, who with one accord turned away, as if they had not seen her. The Comte took his wife's arm ceremoniously and moved away from the contamination of her presence.

The fat prostitute stopped in amazement; then, plucking up courage, addressed a respectful "Good morning, Madame," in a low voice to the manufacturer's wife. The latter merely gave a supercilious nod, accompanied by a stare of outraged virtue. Everybody seemed busy about something and gave her a wide berth, as if she were infectious. Then they made a rush for the coach, where she arrived last, and in silence took the seat she had occupied on the first part of the journey.

They did not seem to see her or recognize her; but Mme. Loiseau, with an angry glance in her direction, said in a low voice to her husband: "I'm glad I'm not sitting next to her."

The heavy coach started, and the second part of the journey began.

No one spoke at first. Boule de Suif did not dare to raise her eyes. She was conscious at the same time of anger against all her neighbours and of humiliation at having given way, as if she had been defiled by the embraces of the Prussian, into whose arms their hypocrisy had cast her.

But the Comtesse, turning to Mme. Carré-Lamadon, soon broke the uncomfortable silence.

"I believe you know Mme. d'Étrelles?"

"Yes, she's a great friend of mine."

"What a delightful woman!"

"Quite charming! A most unusual person, and a clever woman too, and an artist to her finger-tips; she sings divinely and draws extremely cleverly."

The manufacturer was chatting to the Comte, and from time to time through the clatter of the coach windows single words were audible—dividend warrant—due date—option—futures.

Loiseau, who had pocketed at the inn the old pack of cards,

greasy from lying about for five years on the tops of badly wiped tables, started a game of bézique with his wife.

The nuns seized the long rosaries hanging from their belts, crossed themselves simultaneously, and suddenly began to move their lips more and more rapidly, the speed of the whispered words increasing, as if they were racing each other to reach the end of their prayers; and from time to time they kissed a medallion, made the sign of the cross again and resumed their rapid interminable mumble.

Cornudet, motionless, was lost in thought.

After three hours' travelling, Loiseau gathered up the cards. "I'm getting hungry," he declared.

Then his wife reached for a parcel done up with string, from which she took out a piece of cold veal. She cut it into thin neat slices and they both set to.

"Suppose we follow suit," said the Comtesse. There was general agreement, and she unpacked the food that had been put up for the two families. In one of those elongated pie-dishes, the lid of which is ornamented with a china hare to indicate that it conceals a hare in aspic, lay a savoury mess, in which white rivers of bacon flowed over the brown flesh of the hare, mixed with other meat finely minced. A large slab of Gruyère cheese, wrapped in a piece of newspaper, bore the words "News in Brief" that had come off on its sticky surface.

The two nuns unwrapped a slice of sausage that smelt of garlic; and Cornudet, burying both his hands at the same time in the capacious pockets of his ulster, brought out of one pocket four hard-boiled eggs, and from the other the crusty end of a loaf. He shelled the eggs, dropping the shells in the straw underfoot, and bit into them, scattering over his huge beard little bits of yolk, which shone in it like stars.

Boule de Suif, in the hurry and confusion in which she had got up, had not had time to think of ordering anything; and she watched all her neighbours placidly eating, speech-

less with anger. In the first surge of her indignation she
had opened her mouth to tell them exactly what she thought
of their behaviour, in a flood of abuse that rose to her lips;
but she could not utter a word, choked with the violence of
her feelings.

No one was looking at her or thinking of her. She felt
overwhelmed by the contempt of these respectable cads,
who had first sacrificed her, and then cast her aside as a thing
unclean, for which they had no further use. Then she
remembered her own big basket, full of good things which
they had guzzled—of her two chickens in aspic, of her meat
pies, her pears and her four bottles of claret. Suddenly her
anger collapsed, like a string breaking when it has been
stretched too tight, and she felt she was going to cry. She
made a terrific effort, stiffening herself and swallowing her
sobs like a small child, but her tears would not be denied
and welled up shining in her eyes, till two great drops over-
flowed and coursed slowly over her cheeks; these were
followed by others streaming like water dripping from a
rock, and falling at regular intervals on the prominent curve
of her bosom. She was sitting bolt upright, staring straight
in front of her, her face pale and set, hoping that no one
would notice her.

But the Comtesse saw her and made a sign to her husband.
He shrugged his shoulders, as if to say: " Well, what about
it? It's not my fault."

Mme. Loiseau smiled triumphantly and whispered:
" She is weeping for her shame."

The two nuns were back at their devotions, having wrapped
up the remains of their sausage in a bit of paper.

Cornudet, who was digesting his eggs, stretched his long
legs under the seat opposite, leant back, folded his arms,
smiled like a man who has just thought of a good joke, and
began to whistle the Marseillaise under his breath.

Every brow darkened. The song of the Republic was

obviously not to his neighbours' taste. They got nervous and jumpy, and looked like dogs about to howl at the sound of a barrel-organ. He noticed this, and went on. Sometimes he even hummed the words:

> O sacred love of home and country,
> Your light shall vanquish tyrants base!
> To loose the chains of slavery,
> The land is all ablaze!

They were now making better pace, the snow being harder; and all the way to Dieppe, through the long tedious hours of the drive over the bad road, through the falling dusk, and later on in the blackness of the night, he kept up his remorseless monotonous whistling with grim obstinacy. He forced his weary exasperated audience to follow the song right through from beginning to end, accentuating the rhythm of the tune, so that they could not fail to recall the words.

Boule de Suif went on crying; and from time to time a sob, which she could not restrain, was audible in the darkness between the verses.

THE MINUET

GREAT tragedies hardly affect me at all. (It was Jean Bridelle who was speaking, an elderly bachelor generally reckoned anything but a sentimentalist.) I have seen active service and I have stepped over dead bodies unmoved. The crude violence of nature or man may bring cries of horror or indignation to our lips, but it does not wring the heart or send the shiver down the spine, as does the sight of certain heart-rending, though trivial, incidents.

A mother's most poignant grief is, I am sure, the loss of her child, as the loss of his mother is for a man. It is an overwhelming shock, a shattering, knock-out blow; but one recovers from a tragedy of this kind as one does from a gaping wound which bleeds freely. Certain encounters, however, certain things sensed or guessed, certain secret sorrows, certain tricks of fate awaken in us a world of painful memories; suddenly there opens before us a chink of that mysterious door leading to the intricate maze of the subconscious mind with its incurable misery, the more deep-seated because apparently not acute, the more agonizing because apparently indefinable, the more enduring because apparently imaginary; there persists in the soul as it were a trail of sadness, an after-taste of bitterness, a feeling of disillusion, which it takes years to dispel.

I can never forget two or three incidents, which no one else, I am sure, would have noticed, but which have inflicted on my soul deep invisible wounds that will never heal.

You probably would not understand the lasting effect on me of these brief emotional experiences; I will tell you one of them. It happened years ago, but I remember it as if it were yesterday. Possibly it is only my imagination that is responsible for the impression it made upon me.

I am fifty; at that time I was a young law student. Rather serious-minded and a bit of a dreamer, philosophically a confirmed pessimist, I avoided noisy restaurants and rowdy company; women bored me. I used to get up early, and one of my greatest joys was a solitary walk about eight o'clock in the Luxembourg garden.

You fellows never knew this garden, did you? It was like some survival from the eighteenth century, as charming as an old lady's gentle smile. Thick hedges separated straight narrow walks, peaceful between two walls of carefully clipped foliage. The gardener's shears remorselessly cut back the branches of the dividing hedges; and here and there one came upon flower-beds or shrubberies as orderly as schoolboys out for a walk, clumps of magnificent rose-bushes or symmetrical rows of fruit-trees.

The whole of one corner of this fascinating garden was devoted to bees. Their thatched hives, cunningly spaced on planks, opened doors no bigger than a thimble to the sunlight; and all along the paths one met the buzzing golden insects, the real denizens of this haunt of peace, flitting up and down the narrow quiet walks.

I used to go there nearly every morning and sit down and read. Sometimes I let my book fall on my knee, to dream and listen to the hum of Paris all around me and enjoy the perfect restfulness of these old-world arbours.

But I soon noticed that I was not the only person to frequent this spot as soon as the gates opened, and sometimes, coming round the corner of a clump, I found myself face to face with a queer little old gentleman. He wore silver-buckled shoes, full-fall knee-breeches and a snuff-coloured frock-coat, with a lace cravat and an astonishing grey beaver hat, with a broad brim, dating back to the Flood.

He was very, very thin, and angular, and he simpered

and smiled all the time. His lively eyes blinked and winked under the ceaseless twitching of his eyelids; and he always carried a magnificent stick with a gold knob, obviously a cherished relic of the past.

At first I was merely surprised at this figure of fun; then I became extraordinarily interested in him, and I used to watch him through the hedges and follow him at a distance, stopping at the corners of the shrubberies to avoid being seen.

Suddenly one morning, thinking himself quite alone, he began making strange movements; first a few little jumps, then a bow, then he executed an *entrechat*, which still showed agility in spite of his spindly legs; then he began a graceful pirouette, hopping and jigging up and down in the oddest way, smiling to an imaginary audience, bowing with his hand on his heart, contorting his poor old body like a marionette, waving pathetically ridiculous greetings to the empty air. He was dancing!

I stood dumbfounded, wondering which of us was mad, he or I. But suddenly he stopped, came forward like an actor to the footlights, and backed with a winning smile, throwing kisses like a leading lady, with his trembling hands, to two rows of clipped shrubs. After that he gravely resumed his walk.

From that day forward I kept my eye on him, and every morning he went through his amazing performance again. I felt an overpowering desire to speak to him. At last, taking my courage in both hands, I raised my hat and addressed him. "A lovely day, Sir!" He bowed: "Indeed yes, Sir! The sort of weather we used to have long ago."

A week later we were friends and he had told me his story. He had been Ballet-master at the Opera in the time of Louis XV. His beautiful walking-stick was a present from the Comte de Clermont. When the conversation turned on dancing, there was no stopping him.

One day found him in confidential mood: "I married La Castris, Sir. I will introduce you, if you like, but she only comes here in the afternoon; you see, this garden is our delight, it is our life, all that remains to us of the past. We feel we could not live without it. There is nothing modern about it; it has distinction, has it not? Here I seem to breathe an air which has not changed since I was young. My wife and I spend all our afternoons here, but I come in the morning as well, for I am an early riser."

Immediately after lunch I returned to the Luxembourg, and soon I saw my friend giving his arm with old-world politeness to a tiny little old lady in black, to whom I was introduced. It was La Castris, the famous ballerina, toast of princes, favourite of the King, idol of all that courtly age, which seems to have left behind a haunting perfume of gallantry in the world.

We sat down on a bench; it was May. The scent of flowers was wafted along the trim walks; the cheerful sunshine streamed through the leaves, splashing us with pools of light. La Castris' black dress seemed drenched with liquid gold.

The garden was deserted; the rumble of traffic could be heard in the distance.

"Could you explain to me," I asked the old dancer, "what the Minuet was like?"

He started. "The Minuet, Sir, is the queen of dances and the dance of queens, if you understand me. Now that Kings are no more, the Minuet has disappeared."

Then in stilted language he began a long, extravagantly enthusiastic panegyric, which was quite incomprehensible. I wanted him to describe the steps with every figure and gesture. But he got hopelessly mixed, nervously exasperated at his own inability, till he gave it up.

Suddenly, turning to his aged companion, who had remained gravely silent, he said: "Élise, I wonder if you would—it would be so sweet of you—would you be willing to show this gentleman what it was by dancing it with me?"

She looked all round anxiously, rose without a word and took up her position facing him.

Then I witnessed a sight I shall never forget. They advanced and retired with childish ceremoniousness, smiled, swayed, bowed, skipped, like two old-fashioned dolls, set in motion by an antiquated mechanism, now slightly defective, constructed long ago by some master-craftsman after the mode of his day. I looked on with conflicting emotions, an indefinable sadness in my heart; it was as if I were the spectator of a scene at once pathetic and ridiculous, the ghostly survival of a vanished age. I wanted to laugh and cry at the same time.

Suddenly they stopped; they had come to the end of the figures of the dance. For a few seconds they stood facing one another; then they fell sobbing into each other's arms.

Three days after that I left for the country and I never saw them again. When I returned to Paris two years later, the garden had been done away with. What became of them without their beloved old-world pleasance, with its maze, its perfume of the past and the delightful nooks and corners of its arbours? Are they dead? Are they wandering about the modern streets in hopeless exile? Do they dance, as gibbering ghosts, a fantastic minuet among the churchyard cypresses, along the paths between the rows of tombstones in the moonlight?

Their memory haunts me like an obsession and tortures me like a festering wound, I can't explain why; but I expect you will consider the whole thing ridiculous.

MADAME HUSSON'S MAY KING

WE had just passed Gisors, where I had been woken up by the porters shouting the name of the station, and I was on the point of going to sleep again when a terrific jolt threw me forward on top of the stout lady opposite. The engine had broken a wheel and toppled over across the track. The tender and the luggage-van, also derailed, were lying by the side of the expiring monster, which was gurgling and groaning, hissing and puffing and spitting: it was just like a horse that has fallen down in the street; with heaving flanks, panting chest and steaming nostrils, its whole body quivers, but it seeems quite incapable of making the slightest effort to get up and go on.

No one was killed or seriously hurt, though there were a few bruises, for the train had not got up speed after the stop; and we looked disconsolately at the maimed iron monster, which would not be able to take us any further and was blocking the line, possibly for a considerable time, as a breakdown train would have to be sent for from Paris.

It was then ten o'clock in the morning, and I at once made up my mind to go back to Gisors and get some lunch.

As I walked along the track, I kept saying to myself: "Gisors, Gisors, I know somebody here. Who on earth is it? I'm sure I've got a friend here." Suddenly a name flashed across my mind: "Albert Marambot." He was an old school friend, whom I hadn't seen for at least twelve years, and who was practising as a doctor in Gisors. He had often written to invite me, and I had always promised to come but had never done so. This time I would take advantage of my opportunity.

I asked the first person I met: "Do you know where Dr. Marambot lives?"

He replied without hesitation in the drawling Normandy accent: "Rue Dauphine." And in fact I saw on the door of the house he pointed out a large brass plate with the name of my old school-fellow. I rang the bell, but the servant, a slow-moving peasant girl with tow-coloured hair, repeated vacantly: "Not at 'ome, not at 'ome."

Hearing the clatter of forks and glasses, I shouted: "Hullo, Marambot!"

A door opened and a stout man with side-whiskers appeared with a napkin in his hand, looking annoyed.

I should never have recognized him; he looked at least forty-five—a living illustration of the effect of life in the country, which makes people heavy and stout and prematurely aged. In a flash, before I had time to shake hands, I realized just how he lived, how his mind worked—his whole philosophy of life. I pictured to myself the heavy meals, which accounted for his paunch, his after-dinner siestas and his torpor, while he slowly digested his food sipping his brandy, and his cursory examination of his patients, while his thoughts wandered to the chicken roasting in front of his kitchen fire. His conversation would be about cooking, cider, brandy and wine, recipes for various dishes and the ingredients of sauces, as was vividly suggested by a glance at the florid puffiness of his face, the coarseness of his lips and his lack-lustre eye.

I said to him: "You don't recognize me. I'm Raoul Aubertin."

He flung his arms round me and nearly crushed the breath out of me, and the first thing he said was:

"You haven't lunched, have you?"

"No, I haven't."

"What luck! I'm just sitting down and I've got an excellent trout."

Five minutes later I was sitting down opposite him.
I asked:

" You're not married? "

" You bet I'm not."

" And you enjoy life here? "

" I'm quite busy, I haven't time to be bored. I've got my patients and my friends. I do myself well and my health is good, I laugh a lot and I enjoy my sport. Altogether it's not so bad."

" You don't find life dull in this little town? "

" No, old man, not when one knows how to fill in one's time. After all, a small town is very much like a big one. Fewer things happen and amusements are less varied, but they mean more to you; you meet fewer people, but you meet them more often. When you know every window in a street, each one means more to you and interests you more than a whole street in Paris.

" A small town is quite amusing, you know—exceedingly amusing. Take this one—Gisors. I know it like the back of my hand from its origins centuries ago down to the present day. You've no idea how entertaining its history is."

" You're a native? "

" I? No; I come from Gournay, its neighbour and rival. Gournay is to Gisors what Lucullus was to Cicero. Here everyone is ambitious; people talk about the pride of Gisors. At Gournay everybody is interested in food, and people talk about the guzzlers of Gournay. Gisors despises Gournay, but Gournay laughs at Gisors. This part of the world is a great joke."

I realized that I was eating something quite out of the ordinary—soft-boiled eggs wrapped in a covering of meat-jelly flavoured with herbs and slightly iced.

To please Marambot, I smacked my lips and said: " This *is* good! "

He smiled.

" Two things are needed for it—good jelly, which isn't easy to come by, and good eggs. How rare good eggs are! The yolk ought to be slightly red and really tasty. I keep two hen-runs, one for eggs and one for the table. I feed my laying hens in a special way, on a theory of my own. In an egg, as in the flesh of a chicken, or in beef or mutton or milk—in everything, in fact—there persists, and one ought to be able to taste, the flavour, the quintessence of the animal's previous feeding. How much better food would be if people took more trouble about that! "

I laughed:

" So you are interested in your food? "

" I should think so! Only fools are not interested in their food. A man is interested in his food in just the same way as he is an artist or a member of one of the learned professions or a poet. The palate, my dear fellow; is a delicate organ, which can be trained, and ought to be treated with respect, just as much as the eye or ear. To have no appreciation of food is to be without an exquisite faculty—the faculty of registering the characteristic excellences of different dishes—just as a man may be unable to appreciate the qualities of a book or a work of art; it is to be without an essential sense, one of those which mark the superiority of man over the beasts; it is to belong to one of the countless classes of weaklings, unlucky people and fools that go to make up the human race—in fact, it is to have an uneducated palate, just as some people have uneducated minds. A man who can't tell a crayfish from a lobster, a herring—that king of fish which embraces all the succulence, all the flavours of the sea—from a mackerel or a whiting, or a bergamot from a duchess pear, is the sort of man who would mistake Balzac for Eugène Sue, a Beethoven symphony for a military march by a regimental bandmaster, or the Apollo Belvedere for the statue of General de Blanmont! "

" Who on earth is General de Blanmont? "

" Oh, of course, you wouldn't know. It's obvious you don't come from Gisors! My dear fellow, I've just told you that the pride of Gisors is proverbial, and never was reputation better deserved. But let's have our lunch first, and then I'll take you round the place and tell you about it."

He stopped talking from time to time to drink half a glass of wine with deliberation, gazing at it affectionately, as he replaced it on the table.

With his napkin knotted round his neck, his cheeks flushed, his eye bright and his whiskers framing his mouth, which was working methodically, he was a really comic sight.

He made me eat till I nearly burst. Then, as I wanted to make my way back to the station, he took me by the arm and dragged me out into the streets.

The town, a typical pleasant country town, dominated by its fortress, the most interesting monument of seventh-century military architecture in France, dominates in its turn a long, green valley, where the heavy Normandy cows browse and chew the cud in the meadows.

The Doctor said to me:

" Gisors, a town with a population of four thousand, close to the borders of the Department of the Eure, is mentioned as early as Caesar's *Commentaries*—Caesaris Ostium, then Caesartium, Caesortium, Gisortium, Gisors. I won't take you to see the Roman camp, traces of which are still clearly visible."

I was laughing and I replied:

" My dear fellow, you seem to me to be the victim of a definite disease that you ought to study as a doctor, called parish-pump parochialism."

He stopped abruptly:

"Parish-pump parochialism is nothing but natural patriotism. It begins with love for my home, extends to my town, and finally includes my province, because I find there the same customs as in my village; but if I love my frontier, if I defend it, if I get angry when my neighbour violates it, it is because I feel that there is a threat to my home, because the frontier, which I don't know, is the way into my province. Yes, I'm a Norman, a genuine Norman. So, in spite of my feeling against the Germans and my desire for revenge, I do not hate and loathe them as I do the English, the real hereditary enemy, the Norman's natural foe, because the English have invaded this country where my forbears lived, looted and laid it waste a score of times, and hatred of this treacherous people has been handed on to me with my life by my father. . . . Look here, there's the General's statue."

"What general?"

"General de Blanmont, of course! We had to have a statue; it's not for nothing that people talk about the pride of Gisors. So we discovered General de Blanmont. Look at this bookseller's window."

He dragged me to a bookseller's shop, where some fifteen volumes, yellow, red or blue, caught the eye.

As I read the titles, I couldn't help roaring with laughter; they were:

"Gisors, its origins and its future, by M. X., member of several learned Societies";

"The History of Gisors, by the Abbé A.";

"Gisors, from Caesar to our own day, by M. B., landed proprietor";

"Gisors and neighbourhood, by Doctor C. D.";

"Glorious Gisors, by a Student."

"My dear fellow," went on Marambot, "not a year passes—not a single year, believe it or not—without a new history of Gisors being published here; we've got twenty-three already."

"And what are the glories of Gisors?" I asked.

"Well, I won't go through the whole list; I'll only mention the high lights. First of all we've got General de Blanmont, then Baron Davillier, the famous ceramic expert, who explored Spain and the Balearic Islands and revealed the magnificent Hispano-Arab porcelain to collectors. In the realm of letters we have the justly renowned journalist, now dead, Charles Brainne, and among our living worthies the distinguished editor of the *Rouen Intelligencer*, Charles Lapierre, and many, many others besides."

We were walking up a long street, slightly uphill; the whole length of it was in the blazing June sun, which had driven everyone indoors.

Suddenly, at the far end of the street, a drunk man staggered into view. He came towards us, lurching forward, with arms swinging and unsteady on his legs, in spurts of three, six or ten quick steps, always followed by a pause. When his short-lived bursts of energy had carried him half-way down the street, he stopped dead, swaying precariously, hesitating between falling down and a new dash forward. Then suddenly he started off uncertainly and bumped into a house, to which he seemed to cling, as if he wanted to get into it through the wall. Presently he turned round with a jerk and stared straight in front of him, his mouth open and his eyes blinking in the sun; at last, pushing off with his back against the wall, he started on his way again.

A small light-brown dog, a half-starved mongrel, followed him, barking, stopping when he stopped and going on again when he went on.

"Hullo!" said Marambot, "there's Mme. Husson's May King!"

I asked in surprise: "Mme. Husson's May King? What do you mean by that?"

The Doctor began to laugh:

"Oh! that's what we call a drunk man here. It comes from an old story, that has now become a local legend, though it's perfectly true."

"Is it an amusing story?"

"Yes, it's extremely amusing."

"Then let me hear it."

"Right you are! Once upon a time there was an old lady in the town called Mme. Husson, very virtuous herself, and self-appointed guardian of virtue in others. You realize I'm giving you the real names, not fictitious ones. Mme. Husson devoted her life to good works, helping the poor and encouraging the deserving; she was short, walked with short, quick steps, wore a black silk wig and was a stickler for politeness and good manners; on very good terms with the Almighty through his representative, Father Malou, she had a profound instinctive horror of vice, particularly of that vice which the Church calls "lechery". Cases of conception before marriage made her see red, exasperating her to such an extent that she was not responsible for her actions.

"Well, it was the period when all the villages round Paris were crowning virtuous girls as May Queens, and it occurred to her that it would be nice to have a May Queen in Gisors.

"She broached the matter to Father Malou, who immediately drew up a list of candidates.

"But Mme. Husson had an old servant called Françoise, as uncompromising as herself.

"As soon as the priest had left, the mistress called her servant and said:

"'Look here, Françoise, here's Father Malou's list of girls suggested for the prize of virtue; I want you to learn all you can of their reputation in the place.'

"And Françoise went into action. She picked up all the gossip, all the stories, all the tittle-tattle, everything suspicious. In order not to forget anything, she wrote it all down in her kitchen account-book among her expenses, and showed it every morning to her mistress, who, after adjusting her spectacles on her thin nose, was able to read:

"'Bread   .   .   .   .   .   2d.
"'Milk   .   .   .   .   .   1d.
"'Butter   .   .   .   .   4d.

" Malvina Levesque got into trouble last year with Maturin Poilu.

" ' Leg of mutton	.	.	.	1s. 0½d.
" ' Salt	.	.	.	.	½d.

" ' Rosalie Vatinel seen in Riboudet wood with Césaire Piénoir by Mme. Onésime, the laundress, on July 20th, at dusk.

" ' Radishes	.	.	.	½d.
" ' Vinegar	.	.	.	1d.
" ' Salts of sorrel	.	.	.	1d.

" ' Joséphine Durdent is not believed to be guilty of misconduct, though she writes to the young Oportun, who is in the Army at Rouen and sent her a present of a hat by the carrier.'

" Not a single girl passed this searching examination without losing marks. Françoise questioned everybody— the neighbours, the tradespeople, the schoolmaster and the Sisters of Mercy at the school, and picked up every item of gossip.

" As there isn't a girl in the world who has not been talked about by some woman, there wasn't a single one found in the neighbourhood with an entirely clean record.

" Now, Mme. Husson insisted that Gisors' May Queen, like Caesar's wife, must be above suspicion, and she was aghast, flabbergasted, in despair, when she saw her servant's kitchen book.

" The area under examination was widened to include the near-by villages, but with no better luck.

" The Mayor was consulted, but his candidates failed. Those nominated by Dr. Barbesol were no more successful, in spite of his detailed scientific guarantees.

" So one morning Françoise, who had just come in from shopping, said to her mistress :

" ' Look, Madame, if you want to give the crown to someone, the only possible person round here is Isidore.'

" Mme. Husson became lost in thought.

" She knew Isidore—the son of Virginie, the fruiterer—quite well. His proverbial chastity had been the joke of Gisors for years, affording a humorous topic of conversation in the town as well as amusement to the girls, who made merry over teasing him.

" He was over twenty, tall, awkward, shy, slow in mind and body; he used to help his mother in the shop, and spent his time cleaning fruit and vegetables, sitting on a chair in front of the door. He had a morbid horror of skirts, which made him cast down his eyes whenever a woman smiled at him in the shop; and this shyness, which was common knowledge, made him the butt of all the mischievous girls in the neighbourhood. Any equivocal remark or broad joke or salacious allusion made him blush so quickly that Dr. Barbesol had nicknamed him ' modesty's thermometer '. ' Was he really as innocent as he seemed? ' wondered the neighbours, with a wink. Was it only an instinctive presentiment of unknown shameful secrets, or was it really a feeling of repulsion for the sordid physical contacts dictated by love, which raised such powerful feelings in the son of Virginie, the fruiterer? All the young scapegraces of the place, as they ran past the shop, used to shout obscenities just for the fun of seeing him lower his eyes; the girls amused themselves by walking up and down in front of him telling dirty stories in order to drive him into the house. The more brazen of them vamped him openly, just for the joke of the thing, arranging to meet him and suggesting all manner of improprieties.

" So Mme. Husson was plunged in deep thought.

" Isidore was certainly a case of unusual virtue, which everyone knew was unassailable. No one, not even the most incredulous sceptic, could possibly have dared to suspect

him of the smallest breach of any part of the moral law.   He
had never been seen in a bar either, or met in the streets after
dark.   He went to bed at eight and got up at four.   He was,
in fact, a paragon of perfection.

" Nevertheless Mme. Husson still hesitated.   The idea of
substituting a May King for a May Queen worried her and
made her slightly anxious, and she decided to consult Father
Malou.

" He replied :   ' What is it that you want to reward?   It
is virtue, is it not, nothing else?   What does it matter to you,
then, whether it is male or female?   Virtue is immortal, it
knows neither country nor sex;   it is simply Virtue.'

" Thus encouraged, Mme. Husson went to find the Mayor.

" He expressed entire approval.   ' We will make an
impressive ceremony of it,' he said, ' and another year, if we
find a girl as deserving as Isidore, we will give the crown to
a girl.   We shall, in fact, be setting a good example to
Nanterre.   Let us not be exclusive, let us welcome virtue,
wherever we find it.'

" When Isidore was told, he blushed scarlet and seemed
pleased.

" The ceremony was accordingly fixed for August 15th,
the feast of the Assumption, and the Emperor Napoleon's
birthday.

" The Town Council had decided to make a big thing of
the ceremony, and a platform had been erected on the Royal
Parade—a delightful extension of the ramparts, where I will
take you presently.

" By a natural revulsion of public feeling, Isidore's virtue,
which had been previously laughed at, had suddenly become
an object of respect and envy, now that it was going to bring
him £20, plus a Savings Bank Book, and more consideration
and reputation than he would know what to do with.   The
girls now regretted their flippancy, their jokes and the
freedom of their behaviour.   And Isidore, though still

modest and shy, wore a slightly self-satisfied air, which proclaimed the pleasure he felt.

" By the evening of August 14th the whole of the Rue Dauphine was gay with bunting. By the way, I have forgotten to tell you how the street got its name.

" It would appear that the Dauphine—one of them, I don't remember which—during a visit to Gisors, had been kept so long at her official reception that in the middle of a triumphal progress through the city she stopped the procession in front of one of the houses in this street and cried : ' What a lovely house ! I should like to go over it. Who does it belong to?' She was told the name of the owner, who was sent for, found and presented to the Princess, shy but proud.

" She left her carriage, entered the house and insisted on going over it from cellar to attic, even remaining locked in alone in one room for some minutes.

" When she came out again, the crowd, flattered by the honour conferred upon one of the citizens of Gisors, shouted : ' Long live the Dauphine !' But some wit composed a ribald little ditty, and the road took the name of the royal Princess, for :

> The Princess, feeling none too well,
> Sans book, sans beadle and sans bell,
> Relieved at last, with drops of water
>   Baptized the quarter.

" But to return to Isidore.

" The route which the procession was to follow had been strewn with flowers, as is done on Corpus Christi Day, and the National Guard paraded under its commanding officer, Major Desbarres, a Grand Army veteran, who could point with pride, by the side of the glass case with the Cross of Honour conferred by the Emperor himself, to a cossack's beard shorn from its owner's chin by a stroke of the Major's sabre during the retreat from Russia. The contingent under his command, moreover, was a crack formation, well known all over the province, and the Gisors Grenadier Company was invited to all the functions of note for fifteen or twenty leagues round. It is said that, when King Louis-Philippe was reviewing the Eure Militia, he halted in amazement in front of the Gisors company and cried: 'Who are these magnificent men?' 'The Gisors contingent,' replied the General. 'Ah! I might have known it,' murmured the King.

" So Major Desbarres marched off with his men, headed by the band, to escort Isidore from his mother's shop.

" After the band had played a short selection under the windows, the May King appeared in person.

" He was dressed from head to foot in white ducks, and wore a straw hat with a small sprig of orange blossom as a cockade.

" The question of his clothes had caused Mme. Husson much anxious thought; she hesitated between the black coat worn by boys at their first communion and an all-white suit. Her confidential adviser, Françoise, had decided her in favour of the white suit by pointing out that the May King would look like a swan.

" Behind him appeared his patroness and sponsor, Mme. Husson, beaming with pleasure. She took his arm as she left the house, and the Mayor fell in on the other side of the May King. The drums rolled. Major Desbarres gave the command: 'Present arms!' and the procession moved off to the church, in the midst of a vast concourse of people who had come in from the neighbouring villages.

" After a short Mass and a moving address from Father Malou, they made their way to the Royal Parade, where the banquet was to be served in a marquee.

" Before they sat down, the Mayor made a speech. This is what he said, word for word. I learnt it by heart, for it is a noble address:

" ' Young man, a worthy lady, beloved by the poor and respected by the rich, Mme. Husson, to whom I should like to express the thanks of the whole neighbourhood, had the idea—the happy and beneficent idea—of establishing in this town a prize for virtue, as a valuable encouragement to all who live in this beautiful district.

" ' You, young man, are the first to be crowned of a line of kings of sobriety and chastity. Your name will remain for all time at the head of the roll of those who have won this award; and I want you to realize that your whole life must be of a piece with this auspicious start. To-day, in the presence of this worthy lady who rewards your behaviour, in the presence of these citizen-soldiers who have paraded to do you honour, in the presence of this vast concourse deeply stirred by the occasion, who have met together to do homage to you, or rather to virtue in your person, you are giving a solemn undertaking to the town and to all of us to continue till your last hour the admirable example of your youth. Never forget, young man, that you are the first seed to be sown in this field of hope; may you bring forth the fruits that we expect of you! '

" The Mayor took three steps forward and, flinging his arms round the sobbing Isidore, pressed him to his heart.

" The May King could not have explained why he was weeping; his feelings were a confused jumble of pride and vague pleasurable emotions.

" Next the Mayor placed in one of his hands a silk purse, in which jingled twenty golden sovereigns, and in the other . . . a Savings Bank Book. And in solemn tones he declared: ' Honour and glory and prosperity to Virtue ! ' Major Desbarres boomed: ' Hear ! hear ! ' The Grenadiers cheered, and the populace applauded, while Mme. Husson wiped a tear from her eye.

" Then they sat down at the table, where the banquet was served.

"It was a magnificent spread, and of inordinate length. Dish followed dish; golden cider and red wine fraternized in neighbouring glasses, to mingle later inside. The clatter of plates, the hum of conversation and the soft music of the band combined to make a continuous low murmur, which faded into the silence of the cloudless sky among the darting swallows. From time to time Mme. Husson straightened her black silk wig, which somehow got tilted rakishly over one ear, as she chatted with Father Malou. The Mayor was talking politics passionately with Major Desbarres, and Isidore went on eating and drinking all the time, as he had never eaten and drunk before. He took a helping, often two, of everything, realizing for the first time how comforting it is to feel one's belly filling up with good things, which one has first savoured on the tongue. He had skilfully undone the top button of his trousers, which were getting uncomfortably tight under the increasing pressure of his stomach: he did not talk much, and, though he was a little worried over the stain of a drop of wine that had fallen on his duck coat, he stopped eating at frequent intervals to raise his glass to his lips, drinking as slowly as possible in order to prolong the enjoyment.

"The moment for the toasts came. They were numerous, and were received with acclamation. Evening was coming on, and they had been at table since noon. Already thin wisps of whitish mist were floating about in the valley, veiling the streams and meadows for the night as if in a sheet; the sun was setting and the cows were mooing in the distance in the fog that covered the pastures. At last it was all over, and the guests were making their way back to Gisors. The procession had broken ranks and was straggling along anyhow. Mme. Husson had taken Isidore's arm, and was giving him much excellent advice in emphatic terms.

"They stopped in front of the fruiterer's shop, and the May King was left at his mother's house.

" She was not yet in. She had been invited by her own family to celebrate her son's triumph, and had lunched at her sister's, after following the procession to the marquee.

" So Isidore found himself alone in the shop in the gathering dusk.

" He sat down on a chair, excited by the wine and his feelings of pride, and looked round him. Carrots, cabbages and onions filled the closed room with a strong smell of vegetables, the harsh tang of the market-garden, with which mingled the sweet penetrating scent of strawberries and the faint elusive perfume of a basket of peaches.

" The May King took a peach and ate it in great mouthfuls, though his stomach was already as tight as a drum. Then suddenly, in a wild burst of elation, he began to dance; and something jingled in his coat.

" In surprise, he put his hands in his pockets and brought out the purse with the twenty pounds, which he had forgotten in his intoxication. Twenty pounds! What wealth! He emptied the gold coins on to the counter and spread them out with a caressing movement, keeping his fingers wide apart so as to see them all the time. There were twenty of them—twenty gold sovereigns. They shone on the wood in the deepening darkness, and he counted them over and over again, putting his finger on each one in turn and murmuring: ' Two, four, six, eight, ten, twelve, fourteen, sixteen, eighteen, twenty.' Then he put them back in the purse, which he replaced in his pocket.

" Who will ever know, who could describe the terrible struggle between good and evil in the May King's soul, Satan's overwhelming attack, his stratagems and the temptations with which he assailed this shy, innocent heart? What suggestions, what imaginings, what longings did the Evil One invent to overcome and bring this virtuous soul to perdition? Mme. Husson's chosen champion seized his hat, which still had its little sprig of orange blossom, and, going out into the lane behind the house, disappeared into the night.

"Virginie, the fruiterer, who had been told that her son was home, returned almost immediately, and found the house empty. She waited, at first without undue anxiety; then, after a quarter of an hour, she made enquiries. The neighbours in the Rue Dauphine had seen Isidore enter the house and had not seen him come out again. They looked for him, but without success. At last his mother, who was beginning to get worried, hurried to the Town Hall, but the Mayor knew nothing beyond the fact that he had left the May King at his own door. Mme. Husson had just gone to bed when she was informed of her protégé's disappearance. She immediately put on her wig again and went personally to Virginie's house. Virginie, who, like all peasants, had little self-control, was in floods of tears, surrounded by her carrots, cabbages and onions.

"An accident was feared, but no one could suggest what had happened. Major Desbarres informed the police, who made a search all round the town; and on the Pontoise road the little sprig of orange blossom was discovered. It was placed on the table round which the authorities were sitting in conference. The May King must have fallen victim to some trick or some plot prompted by jealousy. But how could it have been carried out? What means had been employed to kidnap the guileless youth, and for what purpose?

"Weary of their fruitless search, the authorities went to bed. Virginie sat up alone weeping.

" The following evening, when the Paris coach arrived on its return journey, Gisors learnt, to its amazement, that the May King had stopped it two hundred yards outside the town, got in, paid his fare with a sovereign, pocketed the change, and had quietly alighted in the centre of the capital.

" There was considerable excitement in the place. Letters

passed between the Mayor and the head of the Paris police, but without result.

" Time went on, till a week had passed.

" Then one morning Dr. Barbesol, who was out early, caught sight of a figure in dirty white sitting on a doorstep asleep, with his head against the wall. He went up to him and recognized Isidore. He tried to rouse him without success. The ex-May King was sleeping so soundly that the doctor, unable to wake him, became alarmed as well as surprised, and went to get help to carry the young man to Boncheval's dispensary. When they picked him up, an empty bottle was found on the ground under him; and after smelling it the doctor declared that it had had brandy in it. This indication enabled him to take appropriate measures, which proved successful.

" Isidore was drunk, dead drunk, besotted after a week of dissipation, and not merely drunk, but so filthy that a dustman would have refused to touch him. His beautiful white duck suit had become a greyish-brown, greasy, filthy wreck, torn and revolting. He smelt of the sewer and the gutter and every haunt of vice.

" He was washed, lectured and confined to the house, which he did not leave for a week. He seemed ashamed of himself and contrite. They had not found on him either the purse with the twenty pounds or the Savings Bank Book, or even his silver watch, a treasured heirloom inherited from his father, the fruiterer.

" On the fifth day he ventured out into the Rue Dauphine. Inquisitive glances followed him as he walked along past the houses with lowered head and averted eyes. He passed out of sight, where the road leaves the town to plunge into the valley; but two hours later he reappeared, laughing hoarsely to himself and bumping into the walls. He was drunk, dead drunk.

" He proved incorrigible.

" Turned out of the house by his mother, he became a carman and drove coal-carts for the firm of Pougrisel, which is still in existence.

" His reputation as a drunkard became so great and spread so far that even at Evreux people talked of Mme. Husson's May King, and round here we still use this nickname for our boozers.

" It's an ill wind that blows nobody any good."

Dr. Marambot rubbed his hands as he finished his story. I enquired :

" Did you know the May King yourself? "

" Yes, I had the honour of closing his eyes."

" What did he die of? "

" An acute attack of Delirium Tremens, of course."

We were by this time near the old fortress, a mass of crumbling walls, dominated by the huge tower of Saint Thomas of Canterbury and the so-called Prisoner's Tower. Marambot told me the story of this prisoner, who, by using a nail, had covered the walls of his cell with carving, following the movement of the sunlight, as it came in through the narrow slit window.

Then I learnt that Clotaire II had given the patrimony of Gisors to his cousin Saint Romain, Bishop of Rouen, that Gisors ceased to be the capital of the whole of the Vexin after the Treaty of Saint Clair-sur-Epte, that the town is the most important strategic point in this part of France, and that, in consequence of this importance, it had been taken and retaken on countless occasions. By order of William Rufus, the famous engineer, Robert de Bellesme, built a powerful fortress, which had been attacked later by Louis the Fat, then by the Norman barons, defended by Robert de Candos, finally ceded by Geoffrey Plantagenet to Louis the Fat, recovered by the English through the treachery of the Templars, claimed by both Philippe-Auguste and

Richard Cœur de Lion, burnt by Edward III of England, who failed to take the castle, again stormed by the English in 1419, restored later to Charles VII by Richard de Marbury, captured by the Duke of Calabria, occupied by the League, lived in by Henri IV, and so on and so forth.

And Marambot, waxing enthusiastic, almost eloquent, kept repeating: "What blackguards these English are! And what drunkards too, my dear fellow; they are all May Kings, the hypocrites!"

Then, after a pause, pointing to the narrow stream, shining in the sun, as it wound through the grass-land:

"Did you know that Henry Monnier was one of the most regular fishermen on the banks of the Epte?"

"No, I didn't know it."

"And, Bouffé, my dear fellow, Bouffé, the stained-glass artist, lived here."

"You don't say so!"

"Yes, he did. I don't know how it is you don't know these things."

A VENDETTA

PAOLO SAVERINI's widow lived alone with her son in a tiny cottage on the ramparts of Bonifacio. The town, built on a mountain spur, in some places actually overhanging the sea, faces the low-lying coast of Sardinia across the strait with its bristling reefs. At its foot on the other side it is almost entirely enclosed by a gash in the cliff like a gigantic passage, which serves as its harbour. The little Italian or Sardinian fishing-boats and once a fortnight the old puffing steamer, which runs to and from Ajaccio, come up as far as the first houses, after threading their way between two precipitous walls of rock.

On the white mountain-side the collection of houses makes a whiter patch. They look like the nests of wild birds clinging to the rock looking down on this dangerous channel, into which few ships venture. The wind harasses the sea remorselessly, sweeping the barren coast sparsely covered with coarse grass; it roars down the strait, stripping the land bare on both sides. Patches of whitish foam round the black tips of the countless reefs, which pierce the waves in every direction, look like torn sheets floating and drifting on the surface of the water.

The widow Saverini's house, clinging to the very edge of the cliff, had three windows opening on to this wide desolate view.

She lived there alone with her son, Antoine, and their dog, Frisky, a great raw-boned bitch, with a long, rough coat, of the sheep-dog breed. The young man used her as a gun-dog.

One evening, after a quarrel, Antoine Saverini was treacherously knifed by Nicolas Ravolati, who escaped to Sardinia the same night.

When the old woman received her son's body, brought to her house by the passers-by, she shed no tears, but stood motionless for a long while, gazing at it; then, stretching out her wrinkled hand over the corpse, she vowed vengeance. She refused to let anyone stay with her, and shut herself up with the body and the howling dog.

The animal never stopped howling, standing at the foot of the bed, with head stretched out towards her master and tail between her legs. She stood as still as the mother, who bent over the body with staring eyes, now weeping silently, as she looked at him.

The young man, lying on his back, wearing his home-spun tweed jacket, with holes and rents in the breast, seemed to be asleep; but there was blood everywhere—on his shirt, which had been torn for first-aid dressings, on his waistcoat, on his trousers, on his face and on his hands. There were clots of dried blood on his beard and hair.

His aged mother began to speak to him; at the sound of her voice the dog stopped howling.

"Don't worry, my boy, my poor child, I will avenge you. Do you hear me? It's your mother's promise, and your mother always keeps her word, you know that."

And slowly she bent over him, pressing her cold lips against the dead man's lips. Then Frisky began howling again, uttering a long-drawn-out moan, monotonous, piercing, sinister.

They stayed there, the two of them, the woman and the dog, till morning.

Antoine Saverini was buried next day, and he was soon forgotten in Bonifacio.

He had left neither brother nor near relative, so there was no one to take up the vendetta on his behalf.

His old mother was the only person who never forgot.

Across the strait all day long she could see a white speck

on the coast. It was the little Sardinian village of Longo-sardo, where Corsican bandits took refuge when hard pressed by the police. They were almost the only inhabitants of the hamlet, facing the coast of their own country, and they waited there till it was safe to come back and return to the "maquis". It was in this village, she knew, that Nicolas Ravolati had taken refuge.

Entirely alone she sat all day long at her window and gazed at this village, dreaming of her vengeance. How was she to carry it out? She was a weak woman, with not much longer to live, but she had promised it, she had sworn it on the body. She could not forget or put it off. What was she to do? Now she could not sleep at night; she had no rest, no peace of mind, obstinately determined to find a way.

The dog dozed at her feet and at intervals raised her head and howled into space. Since her master's death, she often howled in this way, as if calling him; she would not be comforted, as if her animal soul also carried an indelible memory.

One night, as Frisky began to howl, the mother had a sudden inspiration, the fierce vindictive inspiration of a savage. She pondered over it all night, and, getting up at daybreak, she went to the church. There she prayed, bowed down on the stone floor, humbling herself before God, seeking help and support, praying that her poor worn-out body might have the strength to avenge her son.

Then she went home. She had in her back yard an old stove-in barrel, which collected the rain-water from the gutters; she turned it upside down, emptied it and fixed it on the ground with stakes and stones; next she chained Frisky in this kennel and went into the house.

That day she spent hours walking up and down restlessly in her room, her gaze always fixed on the coast of Sardinia, the refuge of the assassin.

The dog howled all day and all night. In the morning the old woman took her a bowl of water, but nothing else—no bread or soup.

Another day passed. Frisky slept, weak with hunger. Next day her eyes were shining, her coat bristling and she was tugging furiously at the chain.

Still the old woman gave her no food. The animal, by now maddened with hunger, kept up her hoarse barking. Another night passed. At dawn the widow Saverini went to a neighbour's house and begged two trusses of straw. She took some of her late husband's clothes and stuffed them with the straw to resemble a human body.

Having fixed a stake in the ground in front of Frisky's kennel, she fastened the dummy to it, so that it looked like a man standing there, and made a head out of a roll of old linen.

The dog looked at the straw man in surprise, and stopped howling, in spite of her hunger.

Next the old woman went to the pork-butcher's and bought a long piece of black blood-sausage. Returning home, she lit a wood fire in the yard near the kennel and grilled the sausage. Frisky, maddened, leapt about and foamed at the mouth, her eyes fixed on the grilling meat, the smell of which sharpened her appetite.

At last the old woman made this steaming savoury mess into a scarf round the dummy's neck. She tied it there with string, leaving it for some time, so that it soaked well into the straw. This done, she untied the dog.

With one terrific bound the animal leapt at the dummy's throat, and with her paws on the shoulders began to tear at it. She dropped to the ground with some of the meat in her mouth; then she returned to the attack, burying her teeth in the string, and tore out more bits of sausage, dropped once more to the ground, and again attacked with mad fury. She tore the face to pieces and reduced the whole throat to ribbons.

The old woman, motionless and silent, watched the dog with tense excitement. Then she chained her up again, kept her without food for another two days and repeated the strange performance.

For three months she trained the dog to this kind of fight, making her use her teeth to get her food. Now she no longer chained her up, but set her on the dummy with a gesture.

She had taught her to go for the figure and tear it to pieces, even when there was no food hidden in the neck. Afterwards she rewarded the animal with the sausage she had grilled for her.

Whenever the dog saw the dummy, she immediately quivered all over, and looked towards her mistress, who cried in a shrill voice, pointing: "At him!"

When she thought the time had come, she went to Confession and received the Sacrament one Sunday morning with ecstatic fervour; then, dressing in man's clothes to look like an old ragged beggar, she struck a bargain with a Sardinian fisherman, who took her, together with the dog, across the strait.

She carried a big piece of sausage in a canvas bag. Frisky had had nothing to eat for two days. The old woman kept making her smell the savoury food to excite her.

They reached Longosardo, and the old Corsican woman hobbled along to the baker's and enquired for Nicolas Ravolati's house. He had resumed his old trade as a joiner, and was working alone at the back of his shop.

The old woman pushed open the door and shouted: "Hullo! Nicolas!" He turned round; then, slipping the dog's lead, she cried: "At him! Go for him, tear him to pieces!"

The starving animal leapt at him and seized his throat. The man, throwing out his arms, grappled with the dog

and fell to the ground.   For a few seconds he writhed, kick-
ing the ground with his heels.   Then he lay still, while
Frisky wrenched at his throat, tearing it to ribbons.   Two
neighbours, sitting at their doors, remembered distinctly
seeing an old beggar come out of the shop with an emaciated
black dog; as it walked, it was eating something brown,
which its master gave it.

The old woman returned home in the evening.   That
night she slept soundly.

A DEAL

Two men, Césaire Isidore Brument and Prosper Napoléon Cornu, had been brought before the Assize Court of the Department of the Lower Seine on a charge of the attempted murder by drowning of the woman Brument, the lawful spouse of the first named.

The two defendants were sitting side by side in the usual dock; they were both peasants, the former short and fat, with short arms and legs and a round red pimply face, set directly on his body, which was also round and short, with no neck visible. He was a pig-breeder, resident at Gacheville-la-Goupil in the rural district of Criquetot.

Prosper Napoléon Cornu was thin and of medium height, with unusually long arms. His head was set askew, his jaw was crooked and he had a squint. A blue blouse, as long as a shirt, reached to his knees, and his sparse straw-coloured hair, clinging closely to his skull, gave his face a shabby, dirty, shop-soiled appearance, that was quite repulsive. He had been nicknamed " the Parson ", because he had the knack of imitating to the life the church chants, and even the notes of the serpent. This ability attracted a great many customers to his bar, for he kept the local public-house; they preferred the " Mass according to Cornu " to the genuine article.

Mme. Brument, who was sitting on the witnesses' bench, was a skinny sleepy-looking peasant. She sat motionless, with her hands crossed on her knees, staring straight in front of her with an expressionless face. The Chairman went on with the cross-examination:

" So, Mme. Brument, they came to your house and threw you into a barrel of water. Tell the court exactly what happened. Stand up."

She stood up, straight as a telegraph-pole, with a tight-fitting white cap on her head. She told her story in a drawling voice:

"I was shellin' broad beans, when they comes in. I says to myself: 'What's up wi' 'em? They looks queer, they's got summat on.' They kep' on watchin' me out of the corner of their eyes, 'specially Cornu with 'is squint. I don't like seein' 'em together—them two together's never up to no good. I says to 'em: 'What d'you want along o' me?' They didn't answer. I feels a bit uncomfortable, as you might say."

The defendant Brument interrupted the evidence excitedly to say:

"I were sozzled."

Then Cornu, turning to his accomplice, declared in a booming voice like the bass stop of an organ:

"Say we was both sozzled an' you won't be far out."

The Chairman, severely: "You mean you were intoxicated?"

Brument: "Not a doubt of it."

Cornu: "That might 'appen to any man."

The Chairman, to the victim of the assault: "Go on with your evidence, Mme. Brument."

"Well, Brument 'e says to me: 'D'you want to make five bob?' 'You bet,' I says, for you don't pick up five bob in the street every day. Then 'e says: 'Then keep yer eyes open and do as I does,' an' off 'e goes to the barrel with no top on it, what stands under the gutter in the corner of the yard. Then 'e empties it, an' then 'e drags it into my kitchen an' puts it in the middle of the floor, and then 'e says to me: 'You go an' fetch water and fill it up to the top.'

"So I goes with two buckets to the pond and brings in the water, an' I goes on for an hour bringin' water, 'cos that there barrel's as big as a copper, if you know what I mean, Sir.

" All the time Brument an' Cornu went on 'avin' a drop, then another drop an' another. When one drunk, then t'other drunk, till I says: ' You're both full up—as full as that there barrel.' Then Brument 'e says: ' Don't you worry, get on with the job; yer turn's comin' presently, you'll get what's comin' to you.' I didn't pay no 'eed to what 'e says, seein' as 'ow 'e were tight.

" When the barrel was full right up, I says: ' There y'are.'

" Then Cornu gives me five bob; it wasn't Brument, it was Cornu that gives me the five bob. Then Brument says: ' D'you want to make another five bob?' I says: ' Yes '; I don't get a windfall like that every day. Then 'e says: ' Then get undressed.'

" ' Me get undressed?'

" ' Yes,' says 'e.

" ' 'Ow much am I to get undressed?'

" 'E says: ' If you like, you can keep on yer chemise; we don't mind.'

" Five bob is five bob, so I undresses myself; but I didn't like undressin' in front of them blighters. I takes off my cap, an' then my jacket, an' then my skirt, an' then my shoes. Brument says: ' You can keep yer stockin's on—we won't be 'ard on yer.'

" An' Cornu repeated: ' No, we won't be 'ard on you.'

" Well, there I was, with 'ardly a stitch to my body. Then up they gets; they couldn't 'ardly stand, they was so sozzled, if you'll excuse the word, Sir.

" I says to myself: ' What's their little game?'

" An' Brument 'e says: ' Is that all right?'

" Cornu says: ' Yes, that's all right.'

" Then they takes 'old of me, Brument by the head and Cornu by the feet, the way you takes a sheet to wring it out. Then I sets up a 'owl.

" An' Brument 'e says: ' Shut yer mouth, you slut.'

" An' they lifted me up over their heads an' throwed me

into the barrel of water: it fair turned me blood and froze me bowels.

"An' Brument 'e says: 'Is that enough?'

"Cornu says: 'Yes, that's all right.'

"Brument says: ''Er 'ead ain't in; that'll make a difference.'

"Cornu says: 'Well, push 'er 'ead in.'

"Then Brument 'olds my 'ead under till I was as good as drowned an' the water come in through my nose an' I was 'alf-way to Kingdom come. An' 'e went on pushin' an' I went right in.

"Then 'e must 'ave got frightened, an' 'e pulls me out an' says: 'Now go an' dry yourself, you old scarecrow.'

"I got away an' runs to the priest's 'ouse; 'e lent me one of 'is servant's skirts, for I was stark naked, an' 'e went to look for Mr. Chicot, the country p'liceman, an' 'e went off to Criquetot to fetch the town p'lice, an' they all went with me to the house.

"There we found Brument an' Cornu fightin' like two rams.

"Brument was shoutin': 'I tell you, it's not true; there was twenty-five gallon, if there was a drop; we can't 'ave measured it right.'

"Cornu 'e was shoutin': 'Six buckets, that don't make more than twelve gallon. You can't deny it, it's a fact!'

"Then the sergeant took 'em in charge. That's all what 'appened."

She sat down amid general laughter from the public. The members of the jury looked at one another in amazement. The Chairman proceeded:

"Defendant Cornu, you seem to have been the originator of this disgraceful plot. What have you to say?"

Cornu in his turn got up:

"I were sozzled, Sir."

The Chairman replied sternly:

" I am aware of that. Go on."

" I'm goin' on. Well, Brument come to my place about
nine o'clock an' orders two brandies, an' 'e says to me:
' One's for you, Cornu.' An' I sits down opposite 'im an'
puts the stuff down, an', knowin' my manners, I stands
'im another. Then 'e did the same again, an' so did I, an'
we went on, an' by twelve o'clock we was tight.

" Then Brument began to cry; I couldn't stand that an'
I asks 'im what's up; 'e says: ' I've got to get forty quid
by Thursday.' That was a kick in the pants for me, if you
know what I mean. Then, all of a sudden like, 'e says: ' I'll
sell you my wife.'

" I were sozzled, and I've lost my own wife. So it seemed
a bit of all right to me. I didn't know 'is wife, but a woman's
a woman, ain't she? I asked: ' 'Ow much do yer want
for 'er? '

" 'E thought a moment or pretended to. When a man's
sozzled, 'e don't see things too clear, an' 'e answered:
' I'll sell 'er by the gallon.'

" That didn't surprise me, for I were as pissed as 'e was,
an' I know all about weights an' measures from my business.
A gallon weighs ten pound, so that seemed all right.

" We'd only got to settle the rate. ' It all depends on the
quality of the article,' I says to 'im. ' 'Ow much per fifty
gallon? '

" 'E answers: ' Eighty quid.'

" I jumped like a shot rabbit; then it struck me a woman
wouldn't come to more than about twelve gallon or so.
But I says all the same: ' That's too much.'

" 'E answered: ' I'd be losin' at less; it wouldn't be worth
my while.'

" You see, one isn't a pig-dealer for nothing, one gets to
know a thing or two. But, if that there bacon-merchant
thinks 'e knows 'is stuff, then I'm tellin' you I'm up to snuff
too, seein' as 'ow I sells it, ha, ha! So I says to 'im: ' That

'ud be fair enough, if she was new, but you've used 'er, 'aven't you? So she's second-hand goods. I'll pay you at the rate of sixty quid per fifty gallon, not a penny more. Do you agree?'

" 'E answered: ' Agreed; done!' "

" ' Done!' says I, and off we staggers arm in arm; one must always be ready to do a pal a good turn in this life.

" But then I began to get the wind up; ' 'Ow are you going to find out 'ow many gallon she weighs, unless you put 'er into water?'

" Then 'e tries 'ard to explain 'is plan, an' it weren't so easy neither, seein' as 'ow 'e was sozzled. 'E says to me: ' I'll take a barrel an' fill it right up with water. Then I'll pop 'er in. We'll measure the water that comes out, an' that'll be 'er weight.' I says to 'im: ' That's all very well, I quite see that, but the water as comes out 'll run away; 'ow are you goin' to get it back?'

" Then 'e tells me I'm a mug, an' explains we've only got to fill up the empty part of the barrel again, when the woman's got out. 'Er weight 'll be the amount needed to fill up the barrel again. I reckoned it 'ud be about eight buckets, that makes sixteen gallon. Anyway, 'e's not so stupid as you might expect, even when 'e's sozzled, the crafty dog.

" Well, we went to 'is 'ouse, and I inspected the woman in question. As fine women go, you wouldn't exactly call 'er a fine woman. Anybody can see that, as she's 'ere in court. I says to myself: ' I've been done, but never mind, she'll do; whether they're pretty or ugly, you can use 'em just the same, can't you, Sir? Then I noticed she was as thin as a rake. I says to myself: ' There's not sixteen gallon of 'er'; I'm an expert, bein' in the trade.

" As for what 'appened, you've 'eard it from 'er. I even allowed 'er to keep 'er chemise on and 'er stockin's, though I lost by it. When it was over, she cleared off. I says: ' Look out, Brument, she's skedaddlin'.' 'E answered:

' Never you worry, we'll catch 'er again; she's got to come back to sleep. I'm going to measure 'ow much water's come out.'

" We measured it, and it was less than six buckets, ha, ha ! "

The defendant began to laugh so immoderately that a policeman had to slap him on the back. Recovering himself, he went on :

" Well, the long an' the short of it is, Brument declared : 'The deal's off, it's not enough.' Then I began to 'oller and 'e began to 'oller, then I 'ollered louder; then 'e 'it me an' I 'it back. The scrap went on for ever an' ever Amen— you see, we was both sozzled.

" Then the cops come. They swears at us an' puts on the bracelets an' we was locked up. I claims damages."

With that he sat down.

Brument fully corroborated his accomplice's story. The jury, not knowing what to make of it all, retired to consider their verdict.

They returned in an hour and acquitted both the defendants, after a stern preamble emphasizing the sanctity of marriage and defining the exact limits within which commercial contracts are valid.

Brument left the court and went home in company with his wife, while Cornu returned to his public-house.

THE MODEL

THE little crescent-shaped town of Etretat, with its white cliffs, white shingle and blue sea, was dozing peacefully in the brilliant July sunshine. At the tips of the crescent two arches of rock jutted out into the calm water, the smaller to the north like a dwarf foot, the larger to the south like a giant leg; and beyond it the Needle, tapering upwards from a broad base almost to the height of the cliff, towered skywards.

On the beach along the water's edge a crowd of people were sitting about watching the bathers. The Casino terrace, where another crowd was sitting or strolling along, looked like a flower-bed, with the brightly coloured ladies' dresses and their red and blue silk-embroidered sunshades.

On the promenade at the far end of the terrace there were others enjoying its restful atmosphere, sauntering up and down, far from the chatter of the well-dressed throng.

A young man, Jean Summer, well known as a painter of distinction, was walking beside an invalid chair, in which his young wife was sitting, looking thoroughly miserable. A man-servant was pushing the bath-chair slowly, and the crippled lady was gazing sadly at the brightness of the sky, the cheerful sunlight and the light-hearted crowd.

They neither spoke nor looked at each other.

" Let's stop a minute," said the lady.

They stopped, and the painter sat down on a camp-stool, which the man-servant handed him.

The people passing behind the motionless silent couple looked pityingly at them. Their romance had become a local legend; he had married her, it was said, in spite of her infirmity, touched by her love.

Not far off two young men were sitting on a winch, talking and gazing vacantly out to sea.

"No, it's not true; I know Jean Summer quite well."

"Then why did he ever marry her? She was an invalid at the time, wasn't she?"

"Yes, she was. He married her . . . well, he married her, as a man always does marry, because he was a fool."

"But there must have been some other reason."

"Other reason, my dear man?—there is no other reason. A man is a fool because he is a fool. Besides, as you know, painters specialize in absurd marriages. They nearly always marry a model, who has been somebody else's mistress before—damaged goods in every sense of the word. Why do they do it? Nobody knows. One would have thought that constant association with the type of imbecile we call a model must have sickened them for ever of this kind of female. But not a bit of it. They make them pose, and then they marry them. You ought to read Alphonse Daudet's little book, *Artists' Wives*—a gem of a book, so true to life and so cruel.

"In the case of the couple over there, the accident happened in an unusual way, that was rather tragic. The girl staged a comedy, or rather a melodrama. In fact, she risked everything on a single throw. Was she sincere? Was she in love with Jean? One can never tell in these cases. Who can say how much the element of cruelty and how much that of sincerity ever enters into women's actions? They are always sincere at the moment, but their feelings are always changing. They are passionate, criminal, devoted, heroic or mean, at the bidding of fleeting emotions, of which they are quite unconscious. They are always telling lies, involuntarily, thoughtlessly, automatically; and with all this, and in spite of all this, they have an absolute honesty of emotion and sentiment; they show this by decisions which are violent, unexpected, incomprehensible, irrational, which defeat all our reasoning, our habits of caution and all our selfish calculations. Owing to the unexpectedness and suddenness of their determinations they always remain indecipherable riddles to us men. We are always asking ourselves: Are they sincere, or are they acting a part?

" My dear fellow, they are sincere and insincere at one and the same time, because it is part of their nature to be both to the highest degree and yet to be neither.

" Think of the means the best of them adopt to attain their ends from us. These means are at once complicated and simple. So complicated that we never guess them in advance, and yet so simple that, after falling into the trap, we can't help being surprised at ourselves and saying : ' Well, did she really fool me as easily as that?'

" And they always get their own way, old man, especially when they want to get married.

" But, anyway, this is Summer's story.

" The girl was a model, of course; she used to pose for him. She was pretty and, even more, she was smart, and she had a divine figure according to all accounts. He fell in love with her, as a man always falls in love with any attractive woman whom he sees a lot of. He imagined he really loved her. It is a curious phenomenon. As soon as a man wants a woman, he is genuinely convinced that he will never be able to do without her for the rest of his natural life. He is fully aware that the same thing has happened to him before and that, when desire is satisfied, disgust ensues; he knows that, in order to spend one's whole life with another human being, it is not the transient passion of the primitive animal that is needed, but a kinship of soul, temperament and feeling. He must be able to distinguish, in the midst of the attraction he feels, whether it is the result of purely physical factors, a kind of intoxication of the senses, or of the deeper union of minds.

" Anyhow, he convinced himself that he did love her;

he vowed eternal fidelity a hundred times over and never looked at any other woman.

"She was genuinely attractive, for she had that gift of superficial smartness which comes so easily to many Paris girls. She babbled and chattered and said foolish things that seemed witty by the amusing way she said them. She was never at a loss for a graceful pose, well calculated to please a painter's eye. Whenever she raised her arm or bent down or got into a carriage or shook hands, her every movement was perfectly timed and just right.

"For three months Jean didn't realise that at bottom she was just like all other models.

"They rented a small house at Andressy for the summer.

"I was there one evening, when the first doubts began to force themselves into my friend's consciousness.

"It was a gorgeous night, and we decided to take a stroll along the river. The moonlight was dancing on the shimmering water, its reflexions broken up into golden spangles by the eddies and currents of the broad, sluggish stream.

"We were walking along the bank, slightly intoxicated by the vague feeling of happiness that often comes over one on a perfect evening like this. We felt as though we could perform superhuman feats and fall in love with the fictitious creations of our own poetical imagination; we were oddly aware of the stirring of strange emotions, longings and aspirations. We were silent, thrilled by the calm exhilarating freshness of this perfect night, and the cool moonlight seemed to go right through us, penetrating the body and drowning the soul in a scented bath of contentment. Suddenly Joséphine—that's her name—uttered a cry:

"'Oh! did you see that big fish jump over there?'

"He answered without looking or taking in her words:

"'Yes, darling.'

"She lost her temper:

"'No, you didn't; your back was turned.'

" He smiled:

" ' Yes, you're quite right; it's such a lovely night that I'm not thinking of anything at all.'

" She said no more; but a minute later she felt the need to talk and asked:

" ' Are you going to Paris to-morrow? '

" He declared:

" ' I don't know.'

" She got annoyed again:

" ' I suppose you think it's amusing to go for a walk and never say a word. People who aren't half-wits talk.'

" He made no answer. Then, realizing, with a woman's perverse intuition, that it would exasperate him, she began singing that irritating song that has been dinned into our ears, insulting our intelligence, for the last two years:

'I was gazing at the sky.'

" He murmured:

" ' Do be quiet! '

" She retorted angrily:

" ' Why should I be quiet? '

" He replied:

" ' You're spoiling the evening for us.'

" Then occurred the inevitable scene, the hateful silly scene, with unpremeditated reproaches and tactless recriminations, and then tears; they ran through the whole gamut. At last they went home; he had let her run on without interruption, mesmerized by the beauty of the night and overwhelmed by the storm of her senseless reproaches.

" Three months later he was struggling desperately in the grip of the unbreakable, invisible bonds that such an association weaves round us. She used her emotional hold over him to dominate him and make his whole life a misery. They quarrelled from morning to night, abused each other and fought.

" Finally he made up his mind to end it all and break

away. He sold all his canvases, borrowed money from his friends, raised twenty thousand francs—he had not made his name then—and left them on the chimney-piece with a farewell letter.

" He sought refuge in my house.

" About three o'clock that afternoon there was a ring at the bell; I went and opened the door. A woman faced me, pushed me aside and forced her way into my studio; it was Joséphine.

" He got up as she entered the room.

" She threw the letter with the bank-notes at his feet with a gesture of no little dignity and said curtly:

" ' There's your money; I don't want it.'

" She was trembling and very pale, in a state when she might do anything. As for him, I saw him turn pale too, pale with anger and exasperation, which might easily lead to violence.

" He asked:

" ' What do you want?'

" She replied:

" ' I don't want to be treated like a harlot. You wanted me and you had your will. I asked nothing from you; now you can't cast me off.'

" He stamped his foot:

" ' No, this is too much. If you think you're going to . . .'

" I had seized his arm:

" ' Don't say anything more, Jean; leave it to me.'

" I went up to her and gently, gradually, I talked reason to her, using all the stock arguments that one can employ in such a case. She listened to me motionless, staring in front of her, silent and obstinate.

" At last, having said everything I could and seeing no hope of a happy ending to the scene, I thought of a last argument. I declared:

" ' He still loves you, my dear; but his family want him to marry; you see what I mean.'

" She started:

" 'Ah! I see now . . .' And, turning to him, she went on: ' You're going . . . you're going to marry? '

" He answered bluntly:

" ' Yes.'

" She took a step forward:

" ' If you marry, I shall kill myself . . . you understand that.'

" He shrugged his shoulders:

" ' Very well—kill yourself.'

" ' You say . . . you say . . . say that again.'

" He repeated:

" ' Well, kill yourself, if you want to.'

" She went on, alarmingly pale:

" ' Don't think I don't mean it; I'll throw myself out of the window.'

" He began to laugh, went to the window, opened it and, like a man bowing a guest out of a room, said politely:

" ' This way—after you! '

" She stared at him for a moment with the light of madness in her eyes; then, taking a run as if she were going to jump over a hedge in a field, she dashed past both of us and, clearing the balcony railing, disappeared from sight.

" I shall never forget the effect of that open window on me, when I saw the falling body pass across it; it suddenly looked as wide as the sky and as empty as space. I instinctively shrank back, afraid to look down, as if I should fall out myself.

" Jean stood motionless in a daze.

" The poor girl was carried in with both legs broken; she would never walk again. Her lover, mad with remorse, and perhaps, too, feeling that he owed it to her, took her back and married her.

Well, that's the story, old man."

It was getting dark. The girl, feeling chilly, wanted to go home, and the servant began to push the bath-chair towards the village. The painter walked by his wife's side; they had not said a word to each other for an hour.

THE OLIVE GROVE

I

When the fishermen of the little Provençal port of Garandou, at the head of the Bay of Pisca between Marseilles and Toulon, saw the Abbé Vilbois' boat coming in from fishing, they went down to the beach to help pull her up.

There was no one else on board except the priest, who rowed like a true sailor, with unusual power, in spite of his fifty-eight years. His sleeves were turned up, showing his muscular arms, his cassock was pulled up and gripped between his knees and partly unbuttoned across his chest, his three-cornered clerical hat lay on the thwart at his side, and he was wearing a white topee; he looked like one of those eccentric muscular Christians from the tropics, more at home in a tight corner than at the altar.

From time to time he glanced over his shoulder to make sure he was bringing the boat in at exactly the right place, and resumed his pulling with steady powerful rhythmical strokes, to show these inferior seamen of the south once more how northerners can row.

The boat, running smoothly, touched the sand and slid over it, as if eager to run right up to the top of the beach, with her keel deeply embedded; then she came to a stop, and the five men watching the priest's arrival came up, eager to talk and pleased to see him back, for they liked him.

" Well," said one of them, with a strong Provençal accent, " have you had good sport, Father? "

The Abbé Vilbois shipped his oars, took off his topee and put on his three-cornered hat, turned down his sleeves and buttoned up his cassock; and with all the dignity of his cloth as priest in charge of the village, replied proudly:

" Yes, excellent, three bass, two murry and some rainbow wrasse."

The five fishermen had come up to the boat, and leaning over the gunwale were examining the dead fish with an expert eye, the fat bass, the flat-headed hideous snaky murry and the purple wrasse with their irregular orange-yellow stripes.

One of them said:

" I'll carry them up to your place for you, Father."

" Thank you, my man."

After shaking hands, the priest set off, followed by one of the men, leaving the others to look after the boat.

He walked with long slow strides, which gave him an air of power and dignity. Being still heated after his hard row, he removed his hat from time to time, as he passed under the shade of the olives, in order to let the evening air, which, though still warm, was tempered by a light breeze off the sea, play over his high forehead under its fringe of white hair, straight and close-cropped, suggesting the officer rather than the priest. The village soon came into sight on a knoll in the middle of a broad valley sloping gently down to the sea.

It was a July evening, and the white road lay buried under a pall of dust; the blinding sun, now nearing the jagged crest of the distant hills, magnified the priest's long shadow slantwise across it; his three-cornered hat, distorted, made a black patch which moved over the adjoining meadow and seemed to be climbing up the olive trees in its path for fun and then dropping to the ground again and crawling between the trees.

Under the Abbé Vilbois' feet a cloud of powdery dust, impalpable and fine as flour, which covers all the roads of Provence in summer, rose like smoke round his cassock, blurring it and coating its skirts with a grey tint, which gradually grew whiter. He had now cooled off and was walking with his hands in his pockets, with the slow powerful stride of a mountaineer going uphill. His clear eye scanned the village—his own village, where he had been parish priest for twenty years, the village of his choice, to which he had been appointed through influence and where he expected to die. The church, his own church, rose above the wide cone of houses, crowded round it, with its two square brown stone towers of unequal height, dominating this lovely southern valley, more like the bastions of an ancient fortress than the towers of the House of God. The Abbé was pleased with himself, for he had caught three bass, two murry and several wrasse. This would be another triumph for him in the eyes of his parishioners, who respected him more than anything because he was the strongest man in the place in spite of his age. These innocent vanities gave him intense pleasure. He could sever the stem of a flower with a pistol-shot; he sometimes fenced with his neighbour the tobac-conist, an ex-regimental fencing instructor, and he was the best swimmer on the coast.

Moreover, as the Baron de Vilbois, he had once been a man of fashion, well known as a member of smart society, and he had not taken Holy Orders till the age of thirty-two, after an unhappy love-affair.

A member of an old Picardy family, supporters of the Royalist cause and of the Church, whose sons for several hundred years had gone to the Army, the judicial bench or the Church, his first ambition, fostered by his mother, had been to take Orders ; later, under pressure from his father, he made up his mind simply to come to Paris, study law and then look out for some dignified judicial post.

But while he was finishing his studies, his father died of pneumonia, caught while shooting in the marshes, and his mother never recovered from the shock, and died shortly after. So, having unexpectedly come in for a considerable fortune, he gave up his thoughts of a career and was content to live as a man of means.

He was a good-looking bachelor and he had brains, though his outlook was narrowed by the creed, traditions and principles which he inherited, along with his powerful physique, from a line of small Picardy squires; so he soon became popular, and was a success in serious circles, enjoying life as a strait-laced young man of wealth and position.

But suddenly, after meeting her several times at a friend's house, he fell in love with a young actress, who as quite a junior pupil of the Conservatoire was making a successful début at the Odéon. He fell in love with all the passionate violence of a man accustomed by his upbringing to be single-minded in his enthusiasms. He fell in love, always seeing her in the romantic part which had brought her fame on her first public appearance.

She was pretty, naturally self-willed, looking like an innocent child or, as he put it, like an angel. She succeeded in dominating him completely and turning him into one of those raving lunatics, whose ecstatic happiness is quite irrational, in whom a glance or a woman's skirt kindles an overpowering passion. He made her his mistress and persuaded her to leave the stage, and he loved her for four years with a love that only increased with time. In spite of his name and the honourable traditions of his family, he would certainly have married her in the end, if one day he had not discovered that she had long been unfaithful to him with the friend who had brought them together.

The scene was all the more painful because she was expecting a baby, and he was only waiting for its birth to make up his mind to marry her.

When he held the proofs—certain letters he had found in a drawer—he accused her of infidelity and shameful treachery with all the brutality of the semi-savage that he was.

But she, a child of the Paris gutters, entirely shameless as well as unchaste, was as sure of her hold over the other man as over him; she was moreover quite fearless, like the common women who mount the barricades out of sheer bravado; so she faced him and insulted him. And, as he raised his hand to strike her, she pointed to her womb.

He turned pale and stopped, at the thought that this polluted flesh, the vile body of this unclean creature, carried his child, blood of his blood, within her. Then he rushed at her to crush them both and destroy this double shame. Suddenly panic-stricken, she realized that her last hour had come, and, as she fell to the ground under his blows and saw his foot ready to stamp on her swollen belly with the young life within it, she cried, stretching out her hand to ward off his blows:

"Don't kill me; it's not your child, it's his."

He recoiled, so dumbfounded, so aghast that his rage died within him and he checked himself, as he stammered:

"You . . . you say . . .?"

Suddenly mad with terror at the murderous look in the man's eyes and his wild gestures, she repeated:

"It's not yours, it's his."

Quite overwhelmed, he hissed through clenched teeth:

"You mean, the child?"

"Yes."

"You're lying."

And again he made a movement with his foot as if to crush some vermin, while his mistress, who had struggled to her knees and was trying to get away from him, went on stammering:

"But I tell you, it's his. If it had been yours, shouldn't I have had it long ago?"

This argument struck him; it seemed so obviously the truth. In one of those flashes of intuition, in which all possible reasons appear at the same moment with luminous clarity, irrefutable, cogent, conclusive, he was immediately convinced that he was not the father of the wretched child that this worthless woman carried in her womb; and, as if a weight had been lifted from his mind, his anger suddenly evaporated and he decided to spare the infamous wretch.

He went on in calmer tones:

"Get up, leave this house, and never let me see your face again."

Overwhelmed, she obeyed and left the house. He never saw her again.

He went away too; he went down south, to the sun, and stopped at a village in the middle of a valley on the shores of the Mediterranean. An inn looking on to the sea took his fancy; he engaged a room and stayed there. He lived there for eighteen months, quite alone with his sorrow and his despair; he lived there, tortured with the memories of the woman's unfaithfulness and of her charm, ashamed of the way she had enslaved and bewitched him, and yet longing for her presence and caresses.

He wandered about in the valleys of Provence under the sun which filtered through the silver-grey leaves of the olives, with his poor tormented brain, still unable to free itself of its obsession.

But his old thoughts of religion, the ardour of his early faith, now more controlled, gradually came back to his mind in his utter loneliness. Religion, which had formerly appeared as a refuge from the unknown experiences of life, now seemed a refuge from its deceits and agonies. He had never given up his habit of prayer. In his sorrow he clung to it, and he often went at dusk and knelt down in the darkening church, where the only light was the gleam of the lamp at the east end of the choir, the sacred guardian of the sanctuary and the symbol of the Divine Presence.

There he poured out his troubles before God, his God, and confessed all his unhappiness; he prayed for advice, pity, help, protection, consolation, and into his prayer, repeated daily with increasing fervour, he put each time a more passionate feeling.

The love-wound in his bruised aching heart was still bleeding and throbbing, and he was starved of affection; but gradually, by dint of prayer, by living like a hermit in the ever-increasing practice of piety, by giving himself up to the mystic communion of saintly souls with the Saviour, who consoles and draws the unhappy to Himself, he let the mystical love of God enter into him and drive out the other love.

Then he went back to his early ambition and decided to offer to the Church the broken life he had nearly given her in the innocence of his youth.

Accordingly he was ordained. Through his family and connexions he got himself appointed priest in charge of this hamlet in Provence, to which chance had led him; and having made over most of his private means to charitable objects, only keeping enough to enable him to be useful and help the poor during his life, he took refuge in the tranquil practice of piety and the service of his fellow men.

He was a priest of narrow views but kindly disposition, a sort of religious guide with the mentality of a soldier, forcibly leading into the Church's narrow way erring humanity, lost in the jungle of life, where all our instincts, our tastes, our passions are paths to lead us astray. But much of his former self lived on in him; he was still fond of violent exercise and aristocratic sports like fencing and shooting; and he hated women, all of them, with a child's fear of the dangers of the unknown.

II

The sailor following the priest was itching to talk, like any southerner, but for some time he did not dare, for the Abbé was regarded with some awe by his flock. At last he took the plunge:

" Well, are you comfortable in your bungalow, Father? "

This bungalow was one of those tiny cottages in which people from the towns and villages of Provence take refuge in the summer to escape the heat. The priest had rented this shack put up in a field five minutes' walk from his presbytery, which was too small and enclosed in the centre of the parish right up against the church.

Even in the summer he did not always live outside the village; he only went to the cottage for a few days at a time to get away from the other houses and be able to practise with his pistol.

"Yes, my man," said the priest, " I'm very comfortable."

The low building came into sight among the trees, washed pink, slashed and chequered with splashes of light, where the sun came through the branches and leaves of the olives planted in the unfenced field. It looked as if it had sprouted there like a Provençal mushroom.

A tall woman was also to be seen, moving about in front of the door, getting ready a small dinner-table, on which she was laying a single place with methodical slowness, making separate journeys with a plate, a napkin, a piece of bread and a glass. She was wearing the small head-dress of Arles, a pointed cone of black silk or velvet with a white mushroom-shaped cap on top.

When the Abbé came within earshot, he shouted:

" Hullo, Marguerite ! "

She stopped and looked and, recognizing her master, called back:

" Oh! it's you, Father."

" Yes, and I'm bringing you a fine catch; I want you to grill me a bass at once, in butter, mind you, just in butter."

The housekeeper, who had come to meet the men, was examining the fish, which the fisherman was carrying, with an expert eye.

" But we've already got a chicken boiled in rice."

" Never mind. Fish the next day is never a patch on

fish just out of the water. I'm going to have a feast fit for a king; I don't do it very often, and anyway it's a venial sin."

The woman picked out one of the bass and, as she was going away with it, she turned round and said:

"Oh! a man called three times to see you, Father."

He inquired casually:

"A man? What sort of a man?"

"Well, I didn't like the looks of him myself."

"What? Was he a beggar?"

"P'raps, I don't know; I should rather think he was a hobo."

The Abbé Vilbois laughed at this slang word for a criminal or tramp, for he knew how nervous Marguerite was; she couldn't live in the cottage without imagining all day, and especially all night, that they would all be murdered.

He gave a few coppers to the fisherman, who went away, and, as he was saying: "I'll go and have a bit of a wash and brush up", for he kept up the old habits of polite society, Marguerite, who was scraping the back of the bass against the grain with a knife, so that its scales, slightly bloodstained, fell off like tiny silver coins, called to him from her kitchen:

"Look, there he is!"

The Abbé turned towards the road, and saw a man, who from a distance looked shabbily dressed, walking slowly towards the house. He waited for him, still smiling at his housekeeper's nervousness and thinking: "My word! she was quite right; he does look like a hobo."

The stranger was approaching with his hands in his pockets, staring at the priest, not hurrying. He was quite young and had a fair curly beard; and wisps of hair straggled down from under a soft felt hat, so dirty and battered that it was impossible to tell its original colour or shape. He was wearing a long dark-brown overcoat, and his trousers were frayed round the ankles; rope-soled shoes gave him the slinking, surreptitious, noiseless tread of a petty thief.

A few paces from the priest he took off the wreck of a hat that shaded his face with a slightly theatrical gesture, revealing features lined and dissolute but still handsome, with a bald patch on the top of his head suggesting bad health or a misspent youth, for he was obviously not more than twenty-five.

The priest immediately took off his own hat, intuitively guessing that this was no ordinary tramp, no out-of-work labourer or old lag wandering about between two convictions, unable to speak anything but unintelligible thieves' jargon.

" Good day, Father! " said the man.

The priest merely replied " Good day ", unwilling to say " Sir " to this ragged, suspicious-looking individual. The two men looked hard at one another; and the Abbé Vilbois felt uncomfortable under the scrutiny of this tramp, sensing the presence of an unknown enemy, aware of one of those mysterious presentiments of tragedy that make one shiver and freeze the blood. At last the tramp went on:

" Well, do you recognize me? "

Taken aback, the priest answered:

" I? No, certainly not."

" Oh! You don't know me? Look a bit closer."

" It's no use my looking at you; I've never seen you before."

" That's true enough," continued the other ironically, " but I'll show you someone you do know."

He put on his hat again and unbuttoned his overcoat, revealing a naked chest. His trousers were kept up by a red belt above the hips round an emaciated stomach.

From a pocket he took an envelope—one of those nondescript envelopes, dirty and stained, which tramps keep in their coat-lining to hold the papers, genuine or forged, stolen or legitimately come by, which guarantee the holder from arrest by any chance policeman. Out of it he took a photograph, the old-fashioned sort the size of a letter, yellow with age, dilapidated and faded from being carried round in the pocket next to the heat of the body.

Then, holding it up alongside his face, he asked:

" Well, do you know *him*? "

The Abbé took a couple of steps forward to see better, and stood dumbfounded and deadly pale, for it was a photograph of himself taken for *her* in the old days of his love.

He did not answer, not understanding.

The tramp repeated:

" Well, do you recognize *him*? "

The priest stammered:

" Of course I do."

" Who is it? "

" It's me."

" You're sure? "

" Yes, of course."

" Well, now look at the two, your portrait and me."

The unhappy priest had already seen; he had seen that the two men, the man in the photograph and the man laughing beside it, were as like as two brothers, but he was still puzzled and he stammered:

" What do you want of me? "

The tramp retorted in a nasty tone:

" What do I want? Well, first of all I want you to recognize me."

" Who are you? "

" What am I, you mean? Ask the first man you meet on the road, ask your housekeeper; we'll go and ask the local mayor, if you like, and show him this. He'll have a good laugh, I can tell you. You don't want to admit that I'm your son, my Reverend ' Father '."

The old man groaned, throwing up his hands in a biblical gesture of despair:

" It's not true."

The young man went close up to him and faced him :

" Oh! it's not true? Look here, you're a priest; I want no more lies from you, see? "

There was an ugly glint in his eyes; his fists were clenched and he spoke with such vehemence that the priest, backing away from him, wondered which of the two was making the mistake now.

However, once more he insisted :

" I never had a child."

The other retorted :

" And perhaps you'll say you never had a mistress either? "

The old man's emphasis made his curt answer into a proud admission :

" Yes, I had."

" And wasn't your mistress expecting a baby when you turned her off? "

Suddenly the old anger, stifled twenty-five years ago, or rather not stifled but buried deep in the lover's heart, burst the barriers erected by faith, pious resignation and renunciation of the world, and, losing control, he shouted :

" I turned her off because she had been unfaithful to me and was carrying another's child—otherwise I should have killed her and you, Sir, at the same time."

The young man hesitated, surprised in his turn at the priest's obviously sincere rage; then he answered more calmly :

" Who told you it wasn't your child? "

" She told me herself, when she defied me."

The tramp, without questioning the assertion, concluded in the casual tone of a gutter-snipe clinching an argument :

" Well, mother was wrong when she cheeked you, that's all about it."

Regaining his self-control after his outburst with an effort, the priest asked :

" And who told you that you were my son? "

" She did, herself, on her death-bed, Father . . . and then there was this ! "

And he held out the little photograph under the Abbé's eyes.

The old man took it, and slowly, carefully, his heart beating fast with the violence of his feelings, he compared this unknown vagrant with the old picture of himself; and he had no more doubts, he *was* his son.

He felt the stab of an overmastering, agonizing emotion, like remorse for some old crime.. He understood a little and guessed the rest; once more the violent scene of their separation passed before his eyes. It was to save her life, threatened by the man she had wronged, that this deceitful treacherous woman had thrown this lie at him. And the lie had been successful. A son had been born to him, and had grown up into this filthy tramp, who smelt of vice as a he-goat stinks of beastliness. He murmured:

" Let's go for a little walk, we must straighten things out."

The other sneered:

" With pleasure; that's why I'm here."

And they walked on side by side through the olive grove. The sun had set. The chill freshness of the southern twilight was extending its invisible cold mantle over the country-side. The Abbé shivered, and suddenly raising his eyes with the familiar movement of an officiating priest, he saw all round, shimmering against the sky, the delicate silver-grey foliage of the sacred tree, which had spread its scanty shade over Christ's last agony, when for the only time in His life He lost hope.

A short desperate prayer rose within him, uttered with that inner voice which does not issue through the lips but carries the prayer of the pious to the Saviour: "O my God, help me! "

Then he turned to his son:

" So your mother is dead? "

A new pain awoke in him, as he uttered the words "Your mother is dead"; his heart was torn with the strange physical agony of a man who has never succeeded in quite forgetting and is living again through the tortures of the past; but still more, perhaps, now that she was dead, he felt a stirring of the brief ecstatic happiness of his youth, of which nothing now remained but the scar in his memory.

The young man replied:

"Yes, Father, mother is dead."

"Long ago?"

"Yes, it will be three years ago."

A new doubt came over the priest.

"How was it you didn't come and find me sooner?"

The other hesitated.

"I couldn't; I was prevented. But excuse me if I interrupt these confidences, which I will continue later in as great detail as you like, to tell you that I have eaten nothing since yesterday morning."

A surge of pity swept over the old man, and holding out both his hands he cried:

"Oh! my poor boy!"

The young man felt the grip of those powerful hands, which crushed his own thin clammy fingers; then he answered in his usual mocking tone:

"Now I'm beginning to think we shall understand each other after all."

The priest turned for home:

"We'll go and have dinner," he said.

He suddenly remembered, with a little instinctive thrill of pleasure that he could hardly have defined or explained, the splendid fish he had caught himself; with the chicken in rice they would make a grand meal for this unfortunate boy.

The housekeeper from Arles, worried and already disposed to grumble, was waiting at the door.

"Marguerite," shouted the Abbé, "clear the table and

take it into the living-room; and hurry up, and lay places
for two—look sharp about it."

The housekeeper did not move, unable to believe that her
master was going to dine with this gaol-bird.

So the Abbé Vilbois began to clear the table and move
the place laid for himself into the single room on the ground-
floor.

Five minutes later he was seated opposite the tramp, in
front of a tureen, from which a little cloud of steam rose
between the two men.

III

As soon as the plates had been filled, the tramp began to
gulp his soup greedily in hurried mouthfuls. The Abbé's
appetite had gone, and he only drank the tasty cabbage soup
slowly, leaving the bread at the bottom of his plate.

Suddenly he asked:

"What do you call yourself?"

The man laughed, highly pleased with himself, as his
hunger began to abate:

"Father unknown," he said, "I have no surname except
my mother's, which I expect you still remember. On the
other hand, I have two Christian names—pretty inappropriate
ones, too, by the way: Philip Augustus."

The Abbé turned pale and, with a lump in his throat,
asked:

"Why did they give you those Christian names?"

The tramp shrugged his shoulders.

"You should be able to guess that. After leaving you,
mother wanted to make your rival think I was his child,
and he did believe it till I was about fifteen. But about
then I began to grow too like you, and he disowned me,
the rotter. That's how I came to have his two Christian
names—Philip Augustus. If I had had the luck to be like

nobody, or to be simply the son of some third blackguard unknown, I should be calling myself to-day Vicomte Philip Augustus de Pravallon, the son, acknowledged at long last, of the Comte of the same name, senator. As it is, I call myself ' Luckless Tom '."

" How do you know all this? "

" Because they had scenes in front of me—damned nasty ones, too. That soon teaches you what life is like."

A new pain, more agonizing than all he had felt and suffered in the last half-hour, now began to assail the priest. He was beginning to be aware of a feeling of suffocation, which would increase and finally kill him; and it came not so much from the things he heard as from the way they were told and from the face of the debauched ruffian who stressed them. Between this man and himself, between his son and himself, he now began to be conscious of a cesspool of moral filth, which is deadly poison to certain people. Was this vile thing really his son? He couldn't believe it yet; he wanted every possible proof, he wanted to learn everything, hear everything, listen to the whole story, however painful. He thought again of the olives growing round his bungalow, and he murmured for the second time: " O my God, help me! "

Philip Augustus had finished his soup and asked:

" Is that all there is for dinner, Father? "

As the kitchen was outside the house, in a built-on annexe, and Marguerite could not hear her master's call, he used to make his needs known to her by striking a few blows on a Chinese gong hanging near the wall behind him.

So he took the padded stick and struck the circle of metal several times. The first note it produced was low, then it swelled louder, a vibrant, piercing, sinister note, as though the smitten bronze were groaning in pain.

The housekeeper appeared. She was scowling, and she glared angrily at the hobo, as if she had a presentiment, like the instinct of a faithful dog, of the tragedy that had befallen her master. She was carrying the grilled bass, from which rose the appetising smell of melted butter. The Abbé slit the fish from head to tail with a spoon and said, as he offered the back fillet to the child of his youth:

" I caught this myself to-day "—a hint of his pride survived even in his distress.

Marguerite did not leave the room. The priest went on:

" Bring some wine—the good stuff, the white Cap Corse."

She made a gesture almost of revolt, and he had to repeat the order in a stern tone:

" Get along now, two bottles."

For on the rare occasions when he offered a guest a bottle of wine, he had one himself too.

Philip Augustus beamed and murmured:

" That's first-rate, a great idea. It's a long time since I've had a meal like this."

The servant returned in a couple of minutes; they were as long as two eternities to the priest, for a desire to know everything was consuming him, as devouring as hell fire.

The bottles were uncorked, but the housekeeper still stood there, glaring at the man.

" Leave us," said the priest.

She pretended not to hear. He repeated almost roughly:

" I told you to leave us."

At last she left the room.

Philip Augustus fell upon the fish with greedy haste; and his father watched him, more and more surprised and shocked at the degradation written in this face, which was yet so like his own. The little bits which the Abbé Vilbois raised to his lips remained in his mouth, for the lump in his throat prevented him from swallowing; and he chewed each mouthful over and over again, as he sought among all the questions that came into his mind for the one that he was most anxious to have answered first.

At last he murmured:

" What did she die of? "

" T.B."

" Was she ill long? "

" About eighteen months."

" How did she get it? "

" Don't know."

They fell silent. The Abbé was thinking. There were so many things in his mind, which he had long wanted to know; for since the day of the rupture, when he had come so near to killing her, he had had no news. It was true he had had no desire to hear anything more, for he had sternly put her out of his life, both her and his own days of happiness; but he suddenly felt, now that she was dead, a keen desire to know, almost a jealous lover's desire. He went on:

" She wasn't alone? "

" No, she was still living with him."

The old man started.

" With him, with Pravallon? "

" Yes, of course."

And the man who had been betrayed so long ago calculated that the woman who had deceived him had lived for more than thirty years with his rival.

It was almost in spite of himself that he stammered:

" Were they happy together? "

With a sneer the young man replied:

" Oh yes! But they had their ups and downs. It would have been all right without me. I was always spoiling things."

" What do you mean? " said the priest.

" I've already told you. Because he believed I was his son till I was about fifteen. But he was no fool, the old buffer; he discovered the likeness for himself, and then there were scenes. I used to listen at the door. He accused mother of deceiving him; mother retorted: ' It's not my fault. You knew perfectly well, when I came to you, that I had been another man's mistress'—the other man was you."

" So they spoke of me sometimes?"

" Yes, but they never mentioned your name, except at the end, right at the end, in the last days, when mother knew she was dying. They didn't trust me."

" But you discovered pretty soon that your mother's position was irregular?"

" Of course I did; I'm not an innocent child, and I never was, I promise you. As soon as one begins to know the world, one guesses that sort of thing."

Philip Augustus kept on filling his glass and draining it. His eyes were beginning to sparkle; he was getting drunk quickly after his long fast.

The priest noticed it and nearly stopped him; but it occurred to him that intoxication was making his son careless and talkative, and, taking the bottle, he refilled the young man's glass.

Marguerite brought in the chicken in rice. Having put it on the table, she glared at the tramp again and said to her master with an offended air:

" Look at him; he's drunk, Father."

" Don't bother us," replied the priest, " clear out."

She went out, banging the door.

He asked:

" What did she say about me—your mother, I mean?"

" Oh! just the sort of thing a woman always says about a man she has chucked; that you made a nuisance of yourself, that she was tired of you, and that you would have made life impossible for her with your ideas."

" She said that often, did she?"

" Yes, sometimes in veiled language, so that I shouldn't understand, but I guessed everything."

" And how did they treat you in the house?"

" Me? Very well at first, very badly later on. When mother saw I was queering her pitch, she got rid of me."

" How did she do that? "

" How? That was quite easy. I'd been sowing a few wild oats at about sixteen, and so the blighters sent me to a reformatory to get rid of me."

He put his elbows on the table, supporting his face in his cupped hands; he was quite intoxicated now, all restraint drowned in the wine; and he was suddenly seized by one of those irresistible impulses to talk about himself, which lead people to indulge in fantastic boasting, when they are drunk.

He had an attractive smile; there was something feminine about the charm he exercised, a perverse charm, which the priest recognized. He recognized, more, he felt it, this detested, winning charm, his ruin, his undoing long ago. The son was now more like his mother, not in feature so much as by his appealing insincere glances and by the witchery of those hypocritically smiling lips, which seemed to open only to reveal the corruption of his nature.

Philip Augustus went on with his story :

" Ha, ha! After I got to the reformatory I had a devil of a time, and no mistake; things happened to me that a great novelist would pay a lot to know about. Old Dumas with his *Monte-Cristo* never invented stranger adventures than I had."

He paused with the ponderous gravity of a drunk man's reflexions; then he went on slowly :

" If you want a boy to turn out well, you ought never to send him to a reformatory, whatever he may have done, on account of the acquaintances he makes there. I made friends there, and they didn't do me any good. As I was loafing round one evening about nine o'clock with three pals, all of us a bit tight, on the main road near the ford at Folac, we met a carriage, in which everybody was asleep, the man driving and his family—they were people from Martinon on their way home after dinner in town. I take the horse's rein—up it goes on to the ferry—I give the punt a shove out into the middle of the river—that makes a row—the old boy at the reins wakes up—can't see a thing—uses his whip. Off goes the horse—flounders into the water with the carriage —every man jack of 'em drowned! My pals gave me away. At the beginning they had laughed at my practical joke. Of course, we had never thought things would turn out fatally. We only expected they'd get a ducking and we'd get a good laugh.

" After that I went pretty steep to get my own back for the reformatory, which I really didn't deserve. But it's not worth telling you about all my little games. I'll only tell about the last, because that'll please you, I know. I avenged you, Daddy! "

The Abbé looked at his son with terror in his eyes; he had stopped eating.

Philip Augustus was on the point of resuming his story.

" No," said the priest, " not now, wait a moment."

Turning round, he struck the booming Chinese gong. Marguerite came in immediately.

And her master gave his order in such a stern tone that she dropped her eyes, frightened and obedient:

" Bring in the lamp and anything else you've got to put on the table and don't come in again till I sound the gong."

She left the room, returned and put on the table a white china lamp with a green shade, a large piece of cheese and some fruit; then she went out.

The Abbé, steeling himself to listen, said:

" Now, go on."

Philip Augustus calmly took a liberal helping of the cheese and fruit and replenished his glass. The second bottle was nearly empty, though the priest had not touched a drop.

The young man went on, stuttering, in the thick voice of one who has eaten and drunk too much:

"This was my last effort, and a jolly fine one too. I'd gone back home . . . and I was living there in spite of them, because they were afraid of me . . . yes, afraid. I'm an awkward customer, when my back's up . . . I stick at nothing, when my back's up. . . . You know . . . they were living together and yet they weren't. He had two houses, his senator's residence and his love-nest. But he spent most of his time with mother, for she had made herself necessary to him. She knew a thing or two, and she'd got guts too, had mother; she knew how to hold a man, and no mistake. She'd got him body and soul, and she never let him go right up to the end. What fools men are! Well, I'd gone back home and I ruled them by fear. I can wriggle out of a tight corner, when necessary; and when it's a question of guile or trickery, or of treating people rough, for that matter, I'm not frightened of anybody. Well, one day mother got ill and he put her in a lovely place near Meulan, in the middle of a park as big as a forest. It went on for eighteen months, as I told you. Then we realized the end was near. He came down every day from Paris; he was cut up, he really was.

"Well, one morning they'd been jabbering hard together for nearly an hour, and I was wondering what on earth they could be gassing about all that time, when I was called in. And mother said to me: 'I'm going to die, and there's something I want to tell you in spite of the Comte's advice'— she always spoke of him as the Comte—'it's your father's name; he's still alive.'

"I'd asked her hundreds of times . . . yes, hundreds of times . . . for my father's name . . . hundreds of times . . . and she'd always refused to tell me. I believe one day I boxed her ears to make her talk, but it wasn't a bit of good. And then, so I wouldn't worry her any more, she told me you'd died without a penny, that you were a rotter, a mistake of her youth, a young girl's slip and so on. She made such a convincing story of it that I was diddled into believing you were dead.

" 'Well,' she said, ' it's your father's name.' The other fellow, who was sitting in an armchair, interrupted, saying three times: 'You're making a mistake, you're making a mistake, you're making a mistake, Rosette.'

" Mother sat up in bed. I can still see her, with her flushed cheeks and bright eyes, for she was fond of me in spite of everything, and she said to him: ' Then do something for him, Philip'—she used to call him Philip and me Augustus.

" He began to shout like a maniac: ' For this debauched blackguard, this ne'er-do-well, this gaolbird, this . . . this . . . this . . .' and he found as many nasty names to call me as if he'd been thinking of them all his life.

" I was losing my temper, but mother told me to keep quiet, and said to him: ' Do you want him to starve? Because I've got nothing.'

" He replied in a matter-of-fact tone of voice:

" 'Rosette, I've given you fifteen hundred pounds a year for thirty years; that comes to forty-five thousand pounds. Thanks to me, you have been able to live like a woman of means, surrounded by love and, I think I may say, happy. I owe nothing to this worthless scoundrel, who has spoiled our last years; he will get nothing from me. It is useless to press the matter. Tell him the other man's name, if you like. I think it's a mistake, but I wash my hands of the whole thing.'

" Then mother turned to me. I was saying to myself: ' Good, now I shall know my real father; if he's got the dibs, I shall be all right!'

" She went on:

" 'Your father, the Baron de Vilbois, now calls himself

Abbé Vilbois, and is parish priest of Garandou, near Toulon. He was my lover, till I left him for my present one.'

"And then she told me the whole story, except that she had kidded you about her pregnancy. But you can't ever expect women to tell the truth."

He laughed unpleasantly, oblivious of the effect he was producing, revealing all the coarseness of his nature. He took another drink and went on quite cheerfully:

"Mother died two days . . . two days later. We followed the coffin to the cemetery, he and I . . . humorous thought that, isn't it? . . . he and I and three servants . . . that's all. He was crying like a baby . . . we stood side by side . . . just like daddy and daddy's little boy. Then we went back home, just the two of us. I was saying to myself: 'Now I shall have to hop it without a bean.' I'd got exactly two pounds.

"How was I to get my revenge?

"He touched me on the arm and said:

"'I want a word with you.'

"I followed him into his study, and he sat down at his desk, and then, spluttering through his tears, he tells me he doesn't really mean to be as hard on me as he had told mother. He begs me not to make a nuisance of myself to you . . . but that's a question we've got to settle, you and I . . . and he offers me a fifty pound note . . . What was the good of a fifty pound note to me, I ask you . . . a man like me? I see there are others in the drawer—a regular wad of them. The sight of all those notes makes me itch to get at him. I hold out my hand to take the one he was offering me, but instead of taking his charity, I throw myself on him and hurl him to the ground, I grip him by the throat, till his eyes nearly start out of his head. When I see he is just going to pass out, I gag him and truss him up, undress him and turn him over on his face; and then I avenged you . . . ha, ha! . . . magnificently."

Philip Augustus coughed, choking with merriment, and all the time, on his lips, drawn up at the corners in that cruel, humorous pucker, the Abbé Vilbois recognized the old smile of the woman who had been his undoing.

" Then what? " said the priest.

" Then . . . ha, ha ! . . . there was a big fire in the room, it was in December . . . it was during a cold snap she died . . . poor mother . . . a big coal fire. I took a poker . . . and heated it red-hot . . . and I made crosses on his back, eight or ten of them, I don't remember just how many; after that I turned him over and did the same on his belly. A priceless idea, wasn't it, Daddy? That's the way they branded galley-slaves in the old days. He wriggled like an eel; but I'd gagged him well, and he couldn't shout. Then I took the notes, twelve of them— with the one I had that made thirteen . . . and it proved an unlucky number. And I cleared out, telling the servants not to disturb the Comte till dinner-time, because he was asleep.

" I calculated on his keeping his mouth shut for fear of the scandal, as he was a senator. But I was wrong. Four days later I was pinched in a Paris restaurant. I got three years. That's why I couldn't come and find you earlier."

He took another drink, and, stumbling over his words so as to be hardly intelligible, he went on :

" Now . . . Daddy . . . my Reverend Daddy . . . it feels so funny to have a priest for your pa. . . . But you must be kind to your darling boy, because he's something a bit out of the ordinary . . . that was a great joke he played on the old buffer, wasn't it? "

The same wild rage that had driven the Abbé Vilbois mad years ago before his unfaithful mistress was now sweeping over him in the presence of this vile creature.

In the name of God he had given absolution for so many shameful crimes, whispered in the secrecy of the confessional;

now in his own name he felt no pity, no forgiveness, and he never thought of appealing again now to the merciful God, who is ever ready to help; for he realized that no help either from God or man can save the victims of misfortunes like this here on earth.

All the fire of his passionate nature and violent blood, damped down by his Orders, awoke in an irresistible revulsion against this wretch who was his son, against his likeness to himself and also to his mother, the unworthy mother who had conceived him in her own image, and against the fate which had attached this incubus to the father, like the cannon-ball chained to a convict's leg.

He saw everything, the present and the future, with sudden clarity, roused by this shock from twenty-five years of the peace of mind which religion had given him.

Suddenly convinced that he must speak loud to inspire fear and strike terror into this blackguard from the start, he clenched his teeth in his rage and, forgetting all about the man's drunkenness, cried:

" Now that you have told me your story, you've got to listen to me. You will go away to-morrow morning. You will live at a place that I shall name and you will never leave it without orders from me. I will make you an allowance, on which you will be able to live; but it will be a small one, for I have little money. The first time you disobey this order, everything will be over between us and I will deal with you."

Though fuddled with the wine, Philip Augustus understood the threat, and the criminal in him suddenly awoke. He spat out between his hiccups:

" No, Daddy, this won't do . . . you're a priest . . . I've got you and you'll have to sing small like the others."

The Abbé started; his muscles, still powerful in spite of his age, twitched with an overmastering desire to seize this monster, break him like a twig and show him that he had

met his match. He shook the table, pushing it against his
son's chest, and shouted:

"You'd better take care, you'd better take care. . . . I'm
not afraid of anybody either."

The drunk man, losing his balance, rocked on his chair.
Feeling that he was going to fall, and realizing that he was
in the priest's power, he stretched out his hand, with a
murderous glint in his eye, towards one of the knives lying
on the table. The Abbé Vilbois saw the movement, and
gave the table such a violent push that his son fell over
backwards and measured his length on the floor. The
lamp rolled off the table and went out.

For a few seconds only the tinkle of broken glass was
audible in the darkness; then the sounds of a soft body
crawling on the tiled floor. Then silence.

With the breaking of the lamp, sudden darkness enveloped
the two men, so swift, so unexpected, so impenetrable, that
they were dazed as if by some paralysing shock. The
drunk man, cowering against the wall, had ceased to move;
the priest was still in his chair in the blackness, which drowned
his anger. The veil of darkness, which checked his rage,
at the same time stifled the wild passion in his heart; and
other thoughts came to him, black and grim like the
night.

Silence reigned, the oppressive silence of a closed tomb,
in which nothing seemed to live or breathe. No sound
came from outside either—not the rumble of a cart in the
distance, not a dog's bark, not even the whisper of a light
breeze in the branches or round the walls.

This lasted for a considerable time, possibly an hour.
Suddenly the gong boomed; it boomed as the result of a
single sharp heavy blow, followed by the unexpected crash
of a fall and a chair overturned.

Marguerite, listening anxiously, hurried to the room;
but, on opening the door, she started back in terror before

the impenetrable blackness. Then, trembling all over, with
wildly beating heart, she gasped out in a whisper:

"Father, Father!"

No one answered, nothing moved.

"My God, my God!" she thought, "what have they
done, what has happened?"

She dared not go in, she dared not go back and fetch a
light; a wild desire to get away from it all and scream seized
her, though her legs felt so weak that she could hardly stand;
she repeated:

"Father, Father, it's me, Marguerite!"

Suddenly, in spite of her fear, an instinctive desire to help
her master, one of those gallant impulses that sometimes
enable women to do heroic deeds, inspired her faltering
courage, and, running to her kitchen, she came back with
her lamp.

At the door of the room she stopped. First she saw the
tramp, lying against the wall asleep, or apparently asleep,
then the broken lamp, then, under the table, the Abbé
Vilbois' two black shoes and his legs in their black stockings;
he must have fallen backwards, striking the gong with his
head.

Trembling with terror, her hands shaking, she kept
repeating:

"My God, my God! What's happened?"

As she came slowly into the room, she slipped on something greasy and nearly fell.

Bending down, she saw a red stream flowing over the
red-tiled floor, spreading round her feet and pouring towards
the door. She guessed that it was blood.

Mad with terror, she fled, throwing away her lamp so as
not to see any more, and rushed out into the open towards
the village. She ran, bumping into the trees, her eyes fixed
on the distant lights, screaming.

Her piercing cries soared up into the darkness like the

sinister hooting of an owl; she kept screaming: " The hobo, the hobo, the hobo ! "

When she reached the first houses, the men ran out in terror and surrounded her, but she struggled and would not answer their questions, for she no longer knew what she was doing.

At last they realized that some tragedy had happened at the priest's place, and a party armed themselves to go to his help.

In the middle of the olive grove the little pink bungalow was invisible, hidden in the silent depths of the night. Ever since the solitary light of its one illuminated window had gone out like an eye closing, it lay buried in the shadows, lost in the gloom, undiscoverable except by a native of the place.

Soon lanterns could be seen moving swiftly towards it through the trees, close to the ground. They shed long yellow streaks of light over the parched grass, and under their wandering gleams the gnarled trunks of the olives looked like the snaky monsters of hell, twisted and writhing. In the beams of light thrown out far in front into the darkness, a vague pale shape suddenly loomed up, and soon the two square walls of the cottage showed pink in the lantern light. A few peasants carried the lanterns, escorting the policemen with revolvers cocked, the ranger, the mayor and Marguerite, supported by two men, for she was on the point of collapse.

At the door, still wide open and sinister, there was a moment's pause; then the sergeant, seizing a lantern, entered, followed by the others.

The housekeeper had told the truth. Blood, already clotted, covered the floor like a carpet. It had reached as far as the tramp, staining one of his legs and one hand.

Father and son were sleeping, the former the sleep of death with his throat cut, the latter the sleep of intoxication.

The two policemen threw themselves on him, and before he was awake the handcuffs were on his wrists. He rubbed his eyes, stupid and dazed by the wine; and, when he saw the priest's body, a look of terror came into his eyes, as if he didn't understand.

" Why didn't he escape? " said the mayor.

" He was too drunk," replied the sergeant.

And everybody thought the same, for it would not have occurred to anyone that perhaps the Abbé Vilbois might have taken his own life.

ROSE

THE two young women looked as if they had been buried under a rain of flowers; they were alone in the huge landau laden with bouquets so that it resembled a gigantic flower-basket. On the front seat were two satin boxes, full of Nice violets, and on the bearskin rug over their knees lay a heap of roses, mimosa, stocks, marguerites, tuberose and orange-blossom, tied up with silk favours; their frail bodies seemed crushed under the variegated scented mass, above which only their arms and shoulders were visible and a glimpse of their dresses, one blue and the other mauve.

The coachman's whip was hidden in a sheath of anemones, and the horses' traces were swathed in wallflowers, while the spokes of the wheels were wreathed with mignonette; and in place of carriage-lamps two huge round bouquets looked like the staring eyes of some flower-covered monster on wheels.

The landau was driving at a brisk trot along the Rue d'Antibes, preceded, followed and surrounded by a crush of decorated carriages, full of women buried under masses of violets. It was the Cannes Battle of Flowers.

They reached the Boulevard de la Foncière, where the battle takes place. Along the whole length of the immense avenue a double line of decorated carriages was passing and repassing like an endless conveyor-belt. Their occupants were pelting each other with flowers, which flew through the air like balls, striking smiling faces; they rose, and then fell in the dust, to be picked up by a host of little boys.

A dense crowd was packed on the footpaths, kept back by mounted police, riding up and down and roughly push-ing back those on foot, who were trying to see, so that the common herd should not come into contact with the rich. The crowd watched the scene, noisy but well-behaved. The occupants of the carriages were calling to each other, recognizing their friends and pelting them with roses. A coach filled with pretty women dressed as devils in red was much admired. A gentleman in a fancy dress copied from a portrait of Henri IV was energetically throwing a huge bouquet on the end of an elastic string. Thinking they were going to be hit, women hid their faces and men ducked, but the graceful projectile described a curve and returned like an obedient boomerang to its master, who immediately aimed it at a fresh victim.

The two young ladies were lavish with their ammunition, and received in return a hail of bouquets; then, after an hour of the battle, they got a little tired, and told the coachman to follow the coast road round the Golfe Juan.

The sun set behind the Esterels, silhouetting the long, jagged ridge of the mountains against the fiery sky. The calm sea stretched clear and blue to the horizon, melting into the sky, and the squadron anchored in the middle of the bay looked like a school of sea-monsters, motionless in the water, armoured and hump-backed, like animals from the Apocalypse, with slender, feathery masts rising from their decks and eyes that lit up at night.

The young ladies, lying back under the heavy rug, watched the scene languidly. At last one said:

" There are some divine evenings, when everything seems perfect, aren't there, Margot? "

The other answered:

" Yes, it's lovely, but there's just one thing lacking."

"What? I feel blissfully, completely happy."

" Yes, there is. You're forgetting. Even if we are lulled by a sense of complete physical well-being, we always want one thing more . . . before the heart is satisfied."

Her companion smiled:

" A little love, you mean? "

" Yes."

They fell silent, staring in front of them; then the one called Marguerite murmured:

" Without it life is to me unbearable. I must be loved, even if only by a dog. All women are really like that, whatever you say, Simone."

" No, dear, not all. I would rather not be loved at all than by just anybody. Do you imagine, for example, that it would amuse me to be loved by . . . by . . ."

She glanced round the vast expanse of country to find someone by whom she might be loved. After looking all round, her eye caught the two brass buttons on the back of the coachman's livery, and she finished her sentence with a laugh, " by my coachman."

Mme. Margot, with the ghost of a smile, declared in a whisper:

" I assure you it's quite amusing to be loved by a man-servant. It has happened to me two or three times. They roll their eyes so oddly that one wants to die with laughter. Of course, the more hopelessly they are in love, the more severe one has to be; then one day one has to make some excuse to get rid of them, because one would become ridiculous, if anybody noticed it."

Mme. Simone listened, staring straight in front of her; then she said:

" No, I'm quite sure my footman would not satisfy me as a lover. But tell me how you knew they were in love with you."

" I knew it as one does with any man, when they became stupid."

" Men don't seem as silly as all that, when they're in love with me! "

" Oh! they're perfect imbeciles; they can't talk or answer a question or take in anything at all."

"But how did it feel to be loved by a man-servant? Were you excited . . . flattered?"

"Excited, no . . . flattered, yes, a little. You always are a little flattered when a man falls in love with you."

"Oh come, Margot!"

"Yes, dear. Look here, I'll tell you a queer experience I had. You'll see what odd contradictory things happen to one under such circumstances.

"Four years ago in the autumn I was without a lady's-maid. I had tried five or six, one after the other, and they were all complete fools; I had almost given up hope of ever finding one, when I read among the small advertisements in a paper that a girl, who could sew, embroider, and dress hair, was looking for a place and had excellent references. Moreover, she could speak English.

"I wrote to the address given, and next day the girl came to see me. She was rather tall, thin, slightly pale and very shy. She had fine dark eyes and a good complexion, and I took to her at first sight. I asked to see her references; she gave me one in English, for she had been, she said, on the staff of Lady Rymwell, where she had stayed ten years.

"The reference stated that the girl had left entirely of her own accord to return to France, and that during her period of service there had been nothing against her except a little French flightiness.

"The sanctimonious English expression even made me smile, and I engaged her on the spot as my maid.

"She came to me the same day; her name was Rose.

"After a month I was really fond of her.

"She was a treasure, a gem, a paragon.

"She was a genius as a hairdresser, she arranged lace on a hat better than the best milliners and she could even dress-make.

"I was amazed at her skill; I had never had such a maid.

" She dressed me quickly, with a remarkable lightness of touch. I never felt her fingers on my skin, and I dislike nothing so much as the feel of a maid's hands; I soon got into dreadfully lazy habits; it was such a joy to be dressed from head to foot, from my chemise to my gloves, by this tall, shy girl, who was always inclined to blush and never spoke. After my bath she rubbed and massaged me, while I dozed on my sofa. I really regarded her more as a humble friend than as a servant.

" Well, one morning my hall porter, with an air of mystery, asked to speak to me. I was surprised and had him in. He was a most reliable man, who had once been my husband's batman.

" He seemed uncomfortable over what he had got to say; at last he stammered out:

" ' Madame, the local Police Inspector is downstairs.'

" I asked sharply:

" ' What does he want?'

" ' He wants to search the house.'

" Of course, the police have their uses, but I don't like them. Theirs is a low-down job.

" And I replied, angry as well as insulted:

" ' Why does he want to search the house? What's he after? He can't come in.'

" The porter went on:

" ' He asserts that there's a criminal in hiding here.'

" This time I was frightened, and told him to show the inspector up to my room to explain matters. He was quite a gentlemanly person, with the ribbon of the Legion of Honour. He excused himself and begged my pardon; then he told me that I had a convict among my domestics.

" I was dumbfounded, and replied that I could answer for all my servants, and I went through the list:

" ' The hall-porter, Pierre Courtin, an old soldier.'

" ' It's not him.'

" 'The coachman, François Pingau, a countryman from Champagne, the son of one of my father's tenant-farmers.'

" 'It's not him.'

" 'A groom, also from Champagne, the son of a peasant family I know; and then there's the footman you've just seen.'

" 'It's not him.'

" 'Then, Sir, you see there must be some mistake.'

" 'Excuse me, Madame, but I'm quite sure there's no mistake. As the man in question is a desperate character, would you be so kind as to parade your whole staff in front of yourself and me?'

"I refused at first, then I gave way, and sent for all my servants to come up, men and women.

"The inspector just glanced at them and said:

" 'These are not all.'

" 'Excuse me, Sir, the only other is my own maid, a girl you couldn't mistake for a convict.'

"He asked:

" 'May I see her too?'

" 'Certainly.'

"I rang for Rose, who immediately appeared. Hardly had she entered the room, when, on a sign from the inspector, two men, whom I had not seen concealed behind the door, rushed at her, seized her arms and slipped on the handcuffs.

"I uttered a cry of anger and wanted to dash to rescue her. The inspector stopped me:

" 'This girl, Madame, is a man called Jean Nicolas Lecapet, who was condemned to death in 1879 for murder following rape. His sentence was commuted to penal servitude for life. He escaped four months ago. We've been looking for him ever since.'

"I was utterly flabbergasted. I just couldn't believe it. The inspector went on with a smile:

" 'I need only give you one proof. His right arm is tattooed.'

"The sleeve was pulled up. It was true. The policeman added rather unnecessarily : -

"'You can take our word for the other proofs of his sex.'

"And they took my maid away.

"Well, would you believe it, the feeling uppermost in my mind wasn't anger at having been taken in like this, deceived and made to look ridiculous; it wasn't shame at having been dressed and undressed, handled and touched by this man . . . but . . . a deep sense of humiliation as a woman. Do you understand?"

"No, I don't quite."

"Just think; he had been condemned . . . for rape, this young man. . . . Well, I thought of the woman he had raped, and it was that which humiliated me. Do you understand now?"

Mme. Margot did not answer. She was staring straight in front of her at the two brass buttons on the coachman's livery with a strange look in her eyes and that inscrutable smile that women sometimes have.

AT SEA

THE following paragraph recently appeared in the press:

> " *Boulogne-sur-Mer, January 22nd: from our correspondent:*
> " There is consternation among the sea-faring community here, which has been so hard hit during the last two years, at a frightful tragedy a few days ago. The fishing-boat commanded by Captain Javel was driven too far to the west, as it was coming into port, and foundered on the rocks of the breakwater protecting the pier. In spite of the efforts of the lifeboat and the use of the rocket apparatus, four men and the cabin-boy lost their lives. The bad weather continues. Further disasters are feared."

I wonder who this Captain Javel is. Is he the brother of the one-armed Javel?

If the poor fellow who was washed overboard and now lies dead, perhaps under the wreck of his shattered vessel, is the man I am thinking of, he was involved, eighteen years ago, in another tragedy, terrifying, yet simple, like all the tragedies of the deep.

At that time the elder Javel was skipper of a trawler.

The trawler is the best type of fishing-boat. Strongly built to face any weather, and broad in the beam, she is always tossing about on the waves, like a cork; at sea all the time, continually lashed by the heavy, salt-laden Channel gales, she combs the sea tirelessly, with all sail set, dragging over the side a great net, which scours the ocean-bed, sweeping off and bringing up all the creatures that lurk in the rocks —flat fish clinging to the sand, heavy crabs with crooked claws and lobsters with pointed whiskers.

When the breeze is fresh and the water choppy, fishing starts. The net is attached along the whole length of a pole cased in iron, which is lowered by means of two cables working on two windlasses fore and aft. And the boat, drifting to leeward with wind and tide, drags along with her this device for stripping and ransacking the sea-bed.

Javel had his younger brother on board, with a crew of four and a cabin-boy. He had sailed from Boulogne in fine, clear weather to go trawling.

Soon the wind got up and, increasing to gale force, compelled the trawler to run before it. She reached the English coast, but mountainous seas were lashing the cliffs and pounding the beaches, so that it was impossible to make harbour. The little vessel put out again and made for the French coast. The storm still made it impossible to come alongside the piers, the approaches to the harbours being dangerous with flying foam and roaring waves.

The trawler put about once more, rising to the rollers, tossed, battered, drenched with spray, buffeted with deluges of water, but undismayed in spite of everything, for she was accustomed to this sort of heavy weather, which sometimes kept her at sea for five or six days between the two neighbouring countries, unable to make harbour in either.

At last the gale dropped, while she was still some distance out, and, though it was still rough, the skipper ordered the trawl-net to be put down.

So the great net was heaved over the side, and two men forward and two in the stern began to let the cables holding it run out over the windlasses. Suddenly it touched bottom, but, as a huge wave made the boat heel over, the younger Javel, who happened to be forward superintending the paying out of the rope, staggered, and his arm got caught between the cable, momentarily slackened by the heeling of the boat, and the wood of the gunwale over which it passed. He made a desperate effort, trying to raise the rope with his other hand, but the net was already drawing and the tightened cable would not give.

The man cried out in pain. Everyone ran to his help. His brother left the tiller. They tugged at the rope in an attempt to free the limb, which was being crushed. It was useless.

"We must cut it," said one of the sailors, taking from his pocket a large knife, two slashes of which could have saved the younger Javel's arm.

But cutting the cable meant losing the net, and the net was worth money, a great deal of money—fifteen hundred francs; and it was the property of the elder Javel, with whom having was keeping.

In an agony of anxiety he shouted: "No! don't cut it; wait a moment; I'll bring her head up into the wind." And he ran to the tiller and put it hard over.

The boat hardly answered the helm, hampered as she was by the net, which checked her way, and there was also the drag of drift and wind.

The younger Javel had fallen to his knees, with clenched teeth and haggard eyes. He did not say a word.

His brother came back, still afraid that one of the sailors would use his knife. "Wait, wait, don't cut, we'll cast anchor."

The anchor was let go, and the whole length of the chain paid out. Then they began to heave at the capstan to slacken the cables of the net. At last the rope relaxed, and the arm, now useless inside the sleeve of the bloodstained jersey, was freed.

The younger Javel seemed dazed. They took off his jersey, revealing a ghastly sight—a mass of pulped flesh, from which blood was spurting as if under the action of a pump. The man looked at his arm and murmured: "Buggered!"

As the hæmorrhage was making a pool on the deck, one

of the crew cried: " He'll bleed to death; the artery must be tied."

So they took a piece of coarse, brown, tarred string and, putting it round the limb above the wound, they pulled it tight with all their force. The flow of blood gradually lessened and finally stopped altogether.

The younger Javel got up, with the arm hanging limp at his side. He took hold of it with the other hand, raised it, turned it round and shook it. Everything was broken, all the bones shattered; it was only joined to the shoulder by the muscles. He examined it sadly and thoughtfully. Then he sat down on a furled sail, and his comrades advised him to bathe the place to prevent gangrene.

They put a bucket near him, and every few minutes he filled a glass with water and bathed the ghastly wound, letting a trickle of fresh water run over it.

" You'd be more comfortable below," said his brother.

He went below, but came up again an hour later, not liking to be alone. Besides, he preferred the fresh air. He sat down on the sail again and went on bathing his arm.

They were having a good catch. The broad, white-bellied fish were lying about near him, wriggling in their death-throes. He kept his eyes on them, bathing his crushed limb all the time.

As they were just getting back to Boulogne, the wind got up again suddenly; and the little vessel began her mad career once more, pitching and tossing, jarring the poor fellow's injured arm.

Night came on. The weather remained dirty till dawn. When the sun rose, England was in sight, but, as the sea was going down, they set course back for France, beating up against the wind.

Towards evening the younger Javel called his comrades and showed them ugly-looking black marks, where mortification of the mangled portion of the limb was setting in.

The sailors examined it, giving their advice.

" It looks precious like gangrene," opined one.

" You'd better put salt water on it," declared another.

So they brought salt water and poured it over the wound. The injured man turned green, ground his teeth and flinched a little; but he did not cry out.

When the smarting ceased, he said to his brother: " Give me your knife." His brother handed him the knife. " Now hold my arm out straight and keep it stretched."

They did as he asked.

Then he began carving his own flesh. He worked quietly, reflectively, severing the last tendons with the razor-edged blade; and soon there was only the stump left. He uttered a deep sigh and declared: " It was the only thing to do; I was buggered."

He seemed relieved, and was breathing heavily, as he resumed his bathing of the stump.

The night was rough again and they could not make land.

When daylight appeared, the younger Javel picked up his severed arm and scrutinized it carefully. Putrefaction was setting in. His comrades also came to examine it; they passed it round from hand to hand, felt it, turned it over and sniffed it.

His brother said: " You'd better throw it overboard now."

But the younger Javel fired up at that: " No, I won't! It's mine, I'd have you know; it's *my* arm, after all."

He picked it up again and put it between his legs.

" That won't prevent it putrefying," said the elder brother.

The injured man had an inspiration. When they were long at sea, they used to pack the fish in barrels of salt to preserve them.

He asked: " I suppose I couldn't put it into brine?"

" That's an idea," declared the others.

So they emptied one of the barrels which had been filled with the last few days' catch; and they put the arm at the bottom. They heaped salt on the top of it and replaced the fish one by one.

One of the sailors made a joke about it: " We must take care not to sell it at the auction."

And everyone laughed except the two Javels.

The wind was still high. They tacked about in sight of Boulogne till ten o'clock the next morning. The injured man went on bathing his arm.

At intervals he got up and walked from one end of the boat to the other. His brother at the tiller watched him, shaking his head.

At last they made the harbour.

The doctor examined the wound and pronounced it quite healthy. He dressed it carefully and ordered rest. But Javel refused to go to bed till he had recovered his arm, and went back as quickly as he could to the harbour to find the barrel, which had been marked with a cross.

They emptied it in his presence, and he picked up his arm, perfectly preserved in the brine, wrinkled, but free from putrefaction. He wrapped it up in a cloth which he had brought for the purpose and went home.

His wife and children carefully examined father's severed arm, feeling the fingers and removing the grains of salt from the nails; then they sent for the joiner to make a miniature coffin.

Next day the whole crew of the trawler followed the funeral of the severed limb. The two brothers, side by side, headed the procession. The parish sexton carried the coffin under one arm.

The younger Javel gave up the sea. He got a small job at the port, and whenever he talked about the accident later, he would add in a confidential whisper: " If my brother had been willing to cut the trawl rope, of course, I should still have my arm. But with him having's keeping."

THE CAPTURE OF
WALTER SCHNAFFS

EVER since he had entered France with the invading army, Walter Schnaffs had been very sorry for himself. He was stout and had difficulty in marching, being short of wind and always in trouble with his feet, which were very flat and very podgy. Besides, he was a peace-loving, kindly soul, not in the least bellicose or bloodthirsty; he was the father of four children, of whom he was passionately fond, and he had a fair-haired young wife, whose affectionate attentions and kisses he missed desperately badly every evening. He liked getting up late and going to bed early, dallying over good food and drinking beer in beer-shops. He reflected, moreover, that all the pleasures of life disappear with death; and he felt an invincible aversion to cannon, rifles, revolvers and sabres, but above all to the bayonet, well aware that he was incompetent to handle this lightning weapon with sufficient agility to defend his fat stomach.

And while he lay on the ground, wrapped in his greatcoat, among his snoring comrades, he could not banish from his mind the thought of his family at home and the dangers that lay before them; if he was killed, what would happen to the children? Who would support them and bring them up? As it was, they were not well off, in spite of the money he had borrowed before starting, in order to leave them a little ready cash. And sometimes Walter Schnaffs wept.

When the fighting began, his knees always felt so weak that he would have collapsed, if he had not reflected that the whole army would trample on him. His hair stood on end, when he heard the ping of the bullets.

For months he had been living in this state of agonizing terror. His division was advancing on Normandy; and one day he was sent out with a small patrol, whose job was simply to reconnoitre a certain stretch of country and then retire. The countryside seemed entirely peaceful and there was no sign of organized opposition.

The Prussians were making their way unconcernedly along a small valley intersected by deep ravines, when suddenly a heavy burst of fire halted them, killing or wounding a score of their men; and a body of partisans, suddenly emerging from a tiny copse, charged them with fixed bayonets.

At first Walter Schnaffs stood stock still, so surprised and dazed that the thought of flight never even entered his head. Then an irresistible impulse to run away came over him; but he immediately realized that he ran like a tortoise in comparison with the lean Frenchmen, who were getting quite close now, leaping like a herd of goats. So, observing, six yards in front of him, a broad ditch filled with scrub under a covering of dead leaves, he dived into it feet first, as one jumps off a bridge into a river. He passed like an arrow through a thick layer of creepers and sharp rushes which tore his face and hands, and landed heavily in a sitting posture on a heap of stones.

Looking up immediately, he saw the sky through the hole he had made. This tell-tale hole might give him away; so he crawled cautiously on all fours along the bottom of the ditch under a roof of interlacing branches as fast as he could away from the scene of the engagement. Then he stopped and sat down again, crouching like a hare in the tall, dry grass.

For some time he could still hear shots, shouts and groans. Presently the noise of the fighting grew fainter and finally ceased altogether. Silence and peace reigned again.

Suddenly something moved close to him. He started in terror. It was a small bird, which had perched on a branch, rustling the dead leaves. It was more than an hour before Walter Schnaffs' heart stopped thumping.

Night was coming on and it was getting dark in the ditch; the soldier began to think. What was he to do? What was going to become of him? He ought to get back to his lines; but how was he to do it? Where were they? And, if he did, he would have to start all over again the hated life of anxiety, terror, fatigue and discomfort, which he had led since the beginning of the war. He would no longer have the physical strength needed to stand the marching and face the constant danger.

But what was he to do? He could not stay in the ditch and hide till the end of hostilities. Of course not. If he hadn't had to eat, this prospect would not have frightened him unduly; but he had to eat, and eat every day.

And here he was, entirely alone, armed, wearing uniform, in a hostile country, far from those who could protect him. He shivered.

Suddenly he had an inspiration: "If only I were a prisoner!" And he felt a longing—a wild, passionate, overwhelming longing—to be a prisoner of the French. Once a prisoner, the war would be over for him; he would be fed and lodged, safe from bullets and sabres, with nothing to fear, in a comfortable, well-guarded prison. To be a prisoner! That was his idea of bliss!

And in a flash he decided what to do—he would surrender.

He got up, determined to put his plan into execution without a moment's delay. But he stopped short, suddenly assailed by disquieting reflexions and new fears.

Where and how was he to surrender? Where was he to go? He began to imagine horrible things; he saw himself dead.

He would run appalling risks, if he ventured alone in his spiked helmet into the countryside.

Suppose he met peasants? These peasants, seeing a Prussian lost and defenceless, would kill him like a stray dog! They would murder him with their pitchforks, their sickles, their picks and shovels. They would tear him limb from limb and make mincemeat of him in the fury and exasperation of defeat.

Suppose he met the partisans? These fanatical partisans, lawless and undisciplined, would shoot him for fun, just to pass the time, jeering at his look of terror. And he saw himself already put up against a wall looking down twelve rifle-barrels, which seemed to peer at him with wicked little black eyes.

Suppose he met the French army itself? The advance guard would take him for a scout, some tough, cunning fellow reconnoitring alone, and they would fire on him. He could already hear the snipers' shots from the cover of the undergrowth, while he, standing in the centre of a field, slumped to the ground, riddled with bullets; he could feel them entering his body.

He sat down again in despair; there seemed no way out of his dilemma. Night had now come on; all round was silence and darkness. He dared not move, and started at every unknown rustle in the shadows. A rabbit, stamping at the entrance to its burrow, nearly made Walter Schnaffs take to his heels. The hooting of the owls set his nerves twitching and his agony of terror was as painful as a wound. He screwed up his staring eyes in his attempts to pierce the darkness, and every minute he thought he heard the tramp of marching feet close to him.

After what seemed an eternity, in which he suffered the torments of the damned, he saw the sky beginning to lighten through the roof of branches. Then he felt inexplicably better: the tension of his limbs relaxed and he was conscious of a sudden relief. The beating of his heart became normal and he fell asleep.

When he woke up, the sun seemed high in the sky; it must be about noon, he thought. Not a sound broke the depressing silence of the countryside, and Walter Schnaffs suddenly became aware that he was excruciatingly hungry.

He yawned and his mouth watered at the thought of sausages—the excellent ration sausages; and his stomach was beginning to cause him acute discomfort.

He got up, took a few steps, felt his legs tottering, and sat down again to think the matter over. For two or three hours he weighed the pros and cons of his position, changing his mind every other minute; his morale had collapsed and he was thoroughly miserable, the prey of conflicting emotions.

At last he hit on an idea which seemed both reasonable and practical; he would wait till a villager passed alone, unarmed and without lethal tools, and he would run to meet him and give himself up, making it quite clear that he was surrendering.

He removed his helmet, fearing that the spike might give him away, and with extreme caution thrust his head up over the edge of his place of concealment.

There was no one to be seen walking alone. Away to the right in a small village the smoke of the midday meal cooking was curling up into the sky above the roofs. Away to the left he noticed a large turreted mansion at the end of an avenue of trees.

He waited till evening in increasing discomfort, seeing nothing but flights of crows and hearing nothing but the rumbling of his own stomach.

Night fell again.

He lay down at the bottom of his ditch and fell into a feverish sleep, haunted by the nightmares of a starving man.

With the dawn he resumed his watch. But the country was as deserted as it had been the day before; and a new fear entered Walter Schnaffs' mind—the fear of dying of hunger. He pictured himself lying on his back at the bottom of his ditch with both his eyes closed. All kinds of insects approached his body and began to devour it, attacking him simultaneously on all sides, crawling in under his clothes to nibble at his cold skin.   And a crow was pecking at his eyes with its sharp beak.

Then he went mad, imagining that he was about to collapse from weakness and was unable to walk.   And already he was preparing to make a dash towards the village, resolved to risk everything and face whatever came, when he saw three peasants on their way to work, with their pitchforks over their shoulders, and he ducked down again into his hiding-place.

But as soon as darkness began to come on, he crawled cautiously out of the ditch and started off, crouching nervously with beating heart, in the direction of the distant mansion, preferring to go there rather than into the village, which seemed to him as terrifying as a den of tigers.

The ground-floor windows were lit up; one of them was actually open; and a strong smell of cooking issued from it, which immediately penetrated Walter Schnaffs' nostrils, sharpening his appetite. It gave him griping pains and made him pant, drawing him irresistibly and giving him the courage of despair.

Suddenly, not thinking what he was doing, he appeared, wearing his helmet, silhouetted in the frame of the window.

Eight servants were at dinner round a large table.   All at once one of the maids stopped with her mouth open, dropping her glass, with eyes staring.   Every glance followed hers.

They sighted the enemy !

Great heavens, the Prussians were attacking the mansion !

First eight voices in different keys uttered a simultaneous cry of panic; then they all leapt to their feet and began struggling, pushing and fighting, to reach the door at the far end of the room.   Chairs were overturned, the men knocked the women down and trampled on them.   In two seconds the room was completely empty, with the table laden with food facing the astonished Walter Schnaffs, who was still standing outside the window.

After a few moments' hesitation he climbed over the sill and advanced towards the plates. The extremity of his hunger made him shake like a man with fever, but terror still held him back and paralysed him. He listened. The whole house seemed to be quivering; doors were being shut, hurrying steps were audible on the first floor. The Prussian listened anxiously to the confused din; then he heard heavy thuds, as though bodies were landing in the soft earth round the walls, as the occupants jumped down from the first storey.

Soon all movement and all sounds ceased and the mansion became as silent as the tomb.

Walter Schnaffs sat down in front of an untouched plate and began to eat. He took enormous mouthfuls, as though he were afraid of being stopped before he had swallowed enough. With both hands he pitchforked the food into his mouth, which opened wide like a trap-door; his throat swelled, as he bolted mouthful after mouthful. Sometimes he stopped, ready to burst like an overfilled pipe, and took the jug of cider to wash out his gullet, as one flushes a blocked drain.

He emptied every plate, every dish, every bottle. Then, stupid with food and drink, torpid, red in the face, dazed, shaken with hiccups, his mouth all greasy, he unbuttoned his tunic to be able to breathe, incapable of walking a step. His eyes began to close and his ideas became muzzy; he laid his heavy head down on his arms crossed on the table, and peacefully lost consciousness.

The pale light of the moon in its last quarter shone in the sky above the trees in the park. It was the chilly hour before dawn.

Shadows began to move in the undergrowth in considerable numbers and complete silence; and from time to time a steel point caught a moonbeam and glinted in the darkness.

The silent mansion reared up its vast black silhouette. Only in two ground-floor windows were the lights still on.

Suddenly a booming voice shouted:

" Forward, you bastards, charge ! "

Then in a flash the doors, the shutters, the windows were forced by a wave of charging men; they smashed and burst their way in and occupied the house. In a flash fifty soldiers, armed to the teeth, rushed into the kitchen, where Walter Schnaffs was sleeping peacefully, and, thrusting fifty loaded rifles against his chest, knocked him backwards head over heels, seized him and trussed him up with ropes.

He was panting and bewildered, too dazed to understand what was happening, bruised and battered and mad with terror.

Suddenly a stout officer, covered with gold lace, planted his foot on his stomach and shouted: " Surrender, you are my prisoner ! "

The Prussian only understood the word " prisoner ", and groaned, " Ja, ja, ja! "

He was picked up, tied to a chair and examined with eager curiosity by his captors, who were puffing like grampuses. Several of them had to sit down, overcome with excitement and fatigue.

He was smiling too, now that he knew that he was a prisoner at last.

Another officer came in and said to the Colonel:

" The enemy have fled, Sir; several of them seem to have been wounded. We are masters of the field."

The portly officer mopped his brow and shouted: " Victory ! "

And, taking a small business note-book from his pocket, he wrote:

" After a desperate struggle, the Prussians were forced to retire, taking with them their dead and wounded; their casualties are estimated at fifty. Several prisoners have been taken."

The young officer went on:

" What orders do you wish me to give now, Sir? "

The Colonel replied :

" We shall now retire to avoid a counter-attack in superior strength, supported by artillery."

And he gave the order to start.

The column re-formed in the dark under the walls of the mansion, and moved off with Walter Schnaffs in the centre, bound and held by six warriors, revolver in hand. Patrols were sent ahead to reconnoitre the route; the main body advanced cautiously, halting from time to time.

At dawn they reached the little market town of La Roche-Oysel, whose National Guard had accomplished this feat of arms.

The population was waiting in a state of apprehension and intense excitement. When they caught sight of the prisoner's helmet, threatening shouts were raised. The women shook their fists; the older ones were in tears. One very old man hurled his crutch at the Prussian, hitting one of the guard on the nose.

The Colonel shouted :

" Guard the prisoner closely! "

At last they reached the Town Hall. The lock-up was opened and Walter Schnaffs thrust into it, after being untied. Two hundred armed men mounted guard round the building.

Then, in spite of symptoms of indigestion, which had been worrying him for some time, the Prussian, wild with joy, began to dance; he danced madly, stamping with his feet and swinging his arms, shouting at the top of his voice all the time, till he sank exhausted at the foot of the wall.

He was a prisoner! He was safe!

This was how the Château de Champignet was retaken from the enemy after only a six hours' occupation.

Colonel Ratier, the draper, who had been in command of the assault, at the head of the National Guard of La Roche-Oysel, was decorated.

THE PIECE OF STRING

ON all the roads round Goderville the peasants and their wives were making their way in towards the little town, for it was market day. The men were plodding along stolidly, their bodies thrust forward with every movement of their long bandy legs; they were misshapen from their heavy work and all the tedious, back-breaking tasks that make up the life of the agricultural labourer; for the downward pressure on the plough raises the left shoulder and so twists the spine, while the firm stance necessary for reaping makes for bandy legs. Their blue starched smocks, as glossy as patent-leather, were relieved round the collar and wrists with fine white embroidery; they bellied out round the men's bony frames like inflated balloons, with a head, two arms and two legs sticking out.

Some were leading a cow or a calf on a rope, while their wives urged the animal on from behind with branches still covered with leaves. The women were carrying on their arms large baskets, from which protruded the heads of chickens or ducks. They walked with a shorter, brisker step than their menfolk; their spare, erect figures were wrapped in skimpy little shawls, pinned across their flat chests, and their hair was covered by a tight-fitting coif with a cap on top.

From time to time a farm-cart would pass, drawn at a jog-trot by an old pony; in it two men, seated side by side, and a woman at the back holding on to the sides against the violent jolting bobbed up and down grotesquely.

On the square at Goderville there was a confused jostling mass of animals and human beings. The horns of the bullocks and the tall beaver hats of the better-off peasants and the caps of their wives stood out above the crush. And the shrill, piercing, high-pitched voices made a harsh, unceasing babel, above which from time to time rose a great, deep-chested roar of laughter from some cheery soul, or the mooing of a cow tied up to the wall of a house.

Everywhere there was the smell of cowhouses and milk and manure, of hay and sweat, the rank, powerful reek of men and animals, characteristic of those who work on the land.

Master Hauchecorne, of Bréauté, had just reached Goder-ville and was making his way towards the market square, when he caught sight of a small piece of string on the ground. Master Hauchecorne, thrifty, like all true Normans, reflected that it was always worth while picking up anything that might come in useful; so he bent down, with some difficulty, for he suffered from rheumatism. He picked up the bit of thin string off the ground and was preparing to roll it up carefully, when he caught sight of Master Malandain, the saddler, at his shop-door watching him. They had had a difference of opinion in the past over a head-stall, and had been on bad terms ever since, being both of an unforgiving disposition.

Master Hauchecorne felt somehow ashamed at being seen by his enemy like this, looking for a bit of string in the muck. He quickly concealed his treasure trove under his smock, slipping it into his trouser pocket; then he pretended to look for something which he couldn't find, and presently he went on towards the square, leaning forward, bent double with his rheumatism.

He was immediately lost in the shrill-voiced, slow-moving crowd, where everyone was bargaining keenly. The peasants were prodding the cows; they went away and came back again, hesitating, always afraid of being taken in, unable to make up their minds; they watched the seller's expression, trying to fathom his cunning or spot the defects of the animal.

The women, having put down their big baskets at their

feet, had taken out the fowls, which now lay on the ground, tied by the legs, with terror in their eyes and their combs scarlet. They listened to the bids, refused to come down, hard-faced and impassive, or else, suddenly making up their minds to accept the lower price offered, shouted after the purchaser, who was slowly walking away:

"Right you are, Master Anthime; you can have it."

Then gradually the crowd in the square thinned, and, as the midday Angelus rang, those who lived too far away to go home scattered to the inns.

At Jourdain's the big room was as full of diners as the courtyard was of vehicles of every kind—farm-carts large and small, gigs and traps, shandrydans of nameless varieties, brown with dung, shapeless, patched up, raising their shafts to heaven like arms, or tilted forward with their tail-boards in the air.

Quite close to the diners as they sat at table, the vast fireplace, in which a bright fire was blazing, threw out its heat on to the backs of the row on the right. Three spits were turning, laden with chickens, pigeons and legs of mutton; and an appetizing smell of meat roasting and gravy trickling over the browning flesh issued from the fireplace, raised everyone's spirits and made every mouth water.

All the aristocracy of the plough took its meals at Master Jourdain's, innkeeper and horse-dealer, a crafty fellow, who had made his pile. Dishes were brought in and carried out again as empty as the jugs of golden cider. Everybody was talking about the business done, what each had bought and sold. Questions were asked about the prospects for the harvest. The weather was good for the green crops, but rather damp for the wheat.

Suddenly the roll of a drum was heard in the courtyard in front of the house. All the diners got up at once, except a few who were not interested, and ran to the door or the windows, with their mouths still full and their napkins in their hands.

When he had finished his roll on the drum, the town-crier read out his notice in a series of jerks, with pauses in the wrong places, so that it made nonsense:

"Notice is hereby given to the inhabitants of Goderville and in general to all—those present at the market that there has been lost this morning on the Beuzeville road between—nine and ten o'clock a black leather wallet containing five hundred francs and some business papers. Anyone finding the same is requested to bring it—without delay to the Town Hall or to Master Fortuné Houlbrèque, of Manneville. A reward of twenty francs is offered."

Then the man continued his round. The deep notes of the drum and the town-crier's announcement, now only faintly audible, were repeated a second time in the distance.

Everyone began discussing the occurrence, speculating on Master Houlbrèque's chances of recovering his wallet or the reverse.

At last the meal came to an end.

They were finishing their coffee, when the police sergeant appeared at the door and enquired:

"Is Master Hauchecorne here?"

Master Hauchecorne, who was sitting at the far end of the table, replied:

"Yes, I'm here."

The sergeant went on:

"Master Hauchecorne, will you be so good as to come with me to the Town Hall? The Mayor would like to speak to you."

The peasant, surprised and worried, hurriedly swallowed his brandy, got up, and, even more bent than in the morning, for the first few steps after a rest were particularly painful, started off in the wake of the sergeant, repeating:

"I'm here, I'm here."

The Mayor was waiting for him, sitting in an armchair.

He was the local solicitor—a stout, important man, fond of pompous language.

"Master Hauchecorne," he said, "you were seen this morning to pick up the wallet lost by Master Houlbrèque, of Manneville, on the Beuzeville road."

The peasant, taken aback, looked at the Mayor; he was already frightened at the suspicion that had fallen upon him, without quite knowing why.

"Me? I picked up the wallet, did I?"

"Yes, you."

"On my honour, I knows nought about it."

"You were seen."

"I were seen; who seen me?"

"Master Malandain, the saddler."

Then the old man remembered, understood, and, flushing with anger, cried:

"So, 'e's seen me, 'as 'e, the scoundrel? This is what 'e seen me pick up, this 'ere piece of string; look, Sir!"

And, rummaging in the depths of his pocket, he pulled out the little bit of string.

But the Mayor shook his head incredulously:

"You'll never persuade me, Master Hauchecorne, that Master Malandain, who is a reliable man, mistook a piece of string for a wallet."

The peasant, now in a furious temper, raised his hand and spat on the floor as evidence of his good faith, repeating:

"But it's God's truth, all the same; it's the whole truth and nothing but the truth, s'welp me God!"

The Mayor went on:

"After picking up the object, you even went on searching in the mud for some time, in case any coin might have fallen out."

The old fellow was speechless with anger and fright:

"Some folks 'll say any damned thing at all; fancy

telling lies like that to discredit an honest man; some folks 'll say anything."

His protestations were unavailing; the Mayor didn't believe him.

He was confronted with Master Malandain, who repeated and upheld his accusation. They abused one another for an hour. At his own request, Master Hauchecorne was searched and nothing was found on him.

Finally, the Mayor, not knowing what to do, sent him away, warning him that he was going to report the matter to higher authority and ask for instructions.

The news had spread. As he left the Town Hall, the old fellow was surrounded and questioned with a curiosity sometimes genuine, sometimes ironical, but always good-natured. And he began to tell the story of the piece of string. No one believed him; they all merely laughed.

As he walked on, everybody stopped him, and he stopped his acquaintances, beginning his story over and over again, repeating his protestations of innocence, turning out his pockets to show that he had got nothing.

But everybody said: "Go on, you cunning old devil!"

And he lost his temper, working himself up into a fever of nervous exasperation, because no one would believe him; he didn't know what to do and merely went on repeating his story.

It was getting dark and time to be going home. He set out with three neighbours, to whom he pointed out the spot where he had picked up the piece of string. And all the way home he enlarged on the incident.

In the evening he took a turn round the village of Bréauté in order to tell everyone. He met with nothing but incredulity.

He couldn't sleep all night for the worry of it.

Next day, about one o'clock in the afternoon, Marius Paumelle, one of Master Breton's farm hands at Ymauville, brought back the wallet with its contents intact to Master Houlbrèque at Manneville.

The man stated that he had actually found the wallet on the road, but, not knowing how to read, had taken it home with him and given it to his employer.

The news soon spread. Master Hauchecorne heard about it. He immediately went round repeating his story, with the sequel. He was vindicated.

"What got my goat," he would say, "wasn't so much the thing itself, if you understand what I mean, but the lies. There's nothing 'urts so much as to be blamed because somebody has told a lie."

He talked all day about his adventure; he told the story to people he passed on the road, to those who dropped into the local for a drink, and to the congregation, as they came out of church the following Sunday. He stopped total strangers to tell them. His mind was now at rest, but something nevertheless still worried him without his knowing exactly what it was. People seemed amused as they listened to him; they didn't seem convinced, and he was conscious of whispering behind his back.

The following Tuesday he went to the Goderville market, simply in order to tell his story.

Malandain, standing at his door, burst out laughing as he passed. He wondered why.

He accosted a farmer from Criquetot, who didn't let him finish his story, and, digging him in the ribs, shouted at him: "Go on, you cunning old devil!" and turned on his heel.

Master Hauchecorne was still puzzled and was getting more and more worried. Why did they call him "a cunning old devil"?

At dinner in Jourdain's inn he began again explaining what had happened.

A horse-dealer from Montivilliers shouted at him:

"Get along, you old scoundrel! I know all about your little games with your string."

Hauchecorne stammered:

"But the wallet has been found."

The other retorted:

"Shut your mouth, old man; the man who returns a thing isn't always the one who found it. Nobody's any the wiser. Now I've got you guessing!"

The peasant was flabbergasted; at last he understood. He was being accused of having had the wallet returned by a confederate, an accomplice. He tried to protest, but the whole table roared with laughter.

He couldn't finish his meal, and went out amid general mocking laughter.

He went home ashamed and indignant, choking with impotent rage, all the more distressed because, with his typical Norman cunning, he was quite capable of doing what he was accused of having done, and even of boasting of it as a clever trick. His duplicity being so well known, he realized dimly that he would never be able to establish his innocence. And the injustice of the suspicion wounded him deeply.

Then he began telling the story all over again, making it longer every day, adding fresh arguments at every telling, more emphatic protestations, more solemn oaths, which he thought out and elaborated, when he was alone, for he could never get the incident of the piece of string out of his mind. The more involved his defence became, the more closely reasoned his arguments, the less did people believe him.

"That's just the sort of argument a fellow uses when he's lying," people were saying behind his back.

He felt it, and was eating his heart out, exhausting himself in vain attempts to establish his innocence.

He began to fail visibly.

The local wits now used to get him to tell the story of the

string for a joke, as people egg on an old soldier to tell the story of his campaigns.

His mind, seriously affected, was giving way.

Towards the end of December, he took to his bed.

He died early in January, and in his last delirium he kept on protesting his innocence, repeating over and over again :

" A little piece of string . . . just a little piece of string, Sir, . . . look, 'ere it is ! "

HIS CONFESSION

When Captain Hector Marie de Fontenne married Mlle. Laurine d'Estelle, their relations and friends expected the marriage to be a failure.

Mlle. Laurine was slim and pretty; she was fair and slightly built and without a trace of shyness; at twelve she had had the assurance of a woman of thirty. She was one of those precocious little Paris girls who seem born knowing everything; she already had all a woman's wiles, a realistic outlook and the instinctive cunning and adaptability which make certain people appear predestined to trick and deceive others in everything they do. Every action seems thoroughly planned, every step nicely calculated, every word carefully weighed; their whole life is a part they are playing before the world.

She also had charm. She was always laughing, unable to stop or control herself, when she thought anything quaint or amusing. She used to laugh in people's faces in the rudest way, but so attractively that she gave no offence.

She was extremely well off. Her marriage with Captain de Fontenne had been arranged by a priest. Brought up very strictly in a religious house, this officer, when he joined his regiment, took with him the moral standards of the monastery, uncomprising principles and extreme intolerance. He was one of those men who are bound to become either saints or anarchists, the slaves of their ideologies; their beliefs are cast-iron and their convictions impervious to argument.

He was a tall, dark young man, serious, strait-laced and unsophisticated; he had the mentality of a child, as limited in outlook as he was obstinate; one of those men who go through life without ever understanding things below the surface, fine shades or subtle distinctions, who guess nothing, suspect nothing and never conceive the possibility of anyone thinking, believing or acting differently from themselves.

Mlle. Laurine saw him, sized him up at first sight and accepted him as her husband.

They got on together admirably. Quick to adapt herself, she played her cards well and showed discretion; she always managed to behave as was expected of her. She was as ready for good works as for amusements, and went to church and the theatre with equal regularity; she could be sophisticated or strait-laced, and in her serious conversation with her austere husband there was always a hint of irony and a twinkle in her eye. She told him all about her charitable activities with the priests of the parish and the neighbourhood, and her good works gave her an excuse to be out most of the day.

But sometimes, in the middle of an account of some charitable work, she would go off into a fit of uncontrollable hysterical laughter. The Captain sat surprised, puzzled and slightly shocked, in front of his wife, who was speechless. When she had calmed down a bit, he would ask:

"What is the matter with you, Laurine?"

She would answer: "Oh! nothing; I just remembered a funny thing that happened to me," and she told him the first story that came into her head.

Well, during the summer of 1883 Captain Hector de Fontenne took part in the grand Army manœuvres of the 32nd Corps.

One evening, as they were in camp on the outskirts of a town, after ten days in bivouacs in the open, during which they had worked hard and lived hard, the Captain's fellow-officers decided to have a good dinner.

M. de Fontenne at first refused to join them, but later agreed to do so, in view of the surprise caused by his refusal.

His next-door neighbour at dinner, Major de Favre, while

discussing military operations—the only subject in which the Captain was passionately interested—saw to it that his glass was kept well filled. The day had been stifling, with that oppressive, dry heat which raises a thirst; and the Captain drank without thinking, not noticing that he was getting unusually cheerful; the wine went to his head and produced an unaccustomed sense of well-being, arousing new passions, strange longings and vague anticipations.

By dessert he was drunk. He was talking and laughing, excited with the noisy, uncontrolled intoxication of a man who is normally quiet and well-behaved.

A visit to the theatre was suggested to wind up the evening, and he went with his friends. One of them recognized an actress with whom he had had an affair; and a supper was arranged to which some of the ladies of the company were invited.

The Captain woke up next morning to find himself in a strange room in bed with a fair-haired prostitute, who said, when she saw him open his eyes: " Good morning, darling ! "

At first he did not understand, but soon he began gradually to remember things, though rather vaguely.

Then he got up and dressed without a word and emptied his purse on the mantelpiece.

He was overcome with shame, when he found himself standing in full uniform, his sword at his side, in this furnished bedroom with its threadbare curtains and a stained sofa that looked anything but inviting. For a time he could not face going downstairs, where he might meet people, and passing the porter, and, worst of all, going out into the street under the eyes of the passers-by and the neighbours.

The woman kept repeating: " What ever is the matter with you, darling? Have you lost your tongue? You had plenty to say last night. What a mug you are ! "

He bowed formally and, forcing himself to leave the house,

he walked back to his quarters as fast as he could, fully convinced that everybody knew, from his appearance, his bearing and his face, that he had been with a harlot.

He suffered agonies of remorse—the torturing remorse of a man of austere, careful life.

He went to confession and communion; but he still felt miserable, haunted by the thought of his lapse and the consciousness that he was in honour bound to tell his wife what had happened.

He did not see her for a month, as she had been spending the period of the manœuvres with her parents.

She came to him with open arms and a smile on her lips. He received her with the embarrassed constraint of a guilty conscience, and hardly said a word all day.

When they were alone, she asked him:

"What's the matter with you, my dear? You're quite changed." He answered awkwardly:

"There's nothing the matter, darling, absolutely nothing."

"Excuse me, I know you pretty well, and I'm sure there is something. You've got something on your mind—something's making you worried and anxious."

"Well, yes, I *have* got something on my mind."

"What is it?"

"I can't tell you."

"You can't tell me? Why not? You make me quite frightened."

"I can give you no reasons. I just can't tell you."

She was sitting on a settee, and he was walking up and down with his hands behind his back, avoiding his wife's eye. She went on:

"Look here, you've got to confess to me; it's my duty to insist, and I demand the truth; it's my right. You can't have secrets from me, any more than I can from you."

Turning his back on her and standing in front of the French window, he insisted:

" My dear, there are some things better not told; my present trouble is one of these."

She got up, walked across the room, took him by the arm and, making him turn round, put both her hands on his shoulders and with an irresistible smile looked up at him and said:

" You know, Marie "—she called him Marie when she was being specially affectionate—" you just can't keep anything from me. I should think you had done something really bad."

He murmured:

" I *have* done something really bad."

She said lightly:

" Oh! it's as bad as that, is it? I *am* surprised at you! "

He answered sharply:

" I don't intend to tell you anything; so it's useless to insist."

But she led him to the armchair, made him sit down and perched herself on his right knee, brushing the curled tip of his moustache with a quick butterfly kiss:

" If you don't tell me, there'll always be something between us."

Tortured by an agony of remorse he murmured:

" If I told you what I've done, you would never forgive me."

" On the contrary, my dear, I should forgive you at once."

" No, you couldn't."

" I promise I will."

" I tell you it's impossible."

" I swear I'll forgive you."

" No, Laurine dear, you couldn't."

" How innocent you are, my dear, not to say childish. By refusing to tell me what you've done, you would make me imagine the worst; I shan't be able to get it out of my mind, and I shall have a grudge against you as much for your silence as for your unknown crime.   Whereas if you make a clean breast of it, I shall have forgotten all about it by to-morrow."

" The fact is. . . ."

He blushed up to the ears and went on solemnly :

" I am making my confession to you as I would to a priest, Laurine."

A ghost of a smile played round her lips, as often happened when he was talking to her, and she said with a hint of mockery in her voice :

" I'm all ears."

" You know, my dear, how little I drink; I only take enough wine to colour the water and I avoid spirits altogether, as you are aware."

" Yes, I know that."

" Well, I must tell you, at the end of the Army manœuvres I let myself go a bit one evening, when I was very thirsty and dead tired, and . . ."

" You got drunk?   For shame, how horrid of you!"

" Yes, I got drunk."

She affected severity :

" You mean, you got blind drunk—you'd better admit it—so drunk you couldn't walk, eh?"

" Oh! no, not as bad as that; I didn't know what I was doing, but I could stand; I talked and laughed; I just went mad."

As he stopped, she asked :

" Is that all?"

" No."

" Well, after that, what?"

" After that I did something dreadful."

She was looking at him anxiously, puzzled, but also genuinely concerned.

" What was it, my dear?"

" We had supper with some actresses; and I don't know how it happened, but I was unfaithful to you, Laurine."

He made this announcement in a serious, solemn voice.

She gave a little gasp, and there was a sudden irresistible twinkle of merriment in her eye. She said:

" You say you were . . ."

And a shrill, staccato, hysterical laugh, three times repeated, interrupted her sentence.

She made an effort to recover herself; but every time she was on the point of speaking, her laughter bubbled up in her throat and burst out; she checked it quickly, but it always got the better of her, breaking out again and again, like the effervescence of an uncorked bottle of champagne, whose froth must overflow. She put her hand over her mouth to stop it and restrain this untimely explosion of merriment, but her laughter broke the barrier, her breast heaved and all her efforts failed to keep back the outburst.

She stammered: " You . . . you . . . were unfaithful to me," and went off into a peal of laughter.

And all the time she was gazing at him with such a strange look of mockery in her eyes, in spite of herself, that he stood tongue-tied and dumbfounded.

Then suddenly, giving up the struggle, she let herself go in an uncontrolled fit of hysterical laughter. Little gasps issued from her mouth, her chest shook, and, with both hands pressed against the pit of her stomach, she had long fits of choking, like a person with whooping-cough.

Every time she tried to recover her composure, a new fit seized her, and every time she tried to speak she became more helpless.

" My poor dear thing! " she gasped, and collapsed again.

He got up, leaving her alone in the armchair, and suddenly turning deathly pale, he said:

" Laurine, this exhibition is worse than unseemly."

She stammered through a burst of laughter:

"I can't help it, I just can't, you're so frightfully funny!"

He went ghastly pale and looked hard at her, as a strange suspicion forced itself upon him. Suddenly he opened his mouth, as if he was on the point of shouting at her, but he said nothing, turned on his heel and left the room, slamming the door behind him.

Laurine, bent double and quite exhausted, was near fainting; her laughter gradually subsided but kept bursting out again from time to time like the embers of a dying bonfire.

TWO FRIENDS

Paris was under blockade, starving and at her last gasp. The sparrows were disappearing from the roofs and the number of rats in the sewers was diminishing. Anything was being eaten.

On a fine morning in January, as he was walking gloomily along the outer Boulevard with his hands in the pockets of his uniform trousers and an empty stomach, M. Morissot, a clock-maker by trade and a gossip by inclination, suddenly stopped in front of a companion in arms, whom he recognized as a friend. It was M. Sauvage, a fishing acquaintance.

Every Sunday before the war, Morissot used to leave home at dawn with a bamboo rod in his hand and a tin box on his back. He took the Argenteuil line, got out at Colombes, and walked to Marante Island. Immediately he reached this place, which was never far from his thoughts, he began fishing, and went on till nightfall.

There every Sunday he used to meet a stout, cheery little man, M. Sauvage, a haberdasher from the street of Our Lady of Loreto, another mad-keen fisherman. They often spent half the day sitting side by side, with their lines in their hands and their feet dangling over the stream; and they had taken a liking to each other.

Some days they didn't speak, sometimes they chatted; but they understood each other perfectly without any words, having similar tastes and identical feelings.

About ten o'clock on a spring morning, when the sun was just beginning to get hot and little wisps of mist were drifting down the calm stream, and the fishing enthusiasts could feel the pleasant spring warmth on their backs, Morissot would say to his neighbour: "Perfect weather, isn't it?" and

M. Sauvage would answer: "Quite perfect." That was all that was needed for them to understand and respect each other.

In the autumn, in the late afternoon, the sky, blood-red in the sunset glow, reflected the shapes of the crimson clouds in the water, staining the whole river red and flushing the horizon; the trees between the two friends, already clad in autumn tints and shivering in the first chill of winter, flamed like fire and gleamed like gold. Then M. Sauvage would look at Morissot and say with a smile: "What an evening!", and Morissot, equally impressed but without taking his eye off his float, would reply: "It's an improvement on the Boulevard, what?"

As soon as they recognized each other, they shook hands warmly, acutely conscious of the changed circumstances in which they met. M. Sauvage murmured with a sigh: "What a mess we're in!" Morissot answered sadly: "And what a glorious day it is! It's the first fine day of the year." The sky was, in fact, a brilliant cloudless blue.

They walked on side by side, thinking regretfully of the past. Morissot went on: "You haven't forgotten our days fishing? Those were good days."

M. Sauvage asked: "When shall we get back to them?"

They went into a little café and had an absinthe together, after which they resumed their walk along the pavements.

Morissot suddenly stopped: "What about another little drink?" M. Sauvage was agreeable: "I don't mind if I do." And they went into another bar.

When they came out, they were quite muzzy in the head, fuddled as people are who have taken alcohol on an empty stomach. It was pleasantly warm and a gentle breeze fanned their faces.

M. Sauvage, his intoxication completed by the warm spring air, stopped:

"Suppose we go?"

"Where?"

" Fishing, of course."

" But where? "

" Why, to our usual island. The French outposts aren't far from Colombes. I know Colonel Dumoulin; they'll let us through, I'm sure."

Morissot quivered with excitement: " Right you are, I'm your man." And they separated to fetch their fishing-gear.

An hour later they were walking side by side along the main road. Presently they reached the villa occupied by the Colonel. He smiled at their whim and agreed to their request. They set off again with their pass.

They soon got through the outposts, crossed the deserted village of Colombes, and found themselves on the edge of the little vineyards that drop down to the Seine. It was about eleven o'clock.

Across the river, Argenteuil looked dead. The high ground at Orgemont and Sannois dominated the whole countryside. The great plain, stretching as far as Nanterre, was empty, with its bare cherry trees and grey fields.

M. Sauvage, pointing to the high ground, murmured: " The Prussians are up there! " And a sudden fear of this deserted bit of country chilled the two friends.

The Prussians! They had never seen any of them, but for months they had felt their presence all round Paris, destroying France, looting, murdering, starving, invisible but irresistible. And a sort of superstitious terror was added to the hatred they felt for their unknown conquerors.

Morissot stammered: "Suppose we ran into some of them, what then? "

M. Sauvage replied with the Puckish humour of the Parisian still there in spite of everything: " We'll offer them a plate of fish to fry."

But they shrank from venturing across the open country, frightened by the silence and emptiness all round them.

At last M. Sauvage made up his mind: " Let's go on, but carefully."

And they went down through a vineyard, crouching and crawling, taking advantage of the cover afforded by the vines, keeping their eyes skinned and listening intently.

There was still a strip of open ground they had to cross to reach the river-bank. They began to run, and, as soon as they got to the steep bank, they hid in the dry rushes.

Morissot put his ear to the ground to make sure that no one was walking about in their neighbourhood. He could hear nothing; they were absolutely alone.

Reassured, they began to fish.

In front, Marante Island, now deserted, concealed them from the far bank. The little restaurant was shut and looked as if it had been closed for years.

M. Sauvage caught the first gudgeon, Morissot the second; and then in quick succession they began to pull in their lines with the little silvery creatures wriggling on the hook—a regular miraculous draught of fishes.

They placed the fish carefully in a close-meshed net-bag, which lay in the water at their feet, and they experienced the thrill of pleasure, the joy one feels at recapturing a long-lost delight.

They felt the cheering warmth of the sun on their backs; they heard nothing and thought of nothing; the rest of the world had ceased to exist for them; they just fished.

Suddenly a dull roar, which seemed to come from underground, made the earth rock. The big guns were starting to thunder.

Morissot turned his head, and over the bank away to the left he saw the lofty outline of Mont-Valérien, its summit wreathed in a white plume of smoke which it had just belched forth.

And immediately a second puff of smoke came from the

top of the fortress, and a few seconds later the growl of another detonation was heard.

Others followed, as at short intervals the hill sent forth its deadly breath, puffing out whitish wisps of smoke, which rose slowly in the windless air and formed a cloud above it.

M. Sauvage shrugged his shoulders: " There they are, at it again."

Morissot, keeping a watchful eye on the feather of his float, as it bobbed up and down, suddenly felt a peace-loving man's anger against these madmen fighting each other, and he growled: " What fools men are to kill each other like that ! " M. Sauvage retorted: " They're worse than wild beasts."

And Morissot, who had just hooked a bleak, declared: " Of course, it'll always be like this as long as there are politicians."

M. Sauvage interrupted him: " The Republic would never have declared war."

Morissot broke in: " With kings one has war abroad, with the Republic one has war at home."

And quietly they began a friendly discussion, settling great political problems with the sane reasonableness of peaceable men of limited outlook, both agreeing on this point, that no one would ever be free. And Mont-Valérien rumbled on ceaselessly, shattering French houses with its shells, dealing death and annihilating life. Many a dream, much joy long looked forward to, many hopes of happiness were being destroyed and wounds inflicted that would never heal in the hearts of women, girls and mothers, far away in other countries.

" Such is life," declared M. Sauvage.

" You'd better call it death," retorted Morissot with a smile.

Then they gave a sudden start of terror, as they became

aware of footsteps behind them; looking round, they saw
four men standing close behind them—four tall men, armed
and bearded, in uniform like men-servants, with flat caps
on their heads, covering them with rifles.

The two lines dropped from their hands and began to
float down the river.

In a few seconds they were seized, marched off, thrown into
a boat and ferried across to the island.

Behind the house, which they had thought deserted, they
saw a score of German soldiers.

A great hirsute giant, who was sitting astride a chair leaning over the back, smoking a porcelain pipe, enquired in
excellent French: " Well, gentlemen, did you have good
sport? "

At that moment a soldier put down at the officer's feet
the net-bag full of fish, which he had carefully brought
along.

The Prussian smiled: " Ah! I see you haven't done so
badly. But that's not what I want to talk to you about.
Listen to me, and don't be alarmed.

" For me, you are two spies sent to keep on eye on me.
I capture you and shoot you. You were pretending to fish
in order to conceal your intentions. You have fallen into
my hands; that's just too bad, but it's war.

" As you came through the advanced posts, you must
have the password in order to get back. Give me that password and I'll spare your lives."

The two friends stood side by side, deathly pale; their
hands trembled a little, but they said nothing.

The officer went on: " No one will be any the wiser;
you will return as if nothing had happened. The secret
will be known only to you. If you refuse, it means death,
instant death. Now choose."

They stood motionless, without a word.

The Prussian went on in a matter-of-fact tone of voice

with a gesture towards the river: "You realize that within five minutes you'll be at the bottom of that water—within five minutes! You must have relations."

Mont-Valérien went on firing.

The two anglers stood there silent. The German gave an order in his own language. He moved his chair, so as not to be too close to the prisoners; and twelve men took up their position twenty yards away, with their rifles at the order.

The officer went on: "I give you one minute, not a second more."

Then he suddenly got up, approached the two Frenchmen, took Morissot by the arm, led him aside and whispered to him: "Quick, the password; your friend will never know; it will look as if I had taken pity on you."

Morissot remained silent.

The Prussian next took M. Sauvage aside and made the same suggestion to him.

M. Sauvage did not answer. They stood side by side again.

The officer gave an order; the soldiers raised their rifles.

Morissot's eye fell accidentally on the net-bag full of gudgeon, lying on the grass a few yards away.

The heap of fish, which were still wriggling, flashed in a gleam of sunlight. He suddenly felt faint. In spite of his efforts, his eyes filled with tears.

He stammered: "Good-bye, M. Sauvage."

M. Sauvage replied: "Good-bye, M. Morissot."

They shook hands, unable to repress the trembling of their limbs.

The officer shouted: "Fire!"

The twelve shots rang out together.

M. Sauvage slumped forward on his face. Morissot, being taller, spun round and fell across his friend's body, face upwards, while blood spurted from the bullet-holes in the breast of his tunic.

The German gave another order.

His men disappeared and soon returned with ropes and stones, which they tied to the feet of the two dead men; they then carried them to the bank.

Mont-Valérien was firing all the time, capped now by a towering cowl of smoke.

Two soldiers took Morissot by the head and the feet, and two others picked up M. Sauvage in the same way. They swung them right back and forward and let go; the bodies described a curve and, weighted by the stones, plunged into the river feet first.

There was a splash, the water foamed and shivered, and soon became calm again, as tiny wavelets spread to the banks.

A little blood was visible on the surface.

The officer, without a trace of emotion, murmured to himself: " Now it's the fishes' turn," and he made towards the house.

Suddenly his eye caught the net-bag with the gudgeon on the grass. He picked it up, examined it, smiled and shouted: " Wilhelm! "

A soldier in a white apron ran up. And the Prussian, throwing him the catch of the two dead men, gave his orders: " Have these little fish fried at once, while they are still alive; they'll be delicious."

And he lit his pipe again.

THE DEVIL

THE peasant was standing facing the doctor at the foot of the death-bed. The old woman, calm, resigned and quite clear in the head, was looking at the two men and listening to what they were saying. She was going to die; she accepted the fact; her time was up, she was ninety-two.

Through the window and door, which were both open, the July sunshine poured in, throwing a hot glow on the brown earth floor, uneven and beaten hard by the wooden clogs of four generations of rustics. The smell of the fields was wafted in, too, by the hot wind, the smell of hay, corn and leaves, scorched by the midday sun. The grasshoppers were clacking loudly, filling the countryside with their strident note, like the noise of the wooden rattles which children buy at fairs.

The doctor, raising his voice, was saying:

"Honoré, you can't leave your mother alone in this condition; she may die at any moment."

And the peasant was repeating in dismay:

"But I've got to get my wheat in, all the same; it's been lying too long already. Just now the weather's perfect. What do you say, Mother?"

The dying woman gave her assent by a glance and nod, still obsessed by the typical avarice of the Norman, urging her son to get his wheat in and leave her to die alone.

But the doctor lost his temper and, stamping his foot, cried:

"You're a heartless brute, do you hear? I forbid you to do it—do you hear? And if you really must get your wheat in to-day, dash it all, go and get Mother Rapet to watch your mother. I insist—do you hear? If you disobey me, I'll let you die like a dog, when your turn comes to be ill—do you hear?"

The peasant, a tall, thin man with slow movements, was in an agony of indecision, torn between fear of the doctor and passionate dislike of spending money; he paused to calculate and stammered:

"How much does Mother Rapet charge for watching?"

The doctor shouted:

"How should I know? It depends on how long you want her. Hang it all, make your own arrangement with her. But I insist on her being here within the hour, do you hear?"

The man made up his mind:

"All right, I'll go; don't be angry, Doctor."

The doctor left, calling out:

"You'd better take care, see, for I don't care a damn for anybody, when I've lost my temper."

As soon as he was alone, the peasant turned to his mother, and, in a resigned voice, said:

"I'm goin' to fetch Mother Rapet; Doctor says I must. Don't fash yourself, I'll be back soon."

And he too left the house.

Mother Rapet, the old laundress, watched by all the dead and dying in the village and the neighbourhood. As soon as she had sewn her clients up in their last winding-sheet, she returned to the iron, with which she ironed the linen of the living. As wrinkled as a last year's apple, bad-tempered, jealous and prodigiously close-fisted, she was bent double, as if her back had been broken by the never-ending movement of her iron over the linen; she might have been described as having an abnormal, cynical passion for death. Her conversation was always about those whose decease she had witnessed, and all the different kinds of death she had seen; and she told the story in minute detail, which never varied, like a shooting man telling of his exploits with the gun.

When Honoré Bontemps entered her house, he found her getting ready some blue for the village girls' collars.

He said:

"Hullo! Good afternoon! I hope I see you well, Mother Rapet."

She turned her head:

"Oh! So so—and yourself?"

"Oh! I'm all right; it's my mother who isn't."

"Your mother?"

"Yes, my mother."

"What's up with your mother?"

"She's just going to kick the bucket."

The old woman took her hands out of the water and the transparent blue drops ran down her fingers, till they fell back into the wash-tub. She asked with sudden sympathy:

"She's that bad, is she?"

"Doctor says she won't last through the afternoon."

"Then she must be pretty bad."

Honoré hesitated. He didn't like to make the suggestion he had in his mind straight out; but, being unable to think of anything to say, he took the plunge:

"How much do you want to watch her till the end? You know we ain't rich; I can't afford a servant. That's what's done in my poor old mother, too much to worry about and too much work. She did the work of ten, though she be ninety-two. They don't make 'em like that to-day."

Mother Rapet answered in a business-like tone:

"There's two prices. Two francs a day and three francs a night for the gentry; one franc a day and two francs a night for the rest. I'll come to you for one and two francs."

But the peasant was thinking. He knew his mother pretty well; he knew the strength and toughness of her constitution. She might last a week, in spite of the doctor's opinion.

He said with decision:

" No! I'd rather you made me a price, a price to see her through to the end. It's a gamble for both of us. Doctor says she'll pop off quite soon. If she does, so much the better for you and so much the worse for me. But if she hangs on till to-morrow or longer, I gain and you lose."

The watcher looked at the man in surprise. She had never taken on a death at contract rates before. She hesitated, attracted by the idea of a gamble, but suspicious that there was a catch somewhere.

" I can't say anything till I've seen your mother," she answered.

" Come along and see her, then."

She dried her hands and followed him at once.

They did not speak on the way. She walked fast, while he took huge strides, as if he was crossing a stream at each step.

The cows, lying in the meadows overcome by the heat, raised their heads sluggishly and mooed feebly towards the two hurrying figures, as if to beg for fresh grass.

As he approached the house, Honoré Bontemps murmured:

" I wonder if it's all over."

And his unconscious hope showed in his voice.

But the old woman was not dead. She was still lying on her back on her truckle bed, with her hands on the purple chintz counterpane—pitifully thin hands, gnarled, like two uncanny, crab-like creatures, knotted by rheumatism, hard work and all the jobs she had done for nearly a hundred years.

Mother Rapet went up to the bed and examined the dying woman. She felt her pulse, sounded her chest, listened to her breathing and asked her questions in order to hear her speak. Then, after further lengthy consideration, she left the room, followed by Honoré. She had made up her mind; the old woman would not last till night. He asked:

" Well? "

The watcher replied:

" Well, she'll last two days, p'raps three. I'll do the job for six francs, all in."

He cried:

" Six francs! Six francs! Are you daft? I tell you mother'll only last five or six hours, no more."

The bargaining lasted a long time, for both were obstinate. At last the watcher made as if to go home and, as time was passing and as the wheat wouldn't get itself in, finally he agreed:

" Very well, I agree to six francs, all in, up to the removal of the body."

" Agreed, six francs."

He strode off to his wheat, which was lying under the blazing harvest sun. The watcher went back into the house.

She had brought her work with her, for all the time she was watching the dying and the dead, she sewed, sometimes for herself, sometimes for the family which was employing her on this double job, paying extra for the sewing.

Suddenly she enquired:

" Have you received the last rites, Mother Bontemps? "

The peasant woman shook her head and Mother Rapet, who was a pious soul, jumped up:

" Good Heavens! Do you mean it? I'll go and fetch the priest."

And she hastened to the priest's house, so fast that the little boys in the square, seeing her almost running, thought that some accident must have happened.

The priest put on his surplice and came at once, preceded by a choirboy ringing a little bell to let people know that the Body of God was being carried through the peaceful summer countryside. The men working in the distance took off their sun-hats and stood still, till the surplice had disappeared behind a farm; the women gathering the corn-

stooks straightened themselves to make the sign of the cross,
the black hens scuttled along the ditches in terror, waddling
towards their usual hole in the hedge, through which they
quickly disappeared; a colt, tethered in a field, took fright
at the sight of the surplice and began to run round in circles
at the end of its rope, lashing out with its heels. The choirboy in his red cassock walked fast; and the priest, with his
head bent sideways and wearing a square biretta, followed
him, murmuring prayers. Mother Rapet brought up the
rear, bent almost double, in an attempt to prostrate herself
as she walked, with hands clasped as if in church.

Honoré saw them pass in the distance. He asked:

" Where's the priest going? "

His paid hand, who had more imagination than his master,
replied:

" 'E's takin' the Blessed Sacrament to your mother, of
course."

The peasant showed no surprise:

" That's quite likely," and he went on with his work.

Mother Bontemps made her confession, received absolution
and took the sacrament; and the priest went away, leaving
the two women alone in the stifling cottage.

Then Mother Rapet began to look at the dying woman,
wondering if it would last long.

Evening was coming on; a cooler air was blowing into
the house in fresher gusts, making a cheap oleograph,
fastened up with two pins, flap against the wall; the little
window-curtains, once white, but now flyblown and yellow
with age, looked as if they were trying to fly away, struggling
in their eagerness to escape, like the old woman's soul.

Motionless, with her eyes open, she seemed to be calmly
awaiting death, which was so near but still delayed. Her
quick breathing made a little whistling noise in her congested throat; it would soon cease and there would be one
woman less in the world, and no one would miss her.

At nightfall Honoré returned. Approaching the bed, he
saw that his mother was still alive and he asked, as he
always did, when she wasn't well:

" 'Ow are you feeling?"

He sent Mother Rapet away, telling her:

" Five o'clock to-morrow morning, without fail."

She answered:

" Right, five o'clock to-morrow morning."

She actually arrived at dawn.

Honoré was eating his soup, which he had made for
himself, before going to work.

The watcher enquired:

" Well, is your mother dead?"

He replied, with a malicious twinkle in his eye:

" No! She seems a bit better."

And he left the house.

Mother Rapet, who was beginning to get anxious, approached the dying woman, whose condition was un-
changed; she was breathing with difficulty, lying inert,
her eyes open and her hands clenched on the counterpane.

And the watcher realized that this might last for two
days, four days or even a week, and fear gripped her miserly
heart, while she felt a surge of anger against the crafty fellow
who had tricked her and against the woman who would
not die.

However, she went about her work and waited, fixing
her eyes on Mother Bontemps' wrinkled face.

Honoré came in for his midday meal; he seemed in good
spirits, almost jovial; after dinner he went out again. He
was certainly getting in his wheat under excellent conditions.

Mother Rapet was getting more and more exasperated;
every minute that passed now seemed to her so much time
stolen, and time was money. She felt a desire, a wild desire,
to seize this obstinate old fool, this stubborn old woman, this
pig-headed old crone by the neck and with one squeeze to

stop for ever the quick faint breathing, which was robbing her of time and money.

But she reflected that this would be risky; and, with a sudden inspiration, she approached the bed.

She asked:

" Have you seen the Devil yet? "

Mother Bontemps murmured:

" No."

Then the watcher began to talk, telling stories to terrify the dying woman's failing mind.

A few minutes before death, she said, the Devil always appeared to the dying. He had a broom in his hand and a cooking-pot on his head, and he uttered loud cries. When he had been seen, it was all over, the dying person had only a few minutes to live. And she enumerated all the people to whom the Devil had appeared in her presence that very year, Joséphine Loisel, Eulalie Ratier, Sophie Padagnau, Séraphine Grospied.

Mother Bontemps, deeply impressed at the end of her story, stirred in bed, moving her hands and trying to turn her head in order to see the back of the room.

Suddenly Mother Rapet disappeared behind the foot of the bed. Out of the cupboard she took a sheet, which she draped round herself; on her head she put the cooking-pot, whose three short curved feet stuck up like three horns; she seized a broom in her right hand and in her left a tin bucket, which she threw up into the air, to make a clatter.

It made a terrific din, as it hit the ground; immediately the watcher, climbing on to a chair, raised the curtain at the foot of the bed and appeared, gesticulating and uttering shrill cries from the inside of the pot, which hid her face, and threatening the old dying peasant woman with the broom like the Devil in a Punch and Judy show.

Terrified out of her senses, Mother Bontemps made a superhuman effort to get up and escape; she even heaved her shoulders and breast out of bed; then she fell back with a great sigh. It was all over.

Mother Rapet calmly put everything back in its place—the broom in the corner against the cupboard, the sheet inside it, the pot in the fireplace, the bucket on the shelf and the chair against the wall. Next, in her best professional manner, she closed the dead woman's staring eyes, put a plate on the bed, poured some holy water into it, dipped the sprig of boxwood that was nailed up over the chest of drawers and, kneeling down, began fervently to recite the prayers for the dead, which from her calling she knew by heart.

When Honoré came home in the evening, he found her praying, and he immediately calculated that she was making a franc out of him, for she had only spent three days and one night, which came to five francs, whereas he had promised to pay her six.

THE DOWRY

No one was surprised when Maître Simon Lebrument married Mademoiselle Jeanne Cordier. Maître Lebrument had just bought the practice of Maître Papillon, the solicitor, and of course that cost money; and Mademoiselle Jeanne Cordier had three hundred thousand francs in ready money, bank-notes and bearer bonds.

Maître Lebrument was a good-looking bachelor and a man of some distinction : he looked like a provincial lawyer, it is true, but he had distinction, and that was not common at Boutigny-le-Rebours.

Mademoiselle Cordier had charm and freshness, though she was a bit awkward and unsmart, but, taken all in all, she was a pretty girl, attractive and presentable.

The wedding caused a great stir in Boutigny, where the young couple were universally admired.

Instead of going away for their honeymoon, they went back to the domestic fireside, having decided just to take a little trip to Paris after a few days alone together.

This arrangement was a great success; Maître Lebrument showed unusual tact, delicacy and refinement in his first relations with his wife. His motto was " Everything comes to him who waits." He was at once patient and ardent, and his conquest was swift and complete.

In four days Madame Lebrument worshipped her husband. She could not let him out of her sight; she had to have him near her all day to fondle and kiss, to stroke his hands, ruffle his beard and pull his nose. She used to sit on his knee and, seizing both his ears, she would say : " Open your mouth and shut your eyes "; he opened his mouth obediently, half closed his eyes and received a long, loving kiss, which sent shivers down his spine. And he in his turn could not satisfy his wife with caresses and kisses, fondling and cuddling her from morning to night and from night to morning.

At the end of the first week he said to his young wife:

"If you like, we'll go to Paris next Tuesday. We'll just be lovers and go to restaurants, theatres, music-halls and everywhere."

She jumped for joy.

"That'll be marvellous; let's go at once."

He went on:

"And we mustn't forget anything; tell your father to have your dowry ready; I'll take it with us and, while we're there, I'll settle with Maître Papillon."

She said:

"I'll tell him to-morrow morning."

And he took her in his arms and started again all the little lovers' games she had come to be so fond of during the last week.

The following Tuesday the father- and mother-in-law saw their daughter and son-in-law off at the station.

The father-in-law said:

"I warn you, it's rash to carry so much money in your brief-case."

And the young lawyer smiled:

"Don't worry, Daddy; I'm used to this sort of thing. You see, in my job I sometimes have as much as a million francs on me. In this way we avoid endless formalities and delays. Don't you worry."

The guard was shouting: "Passengers for Paris, take your seats!"

They hurriedly got into a carriage, where they found two old ladies.

Lebrument murmured to his wife:

"What a bore! I shan't be able to smoke."

She whispered back:

" Yes, it's a bore for me too, but not for the same reason ! "

The train whistled and started. The journey took an hour, during which they didn't talk much, because the old ladies didn't go to sleep.

When they got into the station yard of the Gare St. Lazare, Lebrument said to his wife :

" Let's go and get some lunch on the Boulevard; then we'll come back quietly and pick up our luggage and take it to the hotel."

She immediately agreed :

" Yes, I'd love to lunch at a restaurant.   Is it far ? "

He replied :

" Yes, it's some way, we'll take a bus."

She was surprised :

" Can't we take a cab ? "

He smilingly scolded her :

" That's the way you save money ! A cab for a five-minute journey at half a franc a minute ; you're never satisfied ! "

" You're quite right," she said, a little ashamed.

A large bus with three trotting horses was passing.   Lebrument shouted :

" Hi, conductor !   Stop ! "

The heavy vehicle stopped, and the young lawyer, hustling his wife in, said quickly to her :

" You go inside, I'll go on top; I must have one cigarette before lunch."

She had no time to answer; the conductor, who had seized her by the arm to help her up the step, pushed her into the bus and she collapsed, quite flustered, on to the seat, watching with dazed eyes out of the back window her husband's legs disappearing on to the top.

She sat motionless between a fat man who smelt of tobacco and an old woman who smelt of dogs.

The other passengers were sitting silent in a row—a grocer's boy, a seamstress, an infantry sergeant, a gentleman with gold-rimmed spectacles and a top hat with an enormous brim standing up like a gutter-pipe, two pompous ladies with an ill-tempered expression, whose whole attitude seemed to say: "We are here, but we are really too good for a bus", two nuns, a hatless girl and an undertaker's mute; they looked like a collection of burlesque figures, a museum of grotesques, a series of caricatures of the human face, like those rows of comic dolls one knocks down with balls at a fair.

The jolting of the bus made their heads wobble and shake and their flabby cheeks quivered like jelly; mesmerized by the grinding vibration of the wheels, they had a vacant, dazed look.

The young woman sat there dully:

"Why didn't he come with me?" she wondered, feeling vaguely uncomfortable. "I do think he might have gone without his cigarette."

The nuns signalled to the conductor to stop, and got out one in front of the other, leaving behind them the fusty smell of an old-clothes shop.

The bus went on, and then stopped again; and a cook got in, red in the face and out of breath. She sat down, resting her shopping basket on her knee; a strong smell of washing-up water pervaded the bus.

"It's further than I thought," thought Jeanne.

The mute got out and his place was taken by a coachman, who stank of the stable. The hatless girl's seat was taken by a messenger-boy with smelly feet.

The lawyer's wife felt queer and slightly sick, and was almost crying without knowing why.

Other people got in and out. The bus went on all the time through interminable streets, pausing at the stops and going on again.

"What a long way it is!" said Jeanne to herself. "I do hope he hasn't had a fit of absent-mindedness or gone to sleep. He's been very tired these last few days."

Gradually the bus emptied and she was left absolutely alone. The conductor shouted: "Vaugirard!"

As she didn't move, he repeated: "Vaugirard!"

She looked at him, realizing that his remark was addressed to her, as she was the only passenger left.

The man said for the third time: "Vaugirard!"

Then she asked:

"Where are we?"

He replied in a surly tone:

"Good God, we're at Vaugirard! I've just said so a dozen times!"

"Is it far from the Boulevard?"

"Which Boulevard?"

"Oh! the Boulevard des Italiens."

"We're long past that."

"Well, will you tell my husband?"

"Your husband? Where is he?"

"Why, on the top."

"On the top? There's not been anyone up top for ages."

She started, in a panic:

"What do you mean? It's impossible. He got on with me; he must be there!"

The conductor became offensive:

"Look here, my girl, that's enough. He's not the only pebble on the beach. Clear out, there's nothing doing here; you'll pick up another one in the street."

Tears came into her eyes; she insisted:

"But you're quite wrong, I assure you you're wrong; he had a big brief-case under his arm."

The conductor laughed:

"A big brief-case? Oh! yes, he got off at the Madeleine. Anyhow, he gave you the slip quite neatly, ha! ha!"

The bus had stopped at the terminus. She got out and instinctively, in spite of herself, she glanced at the top; it was entirely empty.

She began to cry, and, not realizing that people could hear her and were staring, said out loud:

" What will become of me? "

The terminus inspector came up:

" What's the matter? "

The conductor answered ironically:

" It's a lady whose husband has given her the slip on the way."

The other replied:

" Oh! is that all? Never mind her; get on with your work; " and he turned on his heel.

Then she began to walk straight in front of her, too frightened and dazed to know what she was doing. Where was she to go? What was she to do? There must be some mistake; he must have just forgotten or lost his memory.

She had two francs in her pocket. Who could she go to for help?

Suddenly she remembered her cousin, Barral, a deputy chief clerk at the Admiralty.

She had just enough for her cab fare and she gave the driver her cousin's address. She ran into him just as he was leaving the house for the Ministry. He was carrying, like Lebrument, a large brief-case under his arm.

She flung herself out of the cab:

" Henry! " she shouted.

He stopped in surprise:

" Jeanne? . . . You here? . . . Alone? What are you doing? Where have you come from? "

She stammered with tears in her eyes:

" My husband has just disappeared.

" Disappeared? Where? "

" On a bus."

" On a bus? Oh! "

And through her tears she told her story.

He listened thoughtfully and asked:

" Was he quite normal this morning? "

" Yes."

" Good! Had he much money on him? "

" Yes, the whole of my dowry."

" Your dowry? All of it? "

" Yes, every penny; he was just going to pay for his practice."

" Well, my dear cousin, I bet that at this moment he's well on the way to Belgium."

She couldn't grasp it yet; she stammered:

" My husband . . . you say. . . ."

" I'm saying he's cleared off with your . . . your money—that's all there is to it."

She stood stock still, choking; at last she murmured:

" Then he's . . . he's a crook! "

And she collapsed, sobbing, into her cousin's arms.

As people were stopping to stare, he gently pushed her into the hall of his house and, with his arm round her waist, he led her upstairs; and when his maid, speechless with astonishment, opened the door, he said:

" Sophie, just run round to the restaurant and fetch lunch for two. I shan't be going to the Ministry to-day."

A NIGHT OUT

MAÎTRE SAVAL, a solicitor at Vernon, was passionately fond of music. Still young, but prematurely bald, and always carefully shaved, he was somewhat portly, as a lawyer ought to be, and wore gold-mounted pince-nez instead of the old-fashioned spectacles; he was an active man, popular with women and fond of good company, and he had a reputation in Vernon for artistic tastes. He played the piano and the violin, and gave musical evenings, at which the latest operatic music was performed.

He even sang a little, though his voice was quite small and lacked power; but he used it with so much taste that, as the last soft note died away, he was always greeted with cries of "Splendid! Exquisite! Amazing! Perfect!"

He had a regular subscription with a music publisher, who forwarded all the new works to him, and he used to send out little invitation cards to a select circle in the town with these words:

"Your presence is requested on Monday evening by Maître Saval, solicitor, to hear the first performance of Saïs in Vernon."

A few officers with good voices took the chorus parts, and two or three local ladies sang as well. The lawyer acted as conductor with such skill that the Director of Music of the 190th Regiment of the Line had said of him one day in the Café de l'Europe:

"Oh! Maître Saval, he's a maestro; it's a pity he didn't take up music professionally."

When his name was mentioned in a drawing-room, there was always someone to declare:

"He's more than an amateur—he's an artist, a real artist."

And two or three others would repeat with complete conviction:

" Yes, he's a real artist," with great emphasis on the " real."

Every time a new work was performed at one of the famous opera-houses in Paris, he went up to hear it.

And so last year he wanted to go as usual to hear *Henry VIII*. He took the fast train which gets to Paris at half-past four, intending to return by the train leaving at 12.35 midnight, in order to avoid a night in a hotel. He had put on evening dress at home, tails and a white tie, which he concealed under his overcoat, turning up the collar.

As soon as he set foot in the Rue d'Amsterdam, he felt blissfully happy; he said to himself:

" The air of Paris is quite different from any other. There's something about it which thrills and excites and intoxicates you, and in some strange way makes you want to dance and do all sorts of other silly things. As soon as I get out of the train, it's just as if I had drunk a bottle of champagne. What a time one could have here surrounded by artists! How happy those lucky people must be, the great men who have made a name in a city like Paris! What a wonderful life they have! "

And he indulged in dreams; he would have liked to know some of the celebrities in order to talk about them in Vernon and spend an evening now and then in their houses when he came to Paris.

Suddenly an idea struck him. He had heard stories about little cafés on the outer boulevards as the meeting-place of painters already famous, writers, even musicians, and he began to walk slowly up the hill towards Montmartre.

He had two hours to kill and he wanted to see for himself.

He strolled along in front of the beer-shops, the resort of the last survivors of the bohemian set, looking at people's faces and trying to guess which were artists. At last he went into The Dead Rat, intrigued by the name.

Five or six women were sitting with their elbows on the
marble-topped tables, talking in low voices about their love
affairs, about the quarrels of Lucie and Hortense, and Octave's
caddish tricks.   They were no longer young and were
either too fat or too thin, looking haggard and worn.   One
guessed that they were losing their hair; and they were
drinking beer like men.

Maître Saval sat down some way from them and waited,
as it was nearly time for the apéritif.

Presently a tall young man came in and sat down near
him.   The proprietress addressed him as M. Romantin.
The lawyer started.   Could it be the Romantin who had
just won a first-class gold medal at the last Salon?

The young man beckoned to the waiter:

" Bring me my dinner at once, and then take round to
my new studio, 15 Boulevard de Clichy, thirty bottles of
beer and the ham I ordered this morning.   We're having a
house-warming."

Maître Saval ordered his dinner at once.   Then he took
off his coat, showing his tails and white tie.

His neighbour appeared to take no notice of him.   He had
picked up a paper and was reading it.   Maître Saval watched
him out of the corner of his eye, desperately anxious to talk
to him.

Presently two young men came in, in red velvet jackets,
with pointed Henry III beards, and sat down opposite
Romantin.

The first said:

" It *is* to-night, isn't it? "

Romantin grasped his hand:

" You've said it, old man; everybody will be there.
Bonnat's coming, and Guillemet, Gervex, Béraud, Hébert,
Duez, Clairin, Jean-Paul Laurens.   It'll be a great show.
And women too, you'll see!   All the actresses; I mean, of
course, all those who are ' resting ' this evening."

The proprietor of the café had come up:

" You have rather a lot of house-warmings, don't you? "

The painter replied:

" You've said it; one every three months, each quarter-day."

Maître Saval could contain himself no longer and said in a hesitant voice:

" Excuse my butting in, Sir, but I heard your name mentioned, and I should immensely like to know if you are really the M. Romantin, whose work I admired so much at last year's Salon."

The artist replied:

" Your humble servant, Sir ! "

The lawyer then paid him a neatly turned compliment, anxious to show that he was a man of education.

The painter was charmed and replied politely, and they proceeded to chat.

Romantin came back to his house-warming, expatiating on the sumptuousness of his party.

Maître Saval asked about all the men who were coming, adding:

" It would be an extraordinary piece of luck for an outsider to meet so many celebrities at one time in the studio of an artist of your calibre."

Romantin, flattered, replied:

" If it would amuse you, do come."

Maître Saval accepted eagerly, reflecting that he could see *Henry VIII* any time.

They had both finished their meal. The lawyer hastened to pay the two bills, eager to return his neighbour's kindness. He also paid for the drinks of the young men in red velvet; then he went out with the painter.

They stopped in front of a long, low building, the first floor of which looked like an immense greenhouse. There were six studios alongside one another facing the boulevard.

Romantin entered first, went upstairs, opened a door, struck a match and lighted a candle.

They were in a huge room, whose only furniture consisted of three chairs, two easels and a few sketches leaning against the wall on the floor.

Maître Saval, in astonishment, remained standing by the door.

The painter announced:

" Here we are; we've got the space, but nothing's been done yet."

And examining the high, bare room, whose ceiling was lost in the darkness, he declared:

" One could do a lot with this studio."

He walked round it, scrutinizing it carefully, and went on:

" I've got a mistress, who might have helped us. Women have a flair for drapery. But I sent her off into the country for the day, so as to get her out of the way for this evening. It's not that I'm tired of her, but she's got no breeding; I should have felt uncomfortable for my guests."

He thought for a moment, then added:

" She's a good girl, but a bit difficult. If she knew I had a party on, she'd scratch my eyes out."

Maître Saval had not moved, he didn't understand.

The artist approached him:

" As I've invited you here, you must give me a hand."

The lawyer protested his willingness to do anything at all to make himself useful.

Romantin took off his coat:

" Well, old man, let's get down to it. We've got to clean up a bit."

He stooped down behind the easel, on which stood the portrait of a cat, and brought out a very decrepit broom.

" Look here, you do the sweeping, while I arrange the lighting."

Maître Saval took the broom, looked at it, and very awkwardly began to sweep the floor, raising clouds of dust.

Romantin stopped him angrily:

" Good God, man! You've not got the faintest idea how to sweep; look here, watch me."

And he began sweeping masses of greyish dirt in front of him, as if he had never done anything else all his life; then he gave the broom back to the lawyer, who imitated his technique.

In five minutes there was such a cloud of dust in the studio that Romantin asked:

" Where are you? I can't see you."

Maître Saval approached him coughing. The painter said:

" How would you set about making a chandelier?"

The other, bewildered, asked:

" What sort of a chandelier?"

" A chandelier to light the room, of course, with candles."

The lawyer didn't understand and answered:

" I don't know."

The painter began to skip about, clicking his fingers like castanets.

" Ah! I've got it, my lord!"

And he went on more calmly:

" Have you got five francs on you?"

Maître Saval replied:

" Yes, certainly."

The artist went on:

" Well, you go and buy me five francs' worth of candles, while I go along to the cooper's."

And he pushed the lawyer out into the street, evening dress and all.

In five minutes they were back, one with the candles and the other with the hoop of a cask. Next Romantin dived into a cupboard and brought out a score of empty bottles, which he fixed round the hoop like a crown. Then he went downstairs to borrow a ladder from the concierge, after explaining that he had got into the old lady's good books by painting the portrait of her cat, which stood on the easel.

Having returned with a stool, he asked Maître Saval:

" Are you a good climber? "

The other, not understanding, said: " Yes."

" Well, climb up on to the stool, and hang this hoop from the ring in the ceiling, and put a candle in each bottle and light them. I tell you, I'm a genius at lighting effects. But, Good Heavens, take off your tails; you look like a flunkey."

The door burst open with a crash and a woman, with eyes blazing, appeared and stopped on the threshold.

Romantin stared at her with terror in his eyes.

She waited a second or two, folded her arms, and then shouted in a shrill, raucous voice, quivering with anger:

" So, you dirty swine, this is why you wanted to get rid of me? "

Romantin said nothing and she went on:

" You rotter! You pretended you were giving me a day in the country. I'll show you how to run your party. Yes, I'll welcome your friends. . . ."

She was getting worked up:

" Yes, I'll throw the bottles and the candles in their faces . . ."

Romantin addressed her in an ingratiating tone:

" Mathilde. . . ."

But she paid no heed and went on:

" Wait a minute, my pretty boy, wait a minute."

Romantin went up to her and tried to take her hand:

" Mathilde. . . ."

But she was now well under way; and she went on pouring out a flood of foul-mouthed abuse and reproaches. Bad language flowed from her lips like an effluent from a cesspool; her words tripped over one another, fighting for utterance. She stuttered and stammered and spluttered, and suddenly out would come an oath or a term of abuse.

He had seized her hands without her noticing it; she didn't seem to see him, she was so busy talking to relieve her feelings.

Suddenly she broke down and sobbed. Tears streamed from her eyes, without stopping the torrent of her abuse. Her words were coming now in a shrill falsetto, now strangled with tears. At last her sobs brought her to a standstill. She started off again two or three times, but choked each time; and finally she stopped in a paroxysm of tears.

He took her in his arms and kissed her hair, genuinely affected.

"Mathilde, darling Mathilde, listen. You must be reasonable. You know, if I'm giving a party, it's only to thank the gentlemen, to whom I owe my medal at the Salon. I can't ask ladies; you ought to realize that. Artists aren't like other people."

She stammered through her tears:

"Why didn't you tell me?"

He replied:

"Only so that you shouldn't be annoyed or hurt. Listen: I'm going to take you home now; you're going to be a good, sensible girl, and stay there quietly and wait for me in your little bed, and I'll come back to you as soon as the party's over."

She murmured:

"All right, but you won't do it again?"

"No, I swear I won't."

He turned to Maître Saval, who had just managed to fix the chandelier:

"My dear fellow, I'll be back in five minutes. If anybody comes while I'm away, you'll do the honours for me, won't you?"

And he dragged Mathilde away, alternately dabbing at her eyes and blowing her nose.

Left alone, Maître Saval finished tidying up the studio. Next he lit the candles and waited.

He waited a quarter of an hour, half an hour, an hour. There was no sign of Romantin. Suddenly on the stairs there was a terrific din, a song shouted by twenty voices in unison and a noise like a Prussian regiment on the march. The tramp of feet made the whole house shake. The door opened and a crowd of people appeared. A stream of men and women in file, arm in arm, stamping, advanced into the studio, like a snake uncoiling; they were chanting:

" Walk up! Walk up! Walk up!

" Nursemaids and soldiers all!

" Walk up! Walk up!"

Maître Saval was standing completely bewildered under the chandelier in his full evening dress. The procession caught sight of him and roared: " A flunkey! A flunkey!" and began to circle round him, enclosing him in a ring of shouting humanity. Then, joining hands, they danced madly round him.

He tried to explain:

" Gentlemen . . . Gentlemen. . . . Ladies. . . ."

But no one listened to him; round and round they went, dancing and singing. At last the dance came to an end.

Maître Saval began:

" Gentlemen. . . ."

But a tall fair young man with a full beard cut him short:

" What's your name, my good man?"

The lawyer, terrified, replied:

" I am Maître Saval."

A voice shouted:

" You mean, Mr. Jeeves!"

One of the women said:

" He's the waiter. Let him alone or he'll lose his temper; he's paid to wait on us, not to be made a fool of."

Maître Saval noticed that each guest had brought his contribution; one had a bottle in his hand, another a meat pie, a third a loaf, a fourth a ham.

The tall fair young man thrust a gigantic sausage into his hands and said:

" Look here, go and lay the supper over there in the corner; put the bottles on the left and the food on the right."

Saval, losing his head, cried:

" But, Gentlemen, I am a solicitor."

There was a moment's silence, then a roar of laughter. One man asked suspiciously:

" How do you come to be here? "

He explained how he had meant to go to the Opera, how he had come from Vernon and got to Paris and how he had spent the evening.

They had sat down round him to listen, ragging him unmercifully and calling him Scheherazade.

Still Romantin did not return. Other guests arrived. Maître Saval was introduced to them, and they all wanted him to begin his story over again; he refused but they insisted. They stuck him on one of the three chairs between two women, who kept his glass full. He drank, laughed and talked; he even sang. He tried to dance with his chair but he fell down.

From that moment everything was a blank. He thought he remembered being undressed and put to bed and feeling very sick.

It was broad daylight when he woke, lying at the bottom of a cupboard in a strange bed. An old woman with a broom in her hand was staring at him angrily. At last she said:

" Come along, you dirty swine! Fancy getting drunk like that! "

He sat up, still feeling slightly sick, and asked:

" Where am I? "

" Where are you, you swine? You're tight. You'd better clear out of this in double quick time."

He tried to get out of bed, but he was stark naked and his clothes had disappeared. He stammered:

" Madame, I . . ."

In a flash it all came back to him. What was he to do? He asked:

" Hasn't M. Romantin come back? "

The concierge shouted:

" Look here, you just clear out; don't let him find you here anyhow."

Blushing scarlet, Maître Saval confessed:

" But I've got no clothes; they have been taken."

He had to wait, explain his predicament, communicate with friends and borrow money to get some clothes. He couldn't start back till the evening.

Now, whenever music is being discussed in the pretty drawing-room of his house at Vernon, he declares with conviction that painting is a very inferior form of art.

MADAME TELLIER'S
ESTABLISHMENT

I

You went there every evening about eleven o'clock, quite naturally, as if it had been a public-house.

The same six or eight always foregathered there, not the fast set, but respectable business men and the young fellows of the town; they drank their glass of Chartreuse and had a bit of fun with the girls, or else chatted soberly with Madame, who was universally respected.

Then they went home to bed before midnight. The younger men sometimes stayed on.

It was a homely sort of house, quite small with yellow walls, at the corner of a street behind St. Stephen's Church; and from the windows could be seen the docks crowded with ships unloading, the great salt-marsh called the Reservoir, and behind it St. Mary's Mound with its old grey chapel.

Madame, who came of good peasant stock from the Department of the Eure, had adopted her present profession exactly as she might have become a dressmaker or a linen-draper. The disgrace attaching to prostitution, so deep and inveterate in towns, does not exist in the Normandy country-side. The peasant considers it a paying job; and he sends his daughter to keep a bevy of prostitutes, just as he would send her to run a girls' boarding-school.

Anyhow, this house had been inherited from its former owner, an old uncle; Monsieur and Madame, who had previously kept an inn at Yvetot, had immediately sold out, thinking the opening at Fécamp more promising; and one fine morning had arrived to take over the business, which was getting into a bad way with no one in charge.

They were a worthy couple, who immediately became popular with their staff and the neighbours.

Monsieur died two years later, of a stroke. His new profession had provided him with an easy livelihood; he took no exercise and became excessively fat, till good living brought on apoplexy.

Since her bereavement Madame had been courted in vain by all the regular clients of the establishment; but her good name was above suspicion, and even the girls in the house had never discovered anything to her discredit.

She was tall, plump and prepossessing. Her complexion, which had become pale in the semi-darkness of a house where the shutters were always kept closed, shone as if it had been thickly varnished. A thin fringe of straggling curls of false hair framed her forehead and gave her a youthful appearance quite out of keeping with the maturity of her figure. Ever cheerful and smiling, she enjoyed a joke, but always with a certain reserve, which her new profession had never been able to diminish. Any coarse expression shocked her; and whenever an ill-mannered young man called her establishment by its proper name, she was annoyed and scandalized. She was a woman of refinement, and, although she treated her girls in a friendly spirit, she repeatedly emphasized the fact that they "were not out of the same basket as herself."

Sometimes on week-days she hired a carriage and went for a drive with some of the girls. They used to run wild on the grassy bank of the stream in the Vale of Valmont. They romped like school-girls on holiday, racing wildly about and playing childish games with all the joy of nuns intoxicated by the fresh air after their life in the cloister. They ate sandwiches on the grass and drank cider, going home at nightfall pleasantly tired and softly sentimental; in the carriage they kissed Madame, as if she were the kindest of mothers, ever ready to spoil them and do anything to make them happy.

The house had two entrances; on the corner was a door, by which labourers and sailors had access to a disreputable sort of bar open in the evenings. Two of the professional personnel of the establishment were ear-marked for the needs of this class of customer. With the help of a waiter called Frederick—a fair, smooth-faced youth, as strong as an ox—they served mugs of wine and bottled beer on rickety marble-topped tables, and encouraged the customers to drink, putting their arms round their necks and sitting on their knees.

The three other girls—there were only five in all—formed a sort of aristocracy, reserved for the company on the first floor, unless they were needed downstairs and there were no visitors upstairs.

The " Jupiter " drawing-room, where the local tradesmen foregathered, had a blue wall-paper adorned with a bold design of Leda reclining with the swan. This room was reached by a spiral staircase with a narrow, inconspicuous door at the bottom opening on the street, over which, behind a grille, a lamp burned all night, like those still lit in some towns at the foot of figures of the Virgin in niches in the walls.

The house, which was damp and old, smelt slightly mouldy. Now and then a whiff of eau de Cologne was wafted along the passages, or the coarse, loud voices of the men seated at the tables on the ground floor echoed through the building through a half-open door like a clap of thunder, bringing an uneasy frown of disgust to the faces of the gentlemen on the first floor.

Madame, who was on friendly terms with her regular customers, never left the drawing-room, and listened with interest to the gossip of the town, which they retailed to her. Her serious conversation made a pleasant change from the inconsequent chatter of the three girls; she afforded a restful interlude to the equivocal banter of the portly gentlemen, who indulged every evening in the mild dissipation of taking their liqueur in the company of girls of easy virtue.

The names of the three first-floor ladies were Fernande, Raphaële and Rowdy Rosie.

The staff being limited in number, each girl had been chosen as a sample, an epitome of one female type, so that every client might find at least an approximation to his ideal.

Fernande represented the blonde type of beauty; she was very tall, so plump as to be almost gross, and flabby, a regular country girl, whose freckles could not be concealed, and whose bobbed tow hair, pale and colourless like combed flax, hardly covered her head.

Raphaële, a Marseilles girl, who had drifted about from one port to another, was cast for the necessary part of the lovely Jewess, thin, with prominent cheek-bones daubed with rouge. Her black hair, shiny with marrow-fat, formed two kiss-curls at the side of her head. Her eyes would have been thought beautiful, if the right one had not had a white speck. Her aquiline nose overhung a powerful jaw, in which two false teeth in the upper row stood out in contrast to those of the lower row, which with age had taken on the mahogany shade of old wood.

Rowdy Rosie, a little dumpling of a girl, all stomach, with tiny legs, had a husky voice, and from morning to night sang snatches from songs, alternately smutty and sentimental, told interminable pointless stories, only stopped talking to eat and eating to talk, was always on the go, like a squirrel, in spite of her weight and spindly legs. Her laugh, a cascade of shrill shrieks, was everlastingly bursting out from every direction, bedroom, attic or bar, all about nothing.

The two ground-floor girls, Louise, nicknamed The Tartlet, and Flora, usually called Dot-and-Carry, because she was a bit lame, were got up, the former as Liberty with a red, white and blue scarf, the latter as a fancy-dress Spanish woman with copper sequins dancing in her ginger hair at each limping step; they looked like two kitchen-maids dressed up for the carnival. Like all such girls with no breeding, they were typical barmaids, neither uglier nor prettier; the sailors called them "The two Beer Pumps."

An uneasy peace, which, however, was rarely broken, reigned among the five women, thanks to Madame's conciliatory tact and unfailing good-temper.

The establishment, the only one of its kind in the town, was extensively patronized. Madame had succeeded in giving it such an air of respectability; she was so pleasant and obliging to everyone, and her kindness of heart was so well known, that she enjoyed what amounted to genuine respect. The regular customers laid themselves out to please her, and were elated when she showed them any special mark of her favour. When they met on business during the day, they would say to each other: "See you again this evening at the usual place," just as one might say: "See you later in the bar after dinner."

In fact, Madame's establishment was an institution, and it was not often that anyone missed the daily rendezvous.

One evening, towards the end of May, the first arrival, M. Poulin, a timber-merchant and ex-mayor, found the door locked. The small lantern behind the grille was not alight; not a sound was audible inside—the house seemed dead. He knocked, first softly, then louder; there was no answer. Then he went back up the street slowly, and as he reached the Market Square he met M. Duvert, a ship-chandler, on his way to the same place. They returned together but were no more successful. Suddenly they heard an uproar quite close, and, making their way round the house, they saw a crowd of English and French sailors banging with their fists against the closed shutters of the bar.

The two tradesmen immediately fled to avoid being involved; but a discreet "hullo" stopped them; it was M. Tournevau, the fish-curer, who had recognized them and was hailing them. They told him the position, which was the more serious for him because, being a married man with a family, his movements were closely watched and he only came on Saturdays "as a safety measure", as he used to say, alluding to the weekly check-up by the Public Health Authorities, of which his friend, Dr. Borde, had told him. It happened to be his evening, so that he would have to miss a whole week.

The three men took a roundabout route to the docks and on the way picked up M. Philippe, Junior, the banker's son, a "regular", and M. Pimpesse, the Collector of Taxes; then the whole party returned by Jews' Lane to make a last attempt. But the exasperated sailors were besieging the house, throwing stones and shouting; and the five first-floor gentlemen beat a hurried retreat and began to wander about the streets.

The party next picked up M. Dupuis, the Insurance Agent, then M. Vasse, Judge of the Commercial Court; and off they went on a lengthy stroll, which brought them first to the pier. There they sat down in a row on the granite parapet and watched the white horses. The foam on the crest of the waves made patches of luminous white in the darkness, disappearing as soon as seen, and the monotonous roar of the sea breaking on the rocks echoed in the night all along the cliff-face. After our crestfallen party had stayed there some time, M. Tournevau remarked: " This is pretty depressing ". " You've said it ", replied M. Pimpesse; and they set off again but without enthusiasm.

After going along the street under the hill, called Underwood Street, they returned by the wooden bridge over the Reservoir, passed close to the railway line, and came out once more in the Market Square, where a dispute broke out suddenly between M. Pimpesse and M. Tournevau, the fish-curer, about an edible mushroom, which one of them asserted he had found in the neighbourhood.

Boredom had made them irritable and they might have come to blows if the others had not intervened. M. Pimpesse went off home in a rage; and immediately a new dispute broke out between the ex-mayor, M. Poulin, and M. Dupuis, the Insurance Agent, about the Collector's salary and his opportunities for making money "on the side". Both parties were indulging in indiscriminate abuse, when a storm of ear-splitting cries burst out, and the mob of sailors, who had got tired of waiting in vain in front of the closed house, emerged on the Market Square. They were walking arm in arm, in file, forming a long line and shouting at the top of their voices. The little party of townsmen took cover in a porch, and the yelling crowd disappeared in the direction of the Abbey. The noise was audible for a long time, growing less and less, like a storm passing away, and at last all was silence again. M. Poulin and M. Dupuis, both still in a towering rage, went off home without saying goodnight to each other.

The other four moved off again, instinctively turning their steps in the direction of Madame's house. It was still shut up, silent and mysterious as the grave. A drunk man, with placid obstinacy, was knocking gently on the front window of the bar and then stopping to call Frederick, the waiter, in a whisper. Finding that he got no answer, he made up his mind to sit down on the doorstep and await events.

Our friends were on the point of going home, when the rowdy party of sailors reappeared at the end of the street. The Frenchmen were bawling the "Marseillaise", the English "Rule Britannia." Surging round the walls on the corner, the wave of coarse humanity rolled on towards the quay, where a scuffle broke out between the two nationalities. In the fight an Englishman had his arm broken and a Frenchman his nose slit open.

The drunk man, who had stayed in front of the door,

was now shedding maudlin tears, like a child who cannot get his way.

At last our party broke up.

Gradually silence returned to the disturbed town. Here and there from time to time the sound of voices was audible, and then died away in the distance.

One man was still wandering about alone—M. Tournevau, the fish-curer, miserable at the thought of having to wait a whole week; he was hoping against hope that something would happen; in his frustration he could not understand how the police could allow an institution of public utility, which they watched and protected, to be closed.

He made his way back to the house, prowling round the walls, trying to find an explanation; and he discovered a notice stuck on the shutter. He quickly struck a wax-vesta and read these words written in a large sprawling hand: " Closed for First Communion ".

Then he went away, convinced at last that there was nothing doing.

The drunk man was asleep by now, stretched at full length on the inhospitable doorstep.

Next day all the " regulars ", one after the other, found some excuse for passing down the street, each with a sheaf of papers under his arm for the sake of appearances; and with furtive glances they all read the mysterious notice: " Closed for First Communion ".

II

The fact is that Madame had a brother who had set up as a carpenter in their native place, Virville, in the Eure. In the days when Madame still kept the inn at Yvetot, she had stood as godmother to this brother's daughter, to whom she had given the name of Constance—Constance Rivet, the latter being her own maiden name. The carpenter, who knew his sister was comfortably off, kept up with her, though they rarely met, being both tied by their businesses and living at some distance from each other.   But as the little girl, who was nearly twelve, was making her first Communion that year, he seized the opportunity to bring them together, and wrote to his sister that he was expecting her for the ceremony. She could not refuse her goddaughter, whose grand-parents were dead, so she accepted.   Her brother, whose name was Joseph, hoped by flattering attentions to induce her to make a will in favour of the child, Madame being childless herself. His sister's business caused him no qualms of conscience; moreover, no one in the place knew anything.   People merely said, when they mentioned her name: " Madame Tellier has got a place at Fécamp ", implying that she had independent means.   Fécamp is at least sixty miles from Virville; and sixty miles across country is a more difficult journey for a peasant than an ocean voyage to the more sophisticated.   The people of Virville had never been further afield than Rouen, and there was nothing to attract the people of Fécamp to a small village of five hundred houses, buried in the depths of the flat country and belonging to a different Department.   Anyhow, they knew nothing about Madame.

But as the date of the Communion drew near, Madame found herself in a serious difficulty.   She had no second-in-command, and was not at all anxious to leave her establishment even for a day.   All the rivalries between the ladies upstairs and those downstairs would inevitably come to a head; moreover, Frederick would certainly get drunk, and when he was drunk he used to knock people about for no reason at all.   Finally she made up her mind to take her whole staff with her, except the waiter, to whom she gave two days off.

When she approached her brother, he raised no objection and undertook to put up the whole party for the night.   So on the Saturday morning the eight-o'clock fast train had Madame and her girls as second-class passengers.

As far as Beuzeville they had the carriage to themselves and chattered like magpies. But at this station a couple got in. The man, an old peasant, was wearing a blue blouse with a smocked collar and broad cuffs, tight at the wrist, relieved by a small pattern in white embroidery; on his head was an old-fashioned top hat whose rusty nap looked as if it had been brushed the wrong way; in one hand he had an enormous green umbrella, and in the other a huge basket, from which the heads of three terrified ducks protruded. The woman in her stiff country clothes had a face like a hen, with a pointed nose like a bird's beak. She sat down opposite her husband and never moved, embarrassed at finding herself in such smart company.

The carriage really did present a dazzling picture of all the colours of the rainbow. Madame, in a long blue silk dress, was wearing over it an imitation French cashmere shawl of a flaming shade of bright red. Fernande was panting in a tartan frock, which had been pulled in by the united efforts of her companions and was forcing up her sagging breasts, till they looked like two india-rubber balls filled with water bobbing up and down under the material.

Raphaële, in a feathered hat looking like a bird's nest, had on a mauve dress with gold spangles, suggestive of the East, to go with her Jewish features. Rowdy Rosie, in a pink skirt with broad flounces, looked like a grossly fat child or a pot-bellied dwarf. The two Beer Pumps sported an amazing get-up, which looked as if it had been made at home out of old window curtains, those old-fashioned curtains with a floral pattern dating from the Restoration.

Now that they were no longer alone, the ladies affected a staid demeanour and began to discuss serious topics to create an impression. But at Bolbec a gentleman got in, with blond whiskers, rings and a gold albert, who stowed several parcels done up in American cloth in the rack above his head. He had a humorous, cheery face. He bowed all round, smiled and enquired without a trace of shyness: " You're being posted to new quarters, ladies? "

This question caused acute embarrassment in the party.

At last Madame recovered herself and replied curtly to avenge the honour of her troop: "You needn't be offensive!"

He apologized: " I'm sorry, I should have said, to a new convent ".

Madame, at a loss for a retort, or perhaps thinking the correction adequate, bowed stiffly and pursed her lips.

Presently the gentleman, who was sitting between Rowdy Rosie and the old peasant, began making faces at the three ducks, whose heads protruded from the large basket; then, when he saw he had attracted attention, he began to tickle the birds under the beak, addressing comic remarks to them in order to break the ice:

" We've left our little p-p-pond! Quack, quack, quack! We're going to make friends with a little spit, quack, quack, quack! "

The wretched birds twisted their necks to avoid his attentions, making despairing efforts to get out of their basketwork prison; suddenly all three in unison uttered a heartrending cry of distress: " Quack, quack, quack, quack! "

This produced a burst of laughter from the ladies. They leant forward, pushing each other in order to get a view; they suddenly became passionately interested in the ducks, and the gentleman surpassed himself in his efforts to attract, amuse and tease.

Then Rosie took a hand, and, leaning over her neighbour's legs, kissed the three birds on the beak. Immediately all the girls had to follow suit, one after the other; and the gentleman made them sit on his knee, jumping them up and down and pinching them: suddenly he adopted the familiar mode of address.

The two peasants, more scared than their ducks, rolled their eyes wildly, not daring to move, and their wrinkled old faces never smiled or even twitched.

Suddenly the gentleman, who was a commercial traveller, offered the ladies braces as a joke, and seizing one of his parcels, opened it. It was a trick; the parcel contained garters.

They were made of silk—blue, pink, crimson, purple, mauve and poppy-red, with metal buckles in the form of two gilt cupids intertwined.

The girls shrieked with joy, examining the samples with the instinctive seriousness of every woman when she is handling anything to do with dress. They exchanged opinions by a glance or whisper, and Madame was enviously handling a pair of orange garters, broader and more imposing than the others—just the thing for a woman in her position.

The gentleman waited, in accordance with his plan of campaign. "Come along, my dears," he said, "you must try them on."

This caused a storm of protests, and they gripped their skirts tight between their legs, as if they were afraid of being assaulted. He bided his time quietly.

"Well," he said, "if you don't want them, I'll pack up again." Then he added slyly: "I'll give away a pair for nothing, any pair you like, to anyone who'll try them on."

But they refused with dignity, sitting bolt upright.

However, the Beer Pumps looked so disappointed that he renewed his offer. Flora Dot-and-Carry, especially, in her desperate anxiety, was visibly weakening.

He pressed his advantage: "Come along, my girl, don't be a coward; look, this mauve pair will match your frock."

So she took the plunge and, pulling up her skirt, revealed a farm-girl's powerful leg in a coarse, ill-fitting stocking.

Bending down, the gentleman adjusted the garter first

below the knee, then above it; and he tickled the girl gently, till she uttered little screams and gave sudden shivers. When he had finished, he gave her the mauve pair and asked: "Who's next?"

There was a unanimous cry: "Me, me!"

He began with Rowdy Rosie, who disclosed a shapeless limb, tubular all the way down, with no ankle, "a regular sausage of a leg", as Raphaële remarked. Fernande was congratulated by the commercial traveller, who waxed eloquent over her Norman pillars. The spindly legs of the lovely Jewess were less admired. Louise, the Tartlet, by way of a joke, let down her skirt over the gentleman's head; and Madame had to intervene to put an end to this unseemly jest. In the end Madame herself stretched out her own leg, a fine Norman leg, well covered and muscular: the commercial traveller, in admiring surprise, greeted this super-calf by gallantly raising his hat with the grace of a modern Bayard.

The two peasants, dumbfounded, stole sidelong glances at the scene from time to time; they looked so exactly like two fowls that the man with the blond whiskers, getting up from his seat, let off a cock-a-doodle-do right in their faces. This was greeted by a new outburst of merriment.

The old couple got out at Motteville with their basket, their ducks and their umbrella; and as they went away, the woman was heard to say to her husband: "There's another batch of whores on their way to that accursed Paris."

The waggish bagman got out himself at Rouen, after a final exhibition of bad taste which forced Madame to put him sternly in his place. She added to point the moral: "That will teach us not to talk to casual acquaintances."

They changed at Oissel, and at a station not much further on they found M. Joseph Rivet waiting for them with a large farm cart filled with chairs and drawn by a white horse.

The carpenter greeted all the ladies politely and helped them

into his cart. Three of them sat on the three chairs at the
back; Raphaële, Madame and her brother on the three
chairs in front; and Rosie, not having a seat, balanced herself
as best she could on the knee of the tall Fernande. Then the
party moved off. But as soon as the old pony broke into
its jerky trot, the cart shook so violently that the chairs began
to jump up and down, tossing the passengers up in the air
first to one side, then to the other, like marionettes. Their
faces were distorted with terror, and they cried out in panic,
till a more than usually powerful jolt reduced them to
sudden silence. They clung to the sides of the vehicle;
their hats fell off backwards, over their faces or on to their
shoulders, while the white horse plodded steadily on, straining
his neck forward with tail erect, a sparse little rat-tail, with
which he swished his haunches from time to time. Joseph
Rivet, with one foot stretched out along the shaft and the
other leg curled up under him, held the reins with elbows
stuck out, while he emitted from his throat at frequent
intervals a clucking sound, which made the steed prick up
its ears and quicken its pace.

On both sides of the road stretched a green expanse of
countryside. Here and there fields of rape in flower formed
great waving yellow patches, from which rose a clean,
powerful scent, at once penetrating and sweet, carried by the
wind over a wide area. In the standing rye cornflowers
were already showing their tiny sky-blue heads. The ladies
wanted to pick them, but M. Rivet refused to stop. From
time to time a whole field seemed to have fallen under a rain
of blood, so many poppies had seeded themselves there.
Through this flat countryside the cart made its way, looking
as if it, too, was carrying a nosegay of even brighter-coloured
flowers, behind the trotting white horse; it was always
disappearing behind the tall trees of a farmstead, to reappear
on the far side of the foliage; it jogged along in the bright
sunshine with its feminine freight in their dazzling dresses

through the fields with their crops alternately green and gold, dotted here and there with red or blue wild flowers.

One o'clock was striking as they reached the carpenter's house. They were dead tired and faint with hunger, having had nothing to eat since their start. Madame Rivet bustled about and helped them down in turn, giving each one a hurried kiss, as she set foot on the ground; she couldn't stop embracing her sister-in-law, in her anxiety to make a good impression. They lunched in the carpenter's shop, which had been cleared of its benches for to-morrow's dinner.

A good omelette followed by a grilled eel, washed down with strong dry cider, restored everyone's spirits; to put them all at their ease, Rivet had drunk the health of each guest himself. His wife did the serving as well as the cooking, bringing in the dishes and clearing them away, whispering to each in turn: " Are you sure you've had enough? " Rows of planks standing against the walls and heaps of shavings swept into the corners gave off a scent of planed wood, the penetrating resinous tang of a carpenter's shop.

They asked for the little girl, but she was in church, and would not be back till the evening.

The party then got up from the table for a stroll in the country.

It was a tiny village with a main road running through it. Ten shops or so bordering this single thoroughfare housed the local tradesmen, the butcher, the grocer, the carpenter, the publican, the cobbler and the baker. The church stood at the end of this sort of village street, surrounded by a small cemetery; and four gigantic lime-trees in front of the west door overshadowed the whole edifice. It was built of knapped flint, in no particular style, topped with a slate bell-tower. Beyond it the open country began again, broken here and there by copses which sheltered the farmsteads.

Rivet, though in his working clothes, had formally given

his arm to his sister, escorting her with dignity. His wife, dazzled by the gold sequins on Raphaële's frock, walked between her and Fernande. The tubby Rosie waddled along behind with Louise the Tartlet and Flora Dot-and-Carry, whose limp was accentuated by her fatigue.

The villagers came to their doors, the children stopped their games, and where a curtain was raised one caught a glimpse of heads in printed calico caps. One old woman with a crutch, who was nearly blind, crossed herself, as if a religious procession was passing; and everyone gazed long at all these lovely town ladies, who had come so far for the First Communion of Joseph Rivet's little girl. The carpenter basked in the reflected glory of universal admiration. As they passed in front of the church, they heard the children singing, their shrill little voices raising a canticle of praise to Heaven; but Madame would not let anyone go in, for fear of distracting the little angels.

After a short stroll in the country, during which Joseph Rivet gave the names and details of the principal estates and the output of each in produce and stock, he brought his party back and made them comfortable in his house.

As the accommodation was very limited, they were split up, two to each room.

Rivet, for this once, would sleep in the workshop on the shavings; his wife would share her bed with her sister-in-law, and in the room next door Fernande and Raphaële would sleep together. Louise and Flora found themselves accommodated in the kitchen on a mattress on the floor, and Rosie had a little dark cupboard to herself at the top of the stairs, opposite the door of a tiny garret, where the child was to spend the night before her First Communion.

When the little girl came home, she was received with a shower of kisses; all the ladies wanted to embrace her with effusive affection, for their profession made them lavish of endearments; it was this which had led them to kiss the ducks in the railway carriage. They all in turn made her sit on their knees, stroked her fair silky hair, and held her tightly in their arms in an ecstasy of instinctive maternal tenderness. Very well-behaved, the child submitted; patient and unconcerned, she was deeply filled with devotional feeling and was still living, as it were, in another world under the spell of the absolution she had received.

Everyone had had a tiring day and they went to bed very soon after dinner. The absolute, almost religious silence of the country fell upon the village—a peaceful, all-embracing hush, reaching to the stars. The girls, accustomed to the noisy evenings at home, where they were never alone, were emotionally affected by the unbroken quiet of the sleeping countryside. They shivered, not with cold but with the loneliness of anxious, troubled hearts.

As soon as they were in bed, each put her arms round her companion as a protection against the all-pervading influence of Nature's deep, peaceful slumber.

But Rowdy Rosie, alone in her dark cupboard, not being used to sleeping without someone in her arms, was conscious of a vague disquiet. She was tossing about on her bed, unable to sleep, when she heard faint sobs like those of a child in tears on the other side of the wooden partition near her head. Frightened, she called in a whisper, and a little voice answered between sobs. It was the little girl, who had always slept in her mother's room, and was afraid in the loneliness of her tiny garret.

Rosie, delighted, got out of bed and quietly, so as not to wake anyone, went and fetched the child. She took her into her own warm bed and hugged her tightly, kissing and cuddling her. She surrounded her with extravagant manifestations of affection, and then, soothed, fell asleep herself. And until the day of her First Communion dawned, the child slept with her head on the prostitute's bare breast.

At five o'clock the little church bell, ringing for the Angelus, woke the ladies, who usually rested after their labours of the night by sleeping right through the morning. The villagers were already up; the women of the place were hurrying from door to door, gossiping eagerly, carefully carrying short muslin dresses starched like cardboard or huge wax candles with a silk bow and a gold fringe round the middle; bits of wax had been cut out so that they could be easily held. The sun, already up, was shining in a cloudless sky, while faint traces of the dawn still showed a pale pink streak along the horizon. Families of hens were strutting in front of their doors, and here and there a black rooster with glossy neck raised his crimson-crested head, flapped his wings and crowed his clarion call to the breezes, to be answered by all the other cocks.

Light carts were coming in from neighbouring villages, discharging on the doorsteps tall Normandy women in black with fichus crossed over the breast and held in place by silver brooches, usually family heirlooms. The men had put on their blue blouses over frock-coats, which were just coming in, or over their old-fashioned green broadcloth tail-coats, whose skirts showed below the blouses.

When the horses had been stabled, the whole length of the main street was lined with a double row of ramshackle country carts, traps, gigs, governess carts, and other vehicles of every shape and age, tilted forward or resting on their tail-boards with shafts in the air.

The carpenter's house was humming like a beehive. The ladies, in dressing-jackets and petticoats, with their hair down their backs—sparse, short hair looking faded and thin—were engaged in dressing the child.

The little girl stood stock still on the table, while Madame Tellier directed the operations of her busy squad. They washed her face, combed her hair, adjusted her cap, put on her dress and with the help of countless pins arranged the pleats of the skirt and took in the waist, which was too large : in fact, they saw that everything was just right.

When they had finished, they made the long-suffering child sit down, telling her not to move; and the excited bevy of girls ran off to dress themselves.

The little church bell began to ring. Its feeble tinkle soared upwards, till it was lost, like a weak voice, drowned in the wide spaces of the blue sky.

The new communicants were now leaving their homes and making their way to the village hall, which housed the two schools and the mayor's office : it stood at one end of the village, while the House of God occupied the other. Their relations, in their Sunday best, looking uncomfortable and moving awkwardly as a result of their life of back-breaking toil, followed their children. The little girls were lost in a cloud of snowy tulle like whipped cream, while the little boys, like miniature waiters, their hair plastered down with grease, walked with their feet far apart so as not to dirty their black trousers.

The reputation of a family was enhanced when a large number of relations from a distance surrounded a child; so the carpenter's triumph was assured. Constance was followed by the Tellier contingent, headed by Madame; the father had his sister on his arm, the mother walked with Raphaële, Flora with Rosie, and the two Beer Pumps brought up the rear. The troop deployed with the dignity of staff officers in full dress. The effect on the village was electric.

At the school the girls fell in under the coif of the kindly Sister of Mercy, the boys under the top-hat of the school-master, a handsome man of commanding presence; then they moved off, chanting a psalm.

The boys, leading the procession, advanced in two long files between the two lines of unharnessed vehicles, the girls following in the same formation; and as the local people respectfully gave pride of place to the ladies from the town, they came immediately behind the little girls, thus continuing the double line of the procession, three on the left and three on the right, their frocks blazing like a firework display.

Their entry into the church dumbfounded the natives, who jostled each other, turned round and pushed to get a good view. Pious women almost forgot to lower their voices, amazed at the sight of ladies more lace-bedizened than the cantors' cottas. The mayor offered his pew—the top pew on the right near the choir—and Madame Tellier took her seat in it with her sister-in-law, while Fernande and Raphaële, Rowdy Rosie and the two Beer Pumps occupied the second pew with the carpenter.

The choir was packed with kneeling children, girls on one side and boys on the other, the long wax candles in their hands looking like lances tilted at every angle.

In front of the lectern stood three men, singing in deep bass voices. They held the sonorous Latin syllables interminably, with an exaggerated lengthening of the A-a of the Amens, supported by the long-drawn note of the serpent, bellowing from its brazen throat. A boy's shrill treble gave the responses. And from time to time a priest, seated in a stall with a square biretta on his head, got up, mumbled something and resumed his seat; whereupon the three cantors started off again, with their eyes fixed on the great plain-song book open in front of them and supported by the outspread wings of a wooden eagle mounted on a re-volving base.

Suddenly there was silence. The whole congregation knelt as one man as the celebrant appeared, a venerable, white-haired old man, bending over the chalice in his left hand. In front of him walked two servers in red cassocks, and behind came a crowd of cantors in clumping shoes, who took their places in two lines on each side of the choir.

A little bell tinkled in the dead silence and the holy office

began. The celebrant moved slowly before the gilded
tabernacle, genuflected and, in a cracked voice quavering
with age, intoned the introductory prayers. As soon as he
had finished, all the cantors and the serpent came in together,
the men in the body of the church joining in less loudly and
more humbly, as it is fitting that a congregation should
sing.

Suddenly the Kyrie Eleison burst forth, uplifted to Heaven
from every breast and heart. Particles of dust and even
splinters of worm-eaten wood fell from the ancient vaulted
ceiling, dislodged by the impact of the voices. The sun,
striking on the slate roof, heated the little church like an oven.
A wave of emotion and eager expectation, as the moment of
the ineffable mystery drew near, swept over the children's
hearts and the mothers felt a tightening of the throat.

The priest, who had been sitting down for some time, went
up the steps to the altar, and, his head bare save for his silvery
locks, with tremulous gestures approached the miracle of
the Mass.

He turned towards the congregation, and, stretching out
his hands, he intoned: " Orate, Fratres; Brethren, let us
pray." Everyone knelt. The old priest now murmured the
words of the supreme mystery; the bell tinkled three times;
the congregation, bending low, invoked the name of God;
the children were faint with anxious anticipation.

At that moment Rosie, her face in her hands, suddenly
remembered her own mother, the village church, her own
First Communion. Memories of the day flooded back;
she was a tiny girl again, lost in her white dress, and she began
to cry. At first she wept silently, the tears welling slowly
from her closed eyes; then with the memories of the past
her emotion overcame her, and with bursting throat and
heaving breast she sobbed aloud. She had taken out her
handkerchief and was wiping her eyes and dabbing at her
nose and mouth to stop her tears. But it was no use. A

hoarse cry tore her throat, answered by two other deep, heartrending sighs, for her two neighbours, Louise and Flora, completely overcome by similar recollections of the past, were also in floods of noisy tears.

Tears being infectious, Madame in her turn soon felt her own eyelids moist, and, turning towards her sister-in-law, saw that the whole of her pew was weeping.

The priest was transforming the elements into the body and blood of Christ. The children were beyond thinking, bowed down to the stone floor in an ecstasy of awe and devotion; and here and there in the church a woman, a mother or sister, caught by the mysterious sympathy of violent emotion and upset by the sight of the smart ladies, whose shoulders were shaking and heaving with sobs as they knelt, was soaking her check calico handkerchief, pressing her left hand against her violently beating heart.

Like the spark which sets fire to a whole ripe corn-field, the tears of Rosie and her friends swept the whole congregation in a flash. Men and women, old men and boys in their smart blouses were all sobbing in a moment; and above them there seemed to hover the supernatural presence of an all-pervading spirit, the miraculous breath of an invisible almighty power.

Then in the chancel the shrill tinkle of the bell rang out; the good Sister of Mercy rapped on her book to give the signal for the Communion, and the children, trembling in a fever of devotion, drew near to the Holy Table.

A row of kneeling figures crowded the altar step; the old priest, with a silver-gilt ciborium in his hand, passed down the line, offering to each between his finger and thumb the consecrated wafer, the body of Christ, Redeemer of the world. They opened their mouths with spasmodic, nervous twitches, their eyes closed and their faces pale; and the long sheet, spread under their chins, quivered like running water.

Suddenly a wave of wild excitement swept the church,

like the murmur of a frenzied crowd, a storm of sobbing and stifled cries. It passed like gusts of wind over bending forest trees. The priest stopped motionless, with a wafer in his hand, paralysed with emotion, murmuring: "God Himself is in the midst of us, manifesting His presence, descending from heaven upon His kneeling people in answer to my prayer." And he whispered prayers wildly, forgetting the words, the prayers of a soul straining to rise to heaven.

He finished the administration in such a state of devotional excitement that his legs would hardly support him, and, when he had himself drunk the Saviour's blood, he prostrated himself in an act of ecstatic thanksgiving.

Behind him the congregation was gradually recovering itself. The cantors, with the confidence born of the dignity of their white surplices, resumed their chanting, though their voices were less assured after their tears; and even the serpent seemed hoarse, as if the instrument itself had been weeping.

The priest raised his hand and signed to them to stop singing, and making his way between the two lines of communicants, who were still in a state of rapturous exaltation, approached the choir screen.

The congregation had seated themselves, with much scraping of chairs, and all were now blowing their noses violently. When they saw the priest there was silence, and he began in a low, hesitating, muffled voice:

"My beloved brethren, my beloved sisters, my children, I thank you from the bottom of my heart; you have just given me the greatest happiness of my life. I felt the presence of God descending upon us in answer to my prayer. And He came, He was here, a real presence, filling your souls and making your eyes overflow. I am the oldest priest in this diocese, I am also to-day the happiest. A miracle has been manifested among us, a true, mighty, sublime miracle. While Jesus Christ was entering for the first time into the bodies of these little ones, the Holy Spirit, the Heavenly

Dove, the Breath of God descended upon you, filled you, dominated you, made you bow down like rushes in the wind."

Then in a stronger voice, turning towards the two pews occupied by the carpenter's party, he went on: " My thanks are especially due to you, my beloved sisters, who have come from afar, and whose presence among us, whose lively faith and manifest piety have set a salutary example to us all. You have been an edification to my parish; your emotion has kindled our hearts; without you perhaps this great day would not have been marked by this truly divine experience. The presence of one sheep of the elect is some-times enough to persuade the Lord to visit His flock."

Words failed him and, after adding: " Grace be with you all, Amen," he went back to the altar to finish the office.

By now everyone was in a hurry to get out. The children themselves were fidgeting, tired after the long emotional strain. Moreover, they were getting hungry, and one by one their relations were going out without waiting for the last gospel, to finish their preparations for the meal.

At the church door there was a jostling, noisy crush and a din of high-pitched voices with the sing-song Normandy accent. Everyone formed up in two lines, and as the communicants came out, each family fell upon its own child.

Constance found herself caught up, surrounded and kissed by all the women of the party. Rosie especially would hardly let her out of her arms. At last she took one hand, while Madame Tellier seized the other; Raphaële and Fernande picked up the long muslin train to prevent it dragging in the dust, while Louise and Flora brought up the rear with Madame Rivet; and the child, quite collected and still possessed by the presence of God within her, set off surrounded by her guard of honour.

The festive board was spread on trestle-tables in the work-shop. The general atmosphere of good cheer throughout the village came in through the door, which opened on the street. Everyone was having a good time; through every window could be seen tables surrounded by guests in their Sunday best, and sounds of revelry came from every house. The peasants in their shirt-sleeves were drinking full mugs of strong cider, and in the centre of each group there were two children, here two girls, there two boys, having their dinner with the family of one of them.

From time to time in the sultry mid-day heat a country cart passed through with an old pony jogging along in the shafts, and the driver in his workaday blouse cast an envious glance on all the festivities that met his gaze.

In the carpenter's house the merriment had a certain air of restraint, the aftermath of the morning's emotions; Rivet alone was in his best form and did not limit his potations. Madame Tellier kept her eye continually on the clock, for, in order not to miss two consecutive days' business, they were to catch the five minutes to four train, which would get them back to Fécamp by early evening.

The carpenter did everything he could to distract her attention, in order to keep his guests till the next day; but Madame would not be put off; with her, business came before pleasure.

Immediately after the coffee, she ordered her staff to get ready as soon as possible; then, turning to her brother, she said: "Now you go and harness the horse at once"; and she went upstairs to finish her own preparations.

When she came down, her sister-in-law was waiting for her to discuss the little girl's future. A long conversation ensued with no definite result. The mother used all her peasant's guile in a forced display of affection, but Madame Tellier, with the child on her knee, refused to commit herself, and only made vague promises; she would not forget her, there was plenty of time; besides, they would be seeing each other again.

Meanwhile the cart did not appear and the girls did not come down; indeed, there was loud laughter upstairs, sounds of a scuffle, little screams and the clapping of hands. Presently, while the carpenter's wife went to the stable to see if the cart was ready, Madame finally went upstairs herself.

Rivet, very drunk and half-undressed, was making vain attempts to assault Rosie, who was incapable with laughter. The two Beer Pumps were holding him back by the arms and trying to restrain him, shocked at this scene after the morning's ceremony; but Raphaële and Fernande were egging him on, convulsed with laughter and holding their sides. They uttered shrill screams at each of the drunk man's vain attempts. Rivet, very angry and red in the face, with his clothes unbuttoned, was making violent efforts to shake off the two women clinging to him, and was tugging with all his might at Rosie's skirt, mumbling: "You slut, so you won't, won't you?" Madame in a towering rage rushed at her brother, seized him by the shoulders and flung him out of the room with such force that he cannoned into the wall across the passage.

A minute later he was heard in the yard, pumping water over his head; and when he appeared with the cart, he was quite sober again.

They went back as they had come the day before, and the little white pony started off at a brisk jog trot.

In the blazing sun the gaiety which had slumbered during the meal broke out. This time the girls were amused by the jolting of the rickety cart; they even pushed their neighbours' chairs over; they screamed with laughter at anything, being especially tickled by the recollection of Rivet's discomfiture.

There was a shimmering heat haze over the fields, dazzling the eye; and the wheels raised two furrows in the dust, which swirled over the highroad far behind the cart.

Suddenly Fernande, who was fond of music, asked Rosie

to sing; and she gallantly plunged into " The Fat Vicar
of Meudon ".   But Madame quickly stopped her, consider-
ing this song unseemly on such a day.   She added: " Sing
us something of Béranger's instead ".   After a few seconds'
hesitation, Rosie made her choice and in her husky voice
began " Grandma ":

> Old Grandma on her birthday night
> Once drank two sips of heady wine;
> Then cried—she was a little tight—
> " What lovers once were mine !
>   My leg was trim to see,
>   So soft and plump my arm;
>   I wasted youth, ah me !
>   What use was all my charm? "

And the girls in chorus, led by Madame herself, took up
the refrain:

> " My leg was trim to see,
>   So soft and plump my arm;
>   I wasted youth, ah me !
>   What use was all my charm? "

" That's the stuff," declared Rivet, excited by the lilt, and
Rosie immediately went on:

> " Fie, Grandma, weren't you always pi? "
> " Dear no ! At fifteen my delights
> I used untaught—I wasn't shy—
> I didn't waste my nights ! "

They all shouted the chorus in unison, and Rivet tapped
with his foot on the shaft and beat time with the reins on the
back of the white pony, which broke into a mad gallop, as
if carried away by the excitement of the music, precipitating
the ladies in a heap one on top of the other at the bottom of
the cart.
They picked themselves up with shouts of laughter.   And

the song went on, shouted at the top of their voices, as they sped through the countryside under the blazing sky, between the ripening crops at breakneck speed, for the pony bolted every time the chorus was repeated and went at full gallop for a hundred yards, to the huge delight of the passengers.

From time to time a stone-breaker straightened his back and through his wire spectacles watched the shouting cartload whirling along in mad career in a cloud of dust.

When they got down at the station, the carpenter waxed sentimental: "It's very sad you're going; we could have had a grand time!"

Madame answered soberly: "There's a time for everything; all days can't be play-days."

Then a happy idea struck Rivet: "Look," he said, "I'm coming to see you in Fécamp next month." And he looked slyly at Rosie with a meaning wink.

"If you do," retorted Madame, "you'll have to behave; come if you like, but you mustn't make a fool of yourself."

He made no answer, and, as the whistle of the train was heard, immediately began to kiss them all round. When it came to Rosie's turn, he made great efforts to find her mouth, which she snatched away every time with a quick sideways movement, laughing with lips closed. He kept his arms round her, but he did not succeed in his object, for the big whip, which he still had in his hand, got in his way, bobbing up and down behind the girl's back in his desperate efforts.

"All passengers for Rouen, take your seats!" cried the guard, and they all got in.

The guard blew a shrill blast on his whistle, answered by a loud whistle from the engine, which noisily spat out its first puffs of steam, while the wheels began to revolve with a visible effort.

Rivet, leaving the platform, ran to the level-crossing to catch a last glimpse of Rosie; and as the carriage with its

human freight passed him, he danced about cracking his whip
and singing at the top of his voice:

> " My leg was trim to see,
> So soft and plump my arm;
> I wasted youth, ah me!
> What use was all my charm?"

His eyes were fixed on a white handkerchief which someone was waving, till it disappeared from view.

III

They slept all the way back in the train, with the sound
sleep of a clear conscience; and when they got home, re-
freshed and ready for the night's work, Madame could not
refrain from remarking: " I'm not sorry; it's good to be
home again."

Supper did not take long; then, having put on their war-
paint, they awaited the arrival of the regular customers, and
the little lighted lantern, as if burning before the Virgin,
informed passers-by that the wandering sheep had returned
to the fold.

The news spread in no time by some unknown means.
M. Philippe, the banker's son, carried kindness to the point
of sending an express message to M. Tournevau, imprisoned
in the bosom of his family.

The fish-curer, it so happened, had several cousins to
dinner, as he always did on Sunday, and they were just
having their coffee, when a man called with a letter in his
hand. In a great state of excitement M. Tournevau tore
open the envelope and went suddenly pale; there were only
these pencilled words: " Cargo of cod located; ship back
in harbour; good chance of a deal for you; come at once."

He put his hand in his pocket and gave the messenger a
threepenny tip; then, blushing to the tips of his ears, he said:

" I must go out ". And he handed his wife the brief mysterious note. He rang the bell, and, when the maid answered it, said: " Quick, my coat and hat! " As soon as he got out of the house, he set off at a run, whistling a tune, and in his impatience the distance seemed twice as long as usual.

Madame Tellier's establishment presented a festive appearance. On the ground floor the loud voices of the men from the harbour made a deafening din. Louise and Flora didn't know whom to serve first; they drank now with one, now with another, fully justifying their nickname of the two Beer Pumps. Everyone was calling for them at once; there were already more than they could cope with, and it looked as though they had a heavy night's work ahead.

By nine o'clock the club-room on the first floor was full. M. Vasse, the Commercial Court judge—Madame's acknowledged, if platonic, suitor—was chatting with her in the corner in a low voice; they were both smiling, as if agreement was imminent. M. Poulin, the ex-mayor, had Rosie sitting astride on his knee, and she, with her face close to his, was running her stumpy fingers through his comic white side-whiskers. She had pulled up her yellow silk skirt, and a piece of bare thigh showed white against the dark cloth of his trousers, and her red stockings were kept up by the blue garters the commercial traveller had given her.

The tall Fernande, lying at full length on the sofa, had both her feet on the stomach of M. Pimpesse, the Tax Collector, and the upper part of her body against young M. Philippe's waistcoat, with her right arm round his neck and a cigarette in her left hand.

Raphaële seemed to be discussing some arrangement with M. Dupuis, the Insurance Agent, and she brought the conversation to an end with the words: " Yes, darling, to-night I won't say No." Then, quickly waltzing across the room by herself, she cried: "Anything you like to-night!"

Suddenly the door opened and M. Tournevau appeared. He was received with acclamation: "Cheers for Tournevau!" And Raphaële, who was still waltzing round, subsided on his breast. He seized her in a close embrace, and, without a word, lifting her off the ground as if she were a feather-weight, he carried her across the drawing-room, made for the door at the end of the room and disappeared with his willing burden up the stairs leading to the bedrooms, amid cheers.

Rosie, who was vamping the ex-mayor, returning his kisses and pulling both his whiskers at the same time to keep his head straight, took the hint. "Come on, follow his lead!" she cried. Then the old buffer got up and, straightening his waistcoat, followed the girl, feeling in the pocket where he kept his money.

Fernande and Madame were left alone with the four men, and M. Philippe cried: "I'll stand champagne; Madame Tellier, send for three bottles."

Fernande, putting her arms round his neck, whispered in his ear: "Do play for us to dance, there's a dear."

He got up, and sitting down at the antiquated spinet standing neglected in a corner, coaxed a husky, sentimental waltz from its wheezy interior. The tall girl put her arm round the Tax Collector and Madame yielded to the embrace of M. Vasse.

The two couples waltzed, kissing as they danced. M. Vasse, who had once been a society dancing man, introduced fancy steps, and Madame, entranced, stole glances at him— glances of encouragement, more discreet and winning than any spoken word.

Frederick brought the champagne. The first cork popped, and M. Philippe played the introductory bars of a quadrille. The four dancers went through the figures as if they were at a smart ball, bowing and scraping with solemn dignity and affected mannerisms.

After which they returned to their glasses.

Presently M. Tournevau reappeared, having had his pleasure, satisfied and beaming. He cried: "I don't know what's come over Raphaële; she's wonderful this evening." When they offered him a glass, he emptied it at a draught, murmuring: "By Jove! there's nothing like bubbly!"

Next M. Philippe struck up a lively polka, and M. Tournevau plunged into the dance with the beautiful Jewess, whirling her round in the air with her feet off the floor. M. Pimpesse and M. Vasse started off again with renewed vigour. From time to time one of the couples stopped by the chimney-piece to toss off a tall glass of the sparkling wine; and this dance looked like going on for ever, when Rosie opened a crack of the door with a candlestick in her hand. She was in bedroom slippers with her hair down and nothing on but her shift; she was very excited and red in the face.

"I want to dance," she cried.

Raphaële asked: "What about your old man?"

She burst out laughing: "Him? He's asleep already; he always goes to sleep at once."

She seized M. Dupuis, who was sitting on the sofa without a partner, and the polka began again.

But the bottles were all empty. "I'll stand one", said M. Tournevau.

"So will I," declared M. Vasse.

"And I too," chimed in M. Dupuis; and everyone applauded.

Things were going with a swing; it was becoming a regular ball. From time to time even Louise and Flora hurried upstairs and danced a few bars of a waltz, while the customers below waxed impatient. Then they ran back to the bar, bitterly regretting that they couldn't stay.

At midnight the dancing was still going on. Now and again one of the girls would disappear, and, when they looked for her as a partner, it was suddenly discovered that one of the men was missing too.

"Where have you been?" asked M. Philippe jocosely, at the exact moment when M. Pimpesse came back into the room with Fernande.

"I've been looking at M. Poulin asleep," answered the Tax Collector.

The witticism was a great success, and all the gentlemen one after the other went upstairs ' to look at M. Poulin asleep,' with one or other of the girls, who were ready for anything that night. Madame turned a blind eye; she was having a long confidential conversation in the corner with M. Vasse, as if she was settling the final details of some deal already decided in principle.

At last at one o'clock the two married men, M. Tournevau and M. Pimpesse, declared that they must be getting home and wanted to pay their bill. Nothing was charged for except the champagne, and that was only six francs a bottle instead of the usual ten. And when they expressed astonishment at this generosity, Madame replied beaming:

"Holidays don't come every day."

PENGUIN POPULAR CLASSICS

Published or forthcoming

Aesop	Aesop's Fables
Hans Andersen	Fairy Tales
Louisa May Alcott	Good Wives
	Little Women
Eleanor Atkinson	Greyfriars Bobby
Jane Austen	Emma
	Mansfield Park
	Northanger Abbey
	Persuasion
	Pride and Prejudice
	Sense and Sensibility
R. M. Ballantyne	The Coral Island
J. M. Barrie	Peter Pan
R. D. Blackmore	Lorna Doone
Anne Brontë	Agnes Grey
	The Tenant of Wildfell Hall
Charlotte Brontë	Jane Eyre
	The Professor
	Shirley
	Villette
Emily Brontë	Wuthering Heights
John Buchan	The Thirty-Nine Steps
Frances Hodgson Burnett	A Little Princess
	The Secret Garden
Samuel Butler	The Way of All Flesh
Lewis Carroll	Alice's Adventures in Wonderland
	Through the Looking Glass
Geoffrey Chaucer	The Canterbury Tales
G. K. Chesterton	Father Brown Stories
Erskine Childers	The Riddle of the Sands
John Cleland	Fanny Hill
Wilkie Collins	The Moonstone
	The Woman in White
Sir Arthur Conan Doyle	The Adventures of Sherlock Holmes
	The Hound of the Baskervilles
	A Study in Scarlet

PENGUIN POPULAR CLASSICS

Published or forthcoming

Joseph Conrad	Heart of Darkness
	Lord Jim
	Nostromo
	The Secret Agent
	Victory
James Fenimore Cooper	The Last of the Mohicans
Stephen Crane	The Red Badge of Courage
Daniel Defoe	Moll Flanders
	Robinson Crusoe
Charles Dickens	Bleak House
	The Christmas Books
	David Copperfield
	Great Expectations
	Hard Times
	Little Dorrit
	Martin Chuzzlewit
	Nicholas Nickleby
	The Old Curiosity Shop
	Oliver Twist
	The Pickwick Papers
	A Tale of Two Cities
Charles Darwin	The Origin of Species
Fyodor Dostoyevsky	Crime and Punishment
George Eliot	Adam Bede
	Middlemarch
	The Mill on the Floss
	Silas Marner
John Meade Falkner	Moonfleet
F. Scott Fitzgerald	The Diamond as Big as the Ritz
	The Great Gatsby
Gustave Flaubert	Madame Bovary
Elizabeth Gaskell	Cousin Phillis
	Cranford
	Mary Barton
	North and South

PENGUIN POPULAR CLASSICS

PENGUIN POPULAR CLASSICS

Published or forthcoming

Charles and Mary Lamb	Tales from Shakespeare
D. H. Lawrence	The Rainbow
	Sons and Lovers
	Women in Love
Edward Lear	Book of Nonsense
Gaston Leroux	The Phantom of the Opera
Jack London	White Fang *and* The Call of the Wild
Captain Marryat	The Children of the New Forest
Herman Melville	Moby Dick
John Milton	Paradise Lost
Edith Nesbit	Five Children and It
	The Railway Children
Francis Turner Palgrave	The Golden Treasury
Edgar Allan Poe	Selected Tales
Sir Walter Scott	Ivanhoe
	Rob Roy
	Waverley
Saki	The Best of Saki
Anna Sewell	Black Beauty
William Shakespeare	Antony and Cleopatra
	As You Like It
	Hamlet
	Henry V
	Julius Caesar
	King Lear
	Macbeth
	The Merchant of Venice
	A Midsummer Night's Dream
	Othello
	Romeo and Juliet
	The Tempest
	Twelfth Night

PENGUIN POPULAR POETRY